reasons
to go
outside

ESME KING

HODDER &
STOUGHTON

First published in Great Britain in 2022 by Hodder & Stoughton
An Hachette UK company

1

A CIP catalogue record for this title is available from the British Library

Hardback ISBN 978 1 529 36282 4
Trade Paperback ISBN 978 1 529 36283 1
eBook ISBN 978 1 529 36284 8

Typeset in Plantin by Manipal Technologies Limited

Printed and bound in Great Britain by Clays Ltd, Elcograf S.p.A.

Hodder & Stoughton policy is to use papers that are natural, renewable
and recyclable products and made from wood grown in sustainable forests.
The logging and manufacturing processes are expected to conform to
the environmental regulations of the country of origin.

Hodder & Stoughton Ltd
Carmelite House
50 Victoria Embankment
London EC4Y 0DZ

www.hodder.co.uk

For Peter, Ethan, Evie, and Milo

Nothing should be out of the reach of hope.
Life is a hope.

Oscar Wilde

1st August 1976

It was the hottest summer for three hundred and fifty years, the driest in more than a century. Newspaper headlines proclaimed the country to be in the grip of a record-breaking heatwave. Under the sun's unrelenting glare, the tarmac on the M1 softened, and swarms of ruby-red ladybirds took the whole nation by surprise. The Thames receded, revealing shores of dank, fetid mud, embedded with the oil drums and shopping trolleys that usually went unseen below the deep, dark water. The capital's landmark had become a tributary of its former self, withered, and reduced. The government declared a state of emergency, standpipes rose out of the pavements, and neighbours stood shoulder to shoulder in the streets with plastic buckets to fill. Queues formed and conversations began about the forest fires that had raged for weeks, dehydrated crops, the threat of rising food prices, and the government's suggestion that everyone should bathe with a friend to save water. Nobody knew when it would come to an end. The unforgettable summer of 1976.

At the height of it, Ray Johnson got in his car and drove Lana Winter and her sixteen-year-old daughter, Pearl, all the way from Godalming to Devon. He stopped only once to buy fuel from a service station. In the close confines of the car, they hardly spoke. This was unusual, almost as unusual as the situation they found themselves in. The quiet was unnerving. It wasn't like Ray not to speak, especially. Pearl's mother had described him as the life and soul of the party when they met, a person other people warmed to instantly. He didn't have children or a wife of his own, Pearl knew, but treated Lana and herself as if they were exactly that. It had been good to see her mother smile again too after her father had left them so suddenly and moved in with a woman who worked in the launderette. But during the journey from Godalming to Devon Ray spoke only to ask Lana if she would light him another one of his cigarettes. On the back seat, Pearl sat among the swirls of dove-grey smoke and concentrated on counting seconds, and then minutes, anything to avoid thinking about the reason they had to leave Godalming. Instead, she focused on the permanently changing landscape outside as the wide motorways and dusty roads gave way to narrow country lanes and sage-coloured fields.

As dusk settled, they reached a town where the cottages were washed in pastel shades of pink, blue and yellow. Each was topped with a bristly thatch. A sign read 'Welcome to Westdown'. Pearl wound down her window and listened to the sound of a jukebox coming from inside a nearby public house, its doors wide open to encourage in a change of air. Outside, there were two hanging baskets containing the desiccated remains of flowers. Pearl guessed petunias. All that was left were their tinder-dry stems trembling in the early evening breeze. Her hair whipped across her face as they drove along the deserted street, so she wound her window back up until it was closed.

Ray pushed his foot on the accelerator pedal and drove out the other side of the town, over a cattle grid and onto an expanse of grassland so vast and impressive Pearl forgot to keep counting seconds. Acres of rugged ground rippled away into the distance under a blazing sunset that burned its indelible stain *of vermillion red and gold on the horizon. In places, the land was scorched the colour of butter and, where it rose in peaks, it was ripped through with sharp-looking rocky outcrops. The undulating hills reminded Pearl of small mountains. Good for climbing up and seeing the view from the top. But she knew, sadly, that she never would. Next to the road, black-faced sheep and wild ponies grazed amiably beside one another on the rough grass. Pearl noticed their fur was covered in patches of dry mud and they looked up only briefly as the car passed, as if a speeding vehicle was nothing to be troubled by.*

'Not much further,' Ray promised. 'Then we'll be there.' Pearl felt relieved. The sooner they reached their new home the better.

He drove on across the moor, taking only one turning off the main road, and after a short distance, pulling up outside a large, stone-built house with a wide front lawn. This had a concrete path running through the centre of it, all the way up to a heavy oak door. Faded blooms of late, lilac wisteria cascaded down one side of the house, and a determined ivy strangled a broken drainpipe on the other. There was a black metal box marked Mail attached to the gate post, and a low, post and rail fence that ringed the boundary.

Ray turned off the car's engine and Lana got out. 'There's nobody else but us,' she said. Pearl listened for a sound. Save for the flap of unseen wings in the towering oak trees nearby, there was nothing. No distant hum of traffic or dogs barking.

'I'll get the suitcases, if you two want to go in,' Ray said helpfully, already lifting the lid of the boot. 'Our furniture will arrive tomorrow in the van. Then Highview will feel more like a home.'

It was just a short distance to the door, through the gate and up the path, but it felt as long as a mile. Pearl kept her head down as she made her way along it, concentrating on the small explosions of emerald-green moss bursting out of the cracks in the concrete. Ahead, Lana unlocked the front door and pushed it open. Pearl didn't stop to think about the terrifying truth of what had happened in Godalming that heatwave summer. To reflect on it, she knew, only served to invite in an unbearable feeling, a fear that threatened to overwhelm her completely and fell her where she stood.

So, as fast as her legs would carry her, Pearl Winter hurried inside.

PEARL

1st August – 43 Years Later

Out on the road, a gang of crows tug at two-day-old roadkill with beaks hooked like daggers. They pull at the sun-baked remains below a dancing circle of flies. This way and that, backward and forward, the dry matter slides. Pearl finds herself squinting in order to see clearly as she has done so many times lately. Her focus is not what it used to be. Almost sixty-year-old eyes. Almost sixty-year-old knees.

Either side of the gate, there is a falling-down section of the fence, and up against it a sweep of tall grass, grown overly thin and longer than is good for it. Pearl reluctantly takes in the sight and notices the sharp brambles advancing over her windowsill. She sees the abundance of sticky chickweed on the ledge, and the gate at the end of the path hanging at a jaunty angle, on account of it having only one hinge. The other lies on the ground, turning ochre with rust in the burning sun. Pearl sighs deeply. If only she could step outside and set the mower in motion, dig up the rampant brambles, and re-attach the hinge to the gate. There is no getting away from it. It is time to make the call she has been putting off for more days than she cares to remember.

In the hallway, on a dark wood table, sits an elephant-grey slab of plastic with extra-large buttons. Next to it is a yellowing pad of A4 paper, flipped open in the middle and revealing the jagged edges of the lined sheets ripped out before. On the open page there is a shopping list, a reminder to have the chimney swept, an order for milk, and a note, all in her mother's unmistakable handwriting: *Should you need help with the garden, my dearest Pearl, please put a postcard in the newsagent's window.* Lana Winter had included a number to call. Seeing the carefully written words, Pearl feels the pain of losing someone so close to her, just as she had done three years previously. It had been unexpected, Lana dying only six years after Ray. It was as if she couldn't bear to continue without the partner she loved. When Lana left Highview for the last time she was wrapped in a pea-green blanket and seated in an NHS wheelchair. Pearl watched the ambulance light flashing its urgency over the dark moor as it disappeared, and for a long time after she stood at the window. The hospital rang the next morning with the news. Lana had passed away in her sleep, unable to fight the chest infection that had plagued her for months. From that moment, Highview had seemed so very quiet. Just Pearl and the crows.

There are few visitors to the house, just the postman with his headphones who knocks infrequently and rarely speaks, and the grocery-delivery driver who arrives briefly and without fail once a week, sometimes a tall man with a limp, sometimes a woman with short, auburn hair and incredibly strong arms. Occasionally there are substitutions on the shopping list. An opportunity to talk; a few words concerning the replacement of wholemeal bread with white, apples for pears, and one time, bananas instead of bleach.

Standing beside the telephone table now, she takes a deep breath, followed shortly after by another. Thinking of the garden once more she decides there is no time to lose. When she makes the call, it rings through while she nervously taps out a beat with her right foot. The rubber sole of her moccasin slippers makes a rat-tat-tat sound on the flagstone floor. *One, two, thr—*

'Good morning, Westdown News.'

'Hello.'

'How can I help?'

'I'd like to place a card in the window . . . for a gardener, please.'

'No problem,' the man replies. 'Is it part-time or full-time you were looking for?'

Pearl thinks of the three-foot grass covering the lawns. 'I'm sorry, I'm not absolutely sure how long the job will take but I think full-time.'

'I'll put five days a week. Monday to Friday?'

'Monday to Friday. Thank you.'

'Monday to Friday with weekends off?' he adds. 'Then you can see how it goes.'

Pearl nods, even though she isn't facing the man. This is going better than she expected.

'And what sort of hourly rate were you thinking of?'

Pearl remembers details about acceptable levels of pay on a government website she'd found on her mother's old computer that sits in a corner of the spare room. It had taken longer to log on to the elderly piece of equipment than to read the information provided about minimum pay scales.

'Nine pounds per hour.'

'Nine pounds,' the man repeats. 'And a mobile number?'

Pearl gazes at the solid-looking telephone on the table before her, fixed securely and firmly in place with four squares of sticky-back plastic. Stationary and immobile.

'I'm afraid I don't have one.'

'Right,' he says, unable to hide the surprise in his voice. 'I can take the landline off the caller display. I'm sorry, but could you just bear with me one moment?'

Pearl loses the newsagent to a woman with an American accent asking about the price of clotted-cream fudge. £10.72 for the small box and £19.80 for the large.

On the line, in his absence, there is the sound of people talking and coughing and the shrill of a buzzer. Pearl imagines a line of customers waiting, all hoping to buy ice creams and cold drinks, sweets, and a copy of the day's newspaper to read in the sun.

'Sorry about that,' the busy man says, returning to the call. 'If I can just take your card details for the payment, then I think that's everything.'

Pearl picks up the debit card from the telephone table and is immediately reminded of Ray's comforting words. *There's an account. Enough money for all the years to come.*

The silver digits making up the long number, expiry date and security pin shimmer in the gloom. She reads them out clearly.

'Your ad'll go up this afternoon,' the man confirms. 'Just as soon as I can get it in the window.'

A woman speaks so close to him Pearl can hear every word. The woman says that he is needed urgently to deal with a delivery of magnums. She is quite insistent. It is such a diverting piece of information Pearl is almost moved to speak up and ask in what quantities the delivery is made. Newsagents selling bottles of Champagne! How times have changed.

'Good luck,' the man says. 'Just give us a call if you need another week and we'll keep it in the window.'

And with a click, he is gone. Pearl looks down at the telephone cord, connecting her connecting her like a plastic umbilical cord to the grey slab. It is still wrapped around her wrist, and so tightly the skin on her hand has turned the colour of blue delphiniums.

She tries to picture the person who might answer her advertisement, the call for help she has put out, somewhat recklessly now she comes to think of it, into the world. Her prayer, when she says it, echoes around the quiet hallway.

'Please let it be someone who won't run a mile when I tell them, someone who might understand why the grass has grown so high without being cut down . . . please let it be someone kind.'

But for the life of her, Pearl can't imagine who such a person could be.

CONNOR

Connor Matthews stands in his bedroom and stares at walls infected with irregular blobs of bright pink paint. It reminds him of when he had chicken pox, aged five. Itchy, irritating chicken pox. The spots on the walls are increasing in number, just like the ones that sprouted on every inch of his body, and are all a different shade from one another, but only marginally. Rocket Ship Rose, Hazy Harlem, and Strawberry Sundae. He checks the names on the corresponding tester pots that are lined up against the skirting board and thinks about throwing them out of the window.

'I see you. You like the new colours, yes?'

When he turns around she is there. Yvo Martens. Belgian. Room invader. His father's girlfriend.

'I cannot decide,' she sighs. 'So many to choose from.'

She is dressed in cycling shorts and a fluorescent long-sleeved cycling top. It matches the neon strips on the downtube of her road bike leant up against the front porch. Now he thinks about it, he's not sure if Yvo is short for something longer. He's not actually sure of very much when it comes to the woman standing uninvited in his room, except that she met his father at the local cycling club a year ago and they share a passion for all things Lycra and two-wheeled. His father, as he'd explained it, had coveted her carbon-fibre frame, and

she his Campagnolo wheels. It had been nauseating to
watch at the time, Donald Matthews acting more like a
lovestruck teenager than a man with a mortgage, a Volvo,
and a receding hairline. And, to make the whole situation weirder, as soon as Yvo had moved in, she'd begun
changing the interior of the house like someone from a
TV makeover show. It had happened so fast. No room
untouched. Like a highly organised, multi-lingual cuckoo,
she had landed in the Matthews family nest, B&Q colour
chart in hand, and immediately made it her own.

'I liked the room as it was,' he says. 'I'm happy with
Magnolia. Just saying.'

'But you will be gone to university soon, no? Then you
will have different walls to look at. You could paint them the
colour you like. And this happy pink,' Yvo says, bending
down and picking up a tester pot marked Flamingo
Fandango, 'it brings joy, I think . . . after all the sadness.'

Connor swallows hard. Has the room become suddenly
darker or is he just imagining it?

'I don't know,' he mumbles, wishing he was anywhere
else but standing here now facing questions about what
happened two years ago. His room feels nothing like the
teenage sanctuary he's sure it's supposed to be, all blackout
curtains, PlayStation consoles and unwritten rules about
knocking before entering.

Yvo looks at him oddly, as if she's thinking about saying
something more. 'I have new paint in the car. . .'

'OK.'

'Your father will be home soon. I think he will like it. And
this one. But I will choose.'

She points to a stain that looks slightly darker than the others. Connor thinks of a name for it. Ten-day-old Dried Blood seems to cover it. He pictures his father walking through the front door after a busy day at the solicitor's practice in town, seeing splats of paint on every available wall. The ones in the hall are bright yellow. Despite the fact they look uncannily like carefully aimed jets of bile, he knows Donald will agree the colours are an improvement and say no more than that. Nothing, in fact, that will change the uncomfortable way things are at number five Fern Crescent. Connor looks around at the pockmarked walls and can't help thinking about the time before two years ago when it wasn't uncomfortable. Then they talked, and went fishing; easy conversations alongside a lake, road trips in the Volvo in search of rivers and waterways they'd read about and looked forward to exploring. Now, their collection of rods and equipment are gathering dust in the garage, and they haven't had the conversation they so obviously need. The one that might just save their fractured relationship.

'I'll go to the car, get the paint and look for some more brushes . . . and the spirit that is white.' Yvo's voice breaks his train of thought. 'I'll be back,' she says, her voice as deep as his father's and not softened any by her accent. It reminds Connor of Arnold Schwarzenegger.

When she has gone, he immediately takes his phone out of his back pocket. There will be enough time. Enough for him to make a call and see if the job is still available. It has been on his mind since he saw it. The postcard in the newsagent's window, hanging at a precarious angle, the sort of half upside-down way that makes you turn your head ninety degrees to read it. He'd stood studying it while the owner was busy shutting up his shop for the evening. Just as the man disappeared from view, the Blu Tack holding it in place had given up its grip and the postcard had slipped down onto the floor behind a display cabinet, amongst the dust and old till receipts.

It had felt like a message, a well-timed lifeline. A job for the summer. An escape from the home that doesn't feel or look like it used to. The home where Yvo and his dad so clearly want to be left alone to get on with the next chapter of their lives, painting walls, riding bikes, and acting as if everything is normal when it isn't.

So, while he has his oddly painted room to himself, Connor telephones the number on the advertisement, and waits anxiously for an answer. He hopes the person who placed the advertisement will be kind because he really needs this job.

NATE

In flat nine Weatherley Gardens, Godalming, sixty-year-old Nate Williams opens the window to let in an evening breeze and lays out his work clothes for the morning. A white shirt, smart navy trousers (both ironed), and an orange tie emblazoned with the TopQuote company logo – *The UK's Number One for All Your Household and Motor Insurance Needs.*

Everything set for the next day, he considers leaving the flat, taking a left at the corner of the road and walking along the main street to the fish and chip shop at the end. It will use up some time, about forty minutes if he walks slowly and includes a chat with the owner, an amiable giant of a man, now in his late seventies, who used to be a bare-knuckle fighter in his youth. Nate thinks about a conversation with the man with no front teeth and LOVE and HAKE tattooed on his knuckles, and he thinks about an enjoyable fish supper. Another night. A Friday or Saturday so he can make something of the weekend if his bank balance allows. TopQuote have increased his wages incrementally over the last forty-two years, but unfortunately not in line with the rising cost of a large cod and chips.

In his kitchenette it is quiet, just the sound of a bus expiring at the stop outside his window. In search of food, he opens the fridge, and his face is illuminated by a stream of golden light. Inside there is a pint of milk, a tub of margarine, half a loaf of bread, and a selection of ready meals for one. Nate gives it some thought. Carbonara it is. He slips off the cardboard sleeve, pierces the clingfilm top and puts the container into the microwave. While it rides the circular merry-go-round inside, he counts his blessings, such as they are. He has a job. Check. He has a roof over his head. Check. Really, that is all he can ask for, Nate decides, having long since given up hope of anything more. Especially love. Love is beyond him. He nods to himself just as the microwave pings, announcing his meal is ready. It will always be beyond him.

When he has finished his Italian-inspired evening meal and drunk a glass of water, Nate changes out of his clothes and into his pyjamas. Like every night, he allows himself a moment to remember the summer of 1976. Then he closes the curtains in his bedroom and goes to bed while it is still light outside.

PEARL

When the telephone rings, Pearl is busy staring at the sunset beyond the kitchen window. She has cramp in her left calf and the beginnings of a twitch in her right eye. Hurrying to the hall, despite the cramp, she feels her heart racing in her chest like a bull confined in a pit. Beside the telephone is Lana's old A4 pad, open at a page of interview questions she has written in case anyone should call.

'Hello. Good evening . . . welcome.'

Much to her dismay and due to the worst case of nerves, Pearl realises she is sounding like someone making the opening announcement of the *Eurovision Song Contest*.

It is a young man's voice that comes rapidly back to her down the line.

'I'm ringing about the card in the newsagent's window.' He stops and Pearl waits. 'Well, it was in the window, but it isn't now,' he says, sounding breathless. 'It fell down the back of the card display.'

Pearl wonders if he might be asthmatic.

'Can I ask where you live?' Question one on the pad is ADDRESS, a sub-heading below the first section marked PERSONAL DETAILS.

'I'm in Westdown – just outside of it,' he offers, readily. 'On the new estate?'

Pearl wonders momentarily what *the new estate* might look like. No doubt Google will shed some light.

'You go through Westdown, out past the farm shop on the right and it's about half a mile on the left. It's called Fern Crescent. Number five.' He is speaking again. 'If you go to the bottom there are several houses. Gravel drive-ways, gardens . . . they all look the same.' The young man stops briefly. 'Sorry, that's probably a lot of useless information. I talk a lot when I'm nervous.'

When she checks her mother's pad, out of all the extremely useful detail the young man has provided, Pearl realises she has only managed to write down the word 'gravel'.

'Anyway, I've got a car,' he says. 'So, I can get to you.'

'I'm up on the moor, a few miles out of Westdown. About eight miles or so,' she replies, already hoping it won't put him off.

'OK,' he says. 'I've got a Fiesta. It's old but reliable.'

Next to the word 'car' on the ageing pad, Pearl rapidly scores a tick in the thinning paper; it goes right through to the page below.

'And your age? I probably should have asked that first,' she says, wishing her heart would stop beating so fast. How long will it keep crashing about inside her?

'Eighteen. I've been doing A-levels at college, but I've finished now . . . for the summer.'

Pearl checks her list, finding listening to information and writing it down all at the same time now it comes to it to be just as hard as patting your head and rubbing your stomach in tandem.

'And gardening experience? The lawns at Highview are very overgrown, and the flower beds are strangled by weeds.'

'My mum taught me how to look after a lawn and plants, and most things you need to care for a garden.'

'And would anyone be able to give you a reference?'

'You mean my mu—?' he begins but is cut short by an interruption on the line – a woman talking about a tester pot for a paint colour called Whispering Watermelon, in a matt *not* a satin, and how it could be the one.

'Can I call you back?' he says. 'Something ... someone ... has come up.'

'Yes . . . of course,' Pearl replies, wondering what would happen if she refused.

'I'm Connor. Sorry, I should have said. Connor Matthews.'

'And I'm Pearl,' she says. 'Pearl Winter . . . Miss.'

'I'll ring back, Miss Wintermiss. Sorry. 'Bye.'

'Goodbye.'

Miss Wintermiss. It has a nice ring to it, but it is a mistake she will need to correct just as soon as they talk again. Honesty is the best policy. She has always believed that.

Outside, a curl of dust is whipped up from the path by an errant breeze while brambles scratch their spiked stems across the window as if trying to break in. Pearl waits for the phone to ring and when the call comes, she quickly picks up the receiver.

'Hello?' She looks down at her list, at the wobbly ticks next to each question and the words 'gravel', 'summer', and 'car'. 'I'd like to offer you the position.'

A relieved sigh whistles down the line all the way from the new estate.

'When would you like me to start? I can be there tomorrow.'

'Would ten o'clock be too early?'

'I'll be there.'

Pearl reads the directions she has written out from memory. *Take the main road across the moor from Westdown, then turn right at the first crossroads, up the hill for a short distance and Highview is on the right.*

After she has given him the details, he says, ''Bye, Miss Wintermiss. See you tomorrow,' and is gone.

In the kitchen, she makes a cup of tea and stands at the French doors, looking out at the rose beds circling the patio, the oak trees beyond the lawn, and the low stone wall that forms a boundary separating Highview from the open moor. Life is about to change. Tomorrow won't just be another day spent listening to Radio Three, scrubbing an already spotless bath and hanging out a minimal amount of clean washing on the indoor airer. Tomorrow will be a very different day to that altogether.

NATE

When he wakes up the next morning, Nate can't shift the feeling that this day is a particularly important one. He checks his leather-strapped wristwatch, lying on the bed-side table. The number in a tiny square window on the right-hand side under its glacial surface confirms it. He looks again. Forty-two years to the day since he'd walked down a side-street off the main road in town and into the cramped office of a small insurance company, in the hope of securing a position. That branch has long since closed down, and the small fledgling company has grown into a multi-million pound conglomerate whose flagship HQ is now an imposing concrete monolith situated on a business park two miles east of Godalming.

Arriving at work, he is greeted by the Floor Supervisor, a young man with greasy hair, halitosis that can reach across a room, and an annoying habit of calling everyone *dude*. He approaches before Nate has had a chance to switch on his computer or pick up his headset.

'Nate, dude, you need to go up to the fifth floor. To HR.'

'Straight away?'

The young man nods. 'That's what the new boss lady says. She made it real clear it was important too. No time to waste. You know what I mean?'

As dude-man walks away, Nate can't help but feel a sense of burgeoning hope about what might be waiting for him on the upper floor. A long-service award, a presentation in person from the management team. He doesn't want to assume anything. He is happy just to get on, but it would make for a good day if his years of service were commemorated in some way, perhaps half an hour or so shaking hands with middle management and accepting a small gift. A moment to reflect on the last four decades of taking calls about car and home insurance, before he returns to his compact cubicle. So, with a spring in his step, Nate heads for the lift.

When the doors open five floors up, a stout woman wearing glasses is standing on the other side. Pale grey eyes stare back at him intently from behind large, round tortoiseshell rims.

'Mr Williams? I'm Marie Simmons, the new Head of HR. Please come this way.'

Nate obediently follows her into an airless side room with scratchy, bright orange carpet tiles on the floor, a desk and two metal chairs with orange fabric seats. One has a small stain on it. Nate thinks about the previous occupant. It has the feel of an interview room straight out of a police procedural drama, even with the prevalence of luminous orange. Nate is confident the tangerine tinge of TopQuote's logo colour extends to every far-flung corner of the building. Even the toilet seats in the men's loo, he's aware, are the same migraine-inducing shade. Nate sits down on the nearest chair and Marie takes the other.

'Can I call you Nathaniel?' she asks, getting settled in her seat. Marie shuffles paperwork already laid out on the desk like a magician preparing to spellbind her audience with an amazing new card trick. 'Or would you prefer Mr Williams?'

'Nate,' he offers. 'Most people call me Nate.'

Marie sits forward and locks her hands together on the desk and for a moment Nate wonders if she is about to begin their meeting with a short prayer. Instead, she says, 'Mr Williams . . . Nate, I'd like to start by asking you to maintain a degree of . . . confidentiality . . . around this meeting. We don't want to cause any undue panic as I'm sure you'd agree.'

He pictures his co-workers sitting glassy-eyed at their terminals and fails to imagine what could provoke the mild-mannered collective into anything even remotely close to a state of alarm.

'This has come from above. Directly,' Marie continues, her eyes shifting heavenwards to the boardroom on the sixth floor before coming back to rest unblinkingly on his. 'We are making changes. Substantial changes, in fact. You might have already heard?'

Nate shakes his head. 'I'm sorry, no.'

'Well then, I'll get right to it,' Marie says, undeterred. 'Call-centre closures are happening all over the country, it's nothing new, and regardless of our reputation for providing years of unrivalled customer service from this very site, unfortunately we must all move with the times.'

Marie takes a moment. Just long enough for Nate to feel the short grey hairs stand to attention on the back of his neck and the room lose what little oxygen it seemed to hold when he walked in.

'In a nutshell,' she says. 'TopQuote is transferring its operation overseas. So, I'm afraid we're having to make some alterations. Unpopular ones. We're talking redundancies on quite a large scale.'

There is the sudden interruption of a burst of animated laughter from a group of office staff in the corridor. The carefree noise leaks into the room, injecting the silence with a note of frivolity that seems at odds with the suddenly sombre mood.

'So,' Marie continues like a woman determined to get to the end of a speech, 'We are speaking to long-service individuals as a priority, and as we don't have anyone else who has worked here for as long as you have, you're first up.'

Nate takes a moment. Unsure he isn't dreaming and about to wake up in flat nine Weatherley Gardens, having overslept for the first time in his working life.

When he speaks, it is with some difficulty that he says the words, 'What happens now?'

Marie holds his gaze. 'We're encouraging employees, wherever possible, to take their leave immediately, to avoid any bad feeling being passed on to the customers.'

Nate trawls through memories of working at his cubicle, headset on, screen-facing; all the queries he has answered about dented cars, leaking ceilings, and accidentally smashed televisions. Not even when a woman had screamed down the phone at him about the criminal hike in cost for the third-party fire and theft policy on her beloved Nissan Micra, had he responded with anything other than utmost courtesy and professionalism.

'Mr Williams?' Marie coughs discreetly.

'It's Nate.'

'Do you have any questions?'

'I don't think so.'

'Right, well, if you'd like to collect your belongings and coat from the staffroom . . .' Marie's rictus smile is a sight to behold.

Nate rises out of the plastic chair feeling like a child dismissed from the classroom for drawing something rude on the blackboard.

'But it's only the morning. Should I go now?'

'Absolutely,' Marie says. 'I'll send on written details of the redundancy payment and a P45.' She stands up and offers him her limp hand across the table. Nate holds it for the briefest of shakes. It's moist and surprisingly cold, like a dead fish.

Before he leaves, she says, as if only just remembering, 'TopQuote would like to take this opportunity to thank you for your many years of service. We pride ourselves on our exemplary record of staff development and well-being. Please make sure you leave your security pass. I can't let you exit the building with it still in your possession. But I am authorised to take it from you now if you prefer.'

Nate looks down at the dizzyingly bright orange lanyard around his neck and the white plastic pass card dangling from the end of it. He slowly lifts the badge over his head and lays it on the desk, the ID photograph taken years before sunny side up and clearly displayed. He uses his last moments in the room to stare at the image, a snapshot from the past, and as he does a young, hopeful Nate Williams stares right back.

CONNOR

The clear bulb that hangs in the centre of the white lamp-shade on the ceiling reminds him of a snowdrop. *Galanthus nivalis.* She'd taught him the botanical names. Mum. He found them easy to remember. No problem. It was just as simple as recalling the lyrics to a favourite song. Much easier, in fact, than the four exam subjects he'd studied in crowded rooms at college, now he comes to think about it. A Level history had never taken root in his mind as effortlessly as the Latin names of plants, the best kind of compost mix to bed-in a hardy perennial, and the ideal time to plant bulbs for flowering in Spring. These things were easier to recall.

Getting up, he crosses to the window and looks out over the back garden of Fern Crescent. It had been her favourite place: outside with her hands deep in the soil, come rain or come shine. The borders are alive with colour: filled with alliums, rudbeckias, geraniums, and lavender. The blooms of deep red, mustard, and purple curl around a circle of freshly mown lawn. There's a small shed in the corner, a wheelbarrow propped up against it, and a compost bin behind. There's a raised bed of herbs too – rosemary, mint, sage. It hadn't taken long to build it from offcuts of old sleepers, using the power drill from the garage. As he stands looking at the garden, the light changes outside. How long will it be before the garden gets a makeover, just like the house? How long before the borders are dug up and concreted over, the grass swapped for something fake and less time-consuming, and the compost bin no longer required? It won't be long, he's sure of it. Good job he's leaving for university in a matter of weeks. Only it doesn't feel that way.

There is a slim cardboard box on his bedside table. It arrived from York. He crosses to it and lifts the already opened lid. Inside is a notepad, pen and drinks bottle, some money-off vouchers for Pizza Hut and a letter from the admissions team welcoming him to the start of his first year. It says the university is pleased to confirm a conditional offer to study law. Three years.

'Soon you will be gone?' Yvo had said enthusiastically at the sight of him standing by the front door with the box in his hands. His father had remained silent, just the slightest movement of his right foot this way and that on the laminated wood flooring giving away the fact that he might be inclined to add something, but then he had found paperwork in the home office that needed his urgent attention. Another moment missed when they could have started a conversation, talked about the way things are, about what had happened to Mum. It's like there's a permanent gulf between them and with each passing day it grows wider.

Not wanting to be late on his first day in a new job, Connor dresses quickly, picks up his phone from the bedside table, grabs his rucksack and heads downstairs. Donald is in the study, hunched over his desk. A tall man with a pronounced stoop, even when sitting down, he looks to his son like someone expecting a pigeon to land on his head. Today he looks no different from any other day, dressed in his self-imposed uniform of checked shirt, cords and smart tie and appearing more like a country vet than the town's only solicitor.

The home office where he can often be found is a compact room at the front of the house, just big enough for a desk by the window, a chair, and a single bookcase filled with cream-coloured folders. Each one contains the details of a problem, a moment in time the client has reached when they don't have any choice but to seek legal advice. Donald says work comes his way courtesy of the three Ds. Divorce, death, and debt. His father, his father's father and his father's grandfather had all been solicitors, all versed in the business of break-ups, inheritance tax, and county court judgements. It's a family tradition. If they could talk freely, father and son, Connor would say he'd prefer to help people in another way, by landscaping a garden filled with colour and interest – a gerbera-lined path to a raised deck, somewhere to retreat to after a hard day's work, or a trickling water feature to draw the eye and relax anyone sitting alongside it. In short, he'd rather be outside. But the chances of father and son talking about paths and ponds, let alone their family of three that used to exist when Mum was around, are slim, he knows. Slim to non-existent.

'I got a job for the summer,' Connor says, leaning against the doorframe of the small room. 'It's up on the moor . . . gardening.'

Donald remains facing away but puts his pen down and takes off his glasses.

'Gardening?'

'Yes.'

'Is it paid?'

'It's nine pounds an hour.'

From the kitchen, there is the sound of Yvo opening and closing cupboard doors loudly, and then a blender whirring into life.

Connor's stomach rumbles.

Donald doesn't seem to notice.

'You must take some time to prepare for York. You'll need to make sure you've made all the necessary arrangements. Yvo will buy a train ticket. You have everything arranged with your finances?' Donald Matthews asks.

'It's all done.' Connor thinks about his student loan, the thousands of pounds he will need to repay one day, the poky room in a terraced house in York he'll share with strangers, and the prospect of years of preparing for a life that leaves him cold. It's a career, for sure, a future indeed. Just not one he would have chosen for himself.

'I should go,' Connor says. 'I don't want to be late.'

'I'll leave you to it then,' Donald replies, picking up his pen and putting his glasses back on.

Connor turns to go, aware as always that his father is as skilled at the art of small talk as he is at white-water rafting. But they must speak soon. About Mum. About going away. About not wanting to take a law degree. Each day it eats away at him. The silence. If only a conversation could begin.

'Donald, your smoothie!' Yvo calls from the kitchen.

Standing in the hall, Connor slips on his trainers and picks up his rucksack from by the door. He can't remember a time when Donald Matthews had anything other than a strong coffee with three sugars in it of a morning, the sort of drink you could stand a spoon up in. He looks back into the office, at his father still bent over his desk. How long will it be before Yvo's changes extend to Donald? How long before he is dressing in chinos and a pale pink polo shirt, wearing loafers, and dyeing his hair an unnatural shade of reddish brown?

Pulling his rucksack over his shoulder, Connor opens the front door and steps out into the morning sunshine. His stomach rumbles again. But breakfast will have to wait.

PEARL

When she opens the door just a fraction, there is a person standing on the other side. He is of slight build with floppy sandy-coloured hair. Two long arms appear from the baggy holes on either side of his voluminous grey T-shirt. There are two equally long legs, wrapped tightly in faded, light blue denim. The denim is ripped in several places as though someone has been given carte blanche to go at them with a pair of extremely sharp scissors.

'Hello . . .' he says. 'I'm Connor.' Through the gaps above and below the trio of thick, high-security chains, Pearl studies his face. A lock of hair falls over one eye, but he does nothing to remove it. She estimates it is just long enough to curl back around one ear if he wanted to.

'I've brought my driving licence,' he says, smiling.

She smiles back. It would be rude not to.

The lock of hair bounces this way and that as he digs about in his back jeans pocket, before producing a rectangle of bubble-gum pink plastic with an image on it. 'It doesn't look like me,' he admits. 'But it is. Honest. They said not to smile in Snappy Snaps . . . the camera shop . . . so I didn't.'

He stops smiling as if to demonstrate the point. 'See?'

Pearl takes the plastic rectangle from him. Without her glasses it's almost impossible to tell. The image is grey and grainy. You can never be sure about people. It's a problem and always has been. She looks down at the name written on the licence and the date of birth. Connor James Matthews. Born 04-10-2000.

Earlier in the morning while the birds were still entertaining the owls with their dawn chorus she had fired up Lana's computer in the spare room and tentatively typed *Teenager* into the search bar. Instantly, the picture of a girl had appeared, eyes rimmed with heavy black make-up and her shoulder-length hair the colour of a raven's back. She wore an indifferent expression as if she had lived a thousand lives already and found none of them to be particularly interesting. Then there had been a multitude of young men, the majority of whom seemed to be having a problem with their trousers. They wore them so low as to reveal the make of their underwear. Under the title *no face no case*, a boy wore a cap pulled down over his eyes. It was a worrisome half-hour spent on the World Wide Web, albeit in the relative security of the spare room with all five dead bolts securing the front door and the comforting sound of Classic FM coming to her from the radio in the kitchen.

Pearl stares out between the chains. Connor Matthews, despite being in need of a satisfying meal, doesn't seem to match the image of a typical teenager according to Google, not by a long shot. He doesn't look anything like the youths she has identified online. He isn't losing his trousers, isn't concealing his identity with a cap, and looks quite pleased to be here.

'Thank you,' she says, realising she has been holding onto the licence for a long time and handing it back. 'I wanted to explain . . . you see, it used to look very different. In its day.'

He looks around. 'I can see how it must have been. It's an amazing place.'

'It's been overgrown for some time now, unfortunately.'

If he wonders why she hasn't donned her wellingtons and attacked the advancing jungle herself, he doesn't say. Looking past him, she can see the grass looks even more wild and untamed than it does when viewed through the window. She can smell the dry earth and taste the fresh air. It would be nice to be out there.

'Shall I get started? Is the mower in the outhouse?' he says.

'Yes, and some cans of petrol,' she replies.

'Hopefully, the weather won't change suddenly.' He flips his head back and looks up to the sky, reminding her of someone shucking an oyster. 'The lawns'll be really tricky to mow if it throws it down.'

'Yes, you're right.' Pearl finds herself nodding in agreement, acutely aware of the moor's wildly unpredictable microclimate. The tendency for the weather to change when you least expect it is legendary. A downpour out of nowhere on a summer's day, or a mist that can appear as quick as you like, cloaking the tops of the tors and causing serious problems for an inexperienced hiker seeking to climb to the summit. The previous week, there had been heavy rain sandwiched between days of wall-to-wall sunshine. The heavens opened and swollen drops of water burst onto the broken path. If she had walked the lawns, as impossible as that would be, her moccasins would have been soaked right through and, without doubt, turned the colour of chopped liver.

When she looks back at her young visitor, he is still standing, looking up to the sky, with his left hand shielding his eyes, as if to make absolutely sure the sun won't disappear.

'The outhouse is unlocked,' she guides him. 'And there's some leather gardening gloves in there, I believe.' Pearl takes in his fragile-looking arms, thinking of the vicious brambles lying in wait for him.

'Then I think that's everything I need.' He hesitates for a moment. 'I just wanted to say a big thanks for giving me the job.'

For a moment, she is stumped for an answer. For forty-three years she hasn't been much use to anyone or anything, unless you count the crows, and do they show any appreciation? Not a chance. She should really explain. But where to start. 'With regard to the garden . . .'

For a moment, her unspoken secret hovers hesitantly between them like a beautiful dragonfly enjoying the still-ness. But unfortunately, the words don't come. 'I should let you get on.'

'In a bit,' he says.

'Yes, of course . . . in a bit,' Pearl replies automatically, realising she's never said such a phrase before and has no idea of its connotations. To be straying so wildly from the vocal norm feels disorientating and quite exhilarating all at the same time.

As he walks away, each long leg covering what seems to her like a great distance, Pearl closes the door and listens for the sound of the mower, rumbling over the path on its cobweb-covered wheels.

Through the French doors leading from the kitchen to the back garden, the ones Ray had installed when they first arrived because he said it would *bring the outside in*, she watches as Connor pulls hard on the cord with his insubstantial arm, forcing the old machine to galvanise itself reluctantly into life. Antiquated equipment started, he moves slowly and surely up and down the lawns, his exposed forearms reddening perceptibly in the sun. He works tirelessly, for one hour and then another. His mother has trained an able apprentice.

When the mowing stops, she watches from the kitchen as he takes a break. He eases his frame onto the freshly mown grass, his long, jeans-covered legs splaying in all directions, reminding her of a new-born giraffe. He stares out to the moor, body unmoving, eyes focused on a spot in the distance as if he's waiting for someone to appear. Melancholy descends on him in this moment when he thinks no one is watching. The sight is so moving she is almost encouraged to risk an early informality: to offer sunscreen for those bare arms, a glass of water with ice, or Ray's old Panama hat to protect his young face from the harsh rays. It is turning out to be a real scorcher.

But there had been a story on the news just this morning, one that reminded her all too readily about the dangers of the outside world and the people who live in it. Recollecting the details makes her pulse quicken. You can never be completely sure of a person's character. Why would she let herself forget that so readily? So, rather than offer Connor Matthews sunscreen and a glass of chilled water, Pearl leaves the French doors firmly locked, turns up the radio, and busies herself with the chores of the day.

1976

'Should we call the doctor?' Lana's words carried out of the front room and up the stairs to where Pearl was sitting at the top in her cotton nightdress. 'Ray, it's been two weeks and she's barely left her room.'

When Ray spoke, he already sounded tired. Defeated even. Not like himself at all.

'We must give her all the time she needs. That's all we can do. Things will change, I'm sure, when she is ready to try.'

Lana began to sob uncontrollably.

I wish I knew what to do. 'My poor Pearl. When I think of what happened that day . . . And now here we are.'

Hearing every word, Pearl pulled her knees up to her chin and hugged her own body for comfort. She named the terrible feeling The Fear. It haunted her and stopped her from going any further than the heavy oak front door. After what happened in Godalming, The Fear had followed her wherever she went like an evening shadow. There was no escaping it.

The next morning, Pearl woke up early. Guilt had swum inside her all night after she'd heard her mother and Ray talking.

It was still early when she opened the front door and forced herself to take a step. Outside, a slight breeze poked under the thin hem of her skirt and made itself felt around the neckline of her top. The road was perfectly still and quiet. The air held a hint of moisture, the possibility of rain and an end to the drought. Ahead there was nothing but green earth and grey clouds.

From the door the path led straight down to the gate, its surface cracked and moss-filled like she remembered it from the day of their arrival. Her fingers tingled with the sensation of pins and needles. Her head felt light. There was an overwhelming sense of doom. Blood rushed in her ears, and her heart thudded in her chest. The disorientating feelings multiplied until she knew, beyond any doubt, leaving the house had been a mistake – she'd been wrong even to consider stepping over the threshold, no matter how much she'd wanted to show her mother and Ray that she could, so that they wouldn't worry. Feeling her head becoming lighter than air, and fearing she might faint, Pearl quickly turned, rushed through the open oak door, and closed it firmly behind her.

Ray had woken early also and watched her from the hallway. This time, he telephoned the doctor without hesitation.

The advice that came back wasn't particularly medical in nature but echoed Ray's thoughts of the night before.

'I'm not surprised she is acting in this way from what you have told me,' the local GP advised. 'She is bound to display unusual behaviour considering what she has been through. Give it some time. Time is a great healer. That's what I would say for now and do contact me again if the situation doesn't improve.'

NATE

Four days later, at just gone three o'clock in the afternoon, Nate opens the door to his flat still wearing his pyjamas. Standing on the other side is Anila Patel, a twenty-six-year-old veterinary assistant who shares the flat next door with her boyfriend, Ryan, who works on the roads.

'Morning, Nate. Sorry to be the bearer of bad news,' Anila says, looking extremely apologetic. 'But they posted this in our pigeonhole downstairs by mistake. I recognised the TopQuote logo as soon as I saw it. Hard to miss it.'

Nate takes the envelope that she hands to him. 'It's good of you to bring it round, Anila. Thanks.'

'Bloody TopQuote, eh?' she sighs. 'Bastards, aren't they?'

Nate nods and opens the envelope, carefully separating the pages of the P45 inside. The document is exactly what he expects it to be, a final confirmation that he has nowhere to go each day and is, without doubt, unemployed. He stares at the piece of mail that has landed in his hands like a live grenade.

'I have got *some* good news, though,' Anila offers optimistically. He looks up at his neighbour's animated face and imagines this must be the way her expression lifts when returning a loved pet, fully repaired, back to its owner. 'Well, maybe not so much *news*,' she says, and Nate's heart sinks just a little. 'My bad. Maybe more like me asking you for a favour is closer to the truth.'

Nate thinks he should get dressed before making a verbal contract. 'Can you hold on a second?' he asks. 'I'll just get a dressing gown. I was having a . . . snooze.'

Anila doesn't question this. He knows she's too polite and too kind to raise the obvious point – that he really should be getting his life back on track rather than moping around his flat all day in his pyjamas watching TV. When Nate returns, fully clothed, she is still waiting patiently in the corridor.

'Sorry about that.'

In the small, open-plan lounge-kitchen-diner that mirrors her own next door, Anila takes a breath before beginning to explain the favour. 'You know the animal rescue centre, the one I've been volunteering at for the last few weeks?'

Nate nods. 'Yes, you mentioned it when I was collecting my post from the lobby last Wednesday.' He'd been wearing his pyjamas in the afternoon then too and had thought, incorrectly, he'd be able to make it to the wooden rack of post slots in the lobby and back again without being noticed.

'They're really short of volunteers right now,' Anila continues, seeming to spare his blushes and not to remember the incident clearly. 'There are too many rescues coming in and not enough staff to cope with the new intake. In short, they need more people. It would be just a few shifts a week . . . starting this weekend . . . if possible. I know it's short notice, Nate, but . . .' She stops talking and he tries to take it all in. 'They're really up against it . . . you know, as a charity. Someone's left because they need a paying job. Can't blame them really.'

Nate nods. 'Of course, it's completely understandable that they would.'

He sees the leaflet in Anila's hand with the words 'Happy Tails Rescue Centre' printed across the top. There's a portly brown Labrador on the front, so close to a tabby cat it looks like they've been Photoshopped into an unnatural position.

'And this has some information,' Anila says, gently handing over the flyer. 'It's all pictures really, and a map. But it gives you an idea,' she adds encouragingly. 'The photo came out a bit odd. Looks like the dog is sitting on top of the cat, if you look at it long enough.'

Nate holds the leaflet in his hand.

'I always wanted a dog as a child,' he says without thinking, the photograph triggering a memory from decades ago. In fact, he'd wanted nothing more.

'That's good then. So, it might be something you would consider?' Anila asks. 'Only I've got my name on the rota for Saturdays, but I was thinking I could show you the ropes tomorrow evening as soon as I've finished at work. Give you a chance to meet the team before starting properly at the weekend?'

Nate feels a twinge of shame about how he has been spending his time. In the days since leaving TopQuote he's barely moved from the sofa, but Anila has been working full-time at the vet's and is now giving up what little spare time she has left to work at the rescue centre as well.

'What time would be best?'

'About five-thirty? I can introduce you to everyone,' Anila says, looking enormously relieved. 'Full disclosure. I should probably say, there are some not-so-great aspects to the job, like clearing up poo and walking dogs in the rain. I wasn't going to mention those at the beginning in case they put you off.'

'Anything other than daytime TV on a loop is a blessing,' Nate replies, feeling an unexpected pinball of exhilaration rocketing around his insides at the thought of joining the outside world all the while wearing proper clothes. He's positive Anila could have mentioned a whole list of dirty disadvantages to the job, from the mundane to the extreme, and not one of them could come close to putting him off.

PEARL

The view from the French doors the next morning is noticeably different from the day before. Connor Matthews is bringing the garden at Highview back to life. The beds of delicate pink roses edging the patio are cleared of the cloying brambles and the soil at their roots dug over to the consistency of a well-baked crumble. The lawns circling the house have all been mowed and the fence repaired where it had been tumbling down.

Pearl watches as he lifts a pile of grass cuttings from the lawn into a wheelbarrow, submerged in a world of his own. It reminds her of the way she is sometimes, so deeply lost in thought there could be a brass band marching past, or an air raid going on overhead, and she'd be completely unaware. Some memories are so hard to forget. Some thoughts are so insistent that they are impossible to ignore.

Crossing to the kitchen cupboard, she removes a baking tin and lifts out the fruits of her early-morning labours. Unable to sleep, she had risen before five, catching her reflection in the bedroom mirror above the dressing table – her short frame covered in a flowing white nightdress reaching down to the floor, she had swept around the kitchen like a ghost. With the radio playing quietly, she mixed butter and sugar, sifted flour and added in eggs to the mixture in her bowl. When the cake had baked and cooled, she had made vanilla buttercream and fetched jam from the larder to layer just the right amount of both between the two halves of light sponge. All that remains now is for the cake to be eaten.

When Connor has finished piling grass into the wheelbarrow, she crosses to the French doors. It is just a single turn of the key that opens them.

He looks up from the cuttings.

'Could I offer you something to eat?'

'I'm all right, thanks, Miss Wintermiss.'

'Yes. About that . . .'

He fixes his attention on her face as if she's about to make an important announcement.

'It's just Winter, I'm afraid. Not a *miss* on the end. Just at the beginning. So, in short, just Winter. Miss. I wanted to be honest about that.' Pearl realises she is tying herself in knots. In trying to explain, she has only made it more complicated. He looks at her and she wonders what he might be thinking.

'OK,' he says. 'Got it.'

'Would you like to come in?'

'Erm . . .no thanks.'

From her position inside, Pearl senses a reticence she hasn't anticipated, as if he may be more worried about coming into her home than she is about accepting him into it.

'I should probably get on,' he says, looking around at the brambles on the ground, and the roses in their beds, before turning back. 'I can see you're busy . . .' Pearl realises he is taking in her light blue cleaning tabard with a small stain of Brasso on the front. She resists the urge to explain that she isn't busy and, in fact, couldn't say that she has been since 1976.

'I've baked.'

He looks at her without speaking.

'And it will go to waste if we don't eat it.' Pearl realises she is sounding desperate now. It reminds her of the first time she talked to the crows, so eager for their company as she was. 'It's Victoria sponge,' she adds, the knowledge that she has not offered him food or water before weighing heavily on her. How the tables have turned. He looks more worried than she is. Just a boy. She can see the tiredness in his eyes and the extent of the sunburn on his arms. The sadness is there too, lingering still. She wonders if it ever leaves him. 'I made the cake this morning . . . especially for you to eat it.' Pearl wonders if this might be a little too much honesty.

But at this, his face unexpectedly breaks into his wide smile. 'Did you say cake?'

'I did,' she says, hopefully. 'You can have more than one slice if you like. I used my extra-large tins.'

'OK, then. Awesome.'

'I'll get some plates.'

When he comes in, he slips off his grass-speckled trainers and leaves them neatly at the door. Any lingering concern she has about his presence in the garden or kitchen is dissipating by the second. Connor Matthews is no threat to anyone or anything it would seem. Unless you are a bramble or an overgrown lawn.

He eats three pieces, dispersing tiny, sugary crumbs onto the kitchen table between mouthfuls as he goes.

'That was so good,' he says, finishing and sweeping a pile of golden crumbs into the palm of his hand and then back onto his plate. 'Proper tasty.'

In contrast, Pearl realises, she hasn't touched a forkful of the piece on her own plate.

'Some water?'

As she pours them a glass from the jug filled and ready, she sees an unexpected visitor alight haphazardly on the patio like a poorly trained fighter pilot, his black feathers ruffled and his wrinkled feet stamping up and down.

'Do they just land on the patio like that all the time?' Connor asks.

Pearl nods. 'They've been here for as long as I can remember, and their parents and grandparents before them . . . they've really been my constant companions since my mother and her partner Ray passed away.'

'I'm sorry,' he says, quietly. 'About your mother and Ray.'

Pearl smiles, thinking only of the good times they'd shared at Highview. 'It was some time ago now. But I do miss them both very much.'

She watches as he studies the crow intently. They look more friendly close up,' he says. 'Where do they wait?'

'The trees beyond the lawn. You'll see them, waiting on the branches, watching for food to be put out. A boiled egg on the patio, monkey nuts on the grass. Sometimes I hear them talking. They like to do that often.' Reaching forward for her glass, she says, 'I realise that probably makes me sound strange.'

'Not really, I mean, not at all, actually,' he corrects himself. 'I think it's quite cool.'

Pearl smiles. 'I'm not sure everyone would see it like that.'

'I'll look for them up in the trees when I'm doing the mowing,' he says.

'Do. They are extremely excited about the goings on in the garden now it's no longer impassable, and the mice don't have a place to hide. Now it looks like a proper garden again.'

Pearl recalls their telephone conversation, the woman who showed her son how to care for a lawn and grow flowers and vegetables.

'If Mrs Matthews would ever like to see where you are working, she'd be more than welcome.'

For a moment, there is nothing but quiet, save for the metronomic tick of the grandfather clock in the front room.

Connor pulls at an imaginary thread on his T-shirt before he says, 'That's not going to be possible.' He looks suddenly lost in another world just like he did earlier when he was sitting on the lawn. 'I wish it was, but it's not.'

CONNOR

He drives across the moor to the church of St Stephen. After their conversation, he'd been upset, and Pearl had encouraged him to leave early and take some time to himself.

'Don't worry. The gardening can wait,' she had said. 'There is no rush.'

Not all employers in the past had been as understanding. Last year he had worked at the restaurant called L'Epoque in town, the one with the fiercely protected five-star TripAdvisor reviews and a head chef who promised to drag any member of staff out of bed if they didn't turn up for their shift, no matter what the reason. It had been a long summer.

After arriving and parking his car alongside, he walks under the steepled porch, through the gate and past gravestones weathered with age; their inscriptions are worn and dusted with lichen, the mustard-yellow stamp that confirms just how long Dorothy Hubert, Albert Collins and William Stevens have lain here. *God Rest Their Souls*.

Today, the graveyard is quiet. At the weekend it's busier. When there are weddings and christenings even more so: friends and families taking photographs under the gate, happy memories being captured on mobile phones, and when the weather changes unexpectedly, beaming brides shielded from the rain by a dozen umbrellas shooting into the sky like popping Champagne corks, or protective parents at christenings holding a hand over their baby's head to avoid it getting wet for the second time in one day. And the procession after a funeral, when mourners leave the church, all dressed in black, their arms linked or hands reaching out and being grasped tightly by another's, before heading to the pub at the bottom of the hill, to toast the life of someone dear to them but now departed. On those days, the church is full of people and sounds. But today it is still and peaceful.

Connor walks on to the back of the graveyard, to where a row of three new headstones form a line in front of a bench. A horse chestnut hangs its branches over from the field behind, providing a welcome canopy of shade. Underneath it, he takes the opportunity to sit down and rest his legs.

These graves are untouched by the dilapidation of time and have more recent dates carved into their pristine surfaces. Baz, Jake, and Sarah.

Baz's headstone is a rectangle of ebony granite rising out of the ground. Since 2011, the loving husband, father and grandfather has remained in the thoughts of his wife Trudi, children Susan, David and Paul, and grandchildren Millie and Ben. Alongside is Jake's grave. His pure white marble stone doesn't have so many names engraved upon it, just those of Hannah and Tim, Mum and Dad. *Sleep tight, our beautiful boy.* A photograph of little Jake, his eyes wide and shining, lies on the ground, wrapped in Clingfilm to protect it from the sun and the rain. His baby face smiles brightly beneath the plastic. Wildflowers lie in bunches, their stems pulled together with strips of pale blue ribbon.

A new addition is a small teddy bear in the same light shade of blue, propped up against the headstone.

The final grave has a border of healing crystals around it. The mauve-coloured stones glisten in the bright afternoon sun. Connor remembers the freezing November day his mum bought them from a shop in Exeter that smelled of incense. 'These ones are for energy,' she said, as they drank coffee afterwards in a café with steamed-up windows that overlooked the cathedral. 'I've been so tired lately, I'm hoping they might help. What do you think?' He'd simply nodded, all the while doubting that a piece of coloured rock could make any real difference. He'd been bored and damp from the rain, sounding, he knew, just like any sixteen-year-old does: disinterested and a little moody. If he'd known then what would happen, he'd have listened, talked, made the most of every single second they had.

> *Sarah Matthews, 39*
> *Beloved Mother and Wife*
> *1978–2017*

He remembers he'd been worrying over his GCSE exams, the day he was called into the principal's office and told he needed to go straight home.

'Come in, Connor.' Mr Underwood had arranged for him to leave his lesson and greeted him at the door to his office. 'I've asked my secretary Gina to sit in with us. I hope you don't mind.'

He had no idea what the Head was talking about.

'We've had a call from your mother. She needs to speak to you. Gina is going to drive you back home.'

'What's happened?' He remembers at the time thinking he'd never been driven home from school by a staff member before.

'Your parents will explain.'

'It's OK, I'll get the bus as usual,' Connor said, feeling uncomfortable about sitting in a car with a woman he had barely said two words to in five years.

The principal paused and then said, 'Not today, Connor.'

Gina dropped him at the entrance to Fern Crescent. When she drove away, she didn't look back. Inside the house it was so echoey he thought nobody was home, but Sarah was sitting very still on the sofa, her face streaked with mascara. His father stood silently by the door. Connor listened to an explanation about specific tests and a scan.

He thought she said the word 'cancer'. It was hard to take it all in. Like a nightmare he couldn't wake up from.

'Months,' she said. 'Maybe weeks.'

He spent the night looking at information on the internet, and when he woke up, his stomach and head felt worse than when he had drunk ten cans of premium-strength lager in Derek's back garden on his birthday. He refused to get the bus to school, but she begged him to live his life as normally as he could.

'Please go in. Let's try and carry on as we were. For now.' Her eyes were red and puffy, and her voice croaky as if she had a bad cold. 'For as long as we can.'

For the first time in his life, he wished for a miracle, prayed to God to make his mum better; things he'd never needed to do before seemed more urgent than ever. He wanted to spend every second he could at home, not at school or travelling on the bus to and from it.

And all the while, his father behaved peculiarly, hardly saying a word.

On the last day of term, Connor stopped at the Co-op in Westdown and bought the most expensive and interestingly flavoured ice creams he could afford with his money from the restaurant. Ones that might encourage her disappearing appetite. Salted Caramel, Honeycomb Crunch, and Belgian Chocolate Brownie.

They sat on the sofa, just the two of them, watched films, talked, and often, because they couldn't help it, cried. Some days he felt raw from emotion as if he'd lived a million years in just a few weeks. He only went out to the supermarket for fresh supplies of Salted Caramel, Honeycomb Crunch and Belgian Chocolate Brownie. The feeling of helplessness grew; she was losing the fight to live, and he knew there was nothing he could do.

Sarah Matthews died on 10 July. It was a Monday.

Alone in the churchyard, he tells her his latest news.

'I started a job, gardening. It's working up on the moor. It's better pay than the restaurant. I get to be outside and save up some money.'

A gentle breeze rustles the leaves of the horse chestnut tree. For a moment, he thinks he hears her reply, but it is a woman talking on her phone as she walks past the church. He used to hear her voice often, after the funeral. She stayed with him, just for a while. In the car, at college, on the bus, at Fern Crescent. He heard her. But not anymore.

Connor closes his eyes and tries to remember a time from the past. A family barbecue in the garden, the tantalising smell of burgers cooking, his father in a chef's hat smiling at his mum, and the sun sitting high above them in a Savlon-blue sky. A happy family. Determined to keep only the best memories alive, he lets the image play over and over in his mind like a film on repeat.

NATE

'Ready?'

'Completely.'

'Thanks for this, Nate. Honestly, don't be put off by what I said about poo and pee because weirdly you do get used to it.'

In the reception area of Happy Tails Rescue Centre, Anila introduces him to Wayne, a stocky, square-jawed man in his early forties with jet-black hair, a manly beard, and a strong handshake. Wayne, Nate soon learns, as well as being a former soldier with years of service also has an encyclopaedic knowledge of reptiles. 'Comes in handy,' he says, 'when we get geckos or bearded dragons in. It happens most just after Christmas. We had a fully grown iguana once. Someone put it in a wheelie bin and just left it there.' Wayne looks like he might want to seriously harm the person who put the iguana in the bin.

After Wayne, Nate is introduced to Katie, a mum of three who is recovering from postnatal depression. She confides in him that Happy Tails has been a lifesaver for her. 'If it weren't for this place, I don't know what I would have done,' she says, her smile grateful and genuine. 'It's good to have a focus when times are tough.'

Nate assures Katie he knows exactly what she means.

'And then that's Claire,' Anila says, pointing out to the car park in the direction of an athletic-looking young woman he estimates to be in her early thirties. The woman's arms are covered in bright, colourful tattoos and her short cap of hair is the colour of Parma Violets. Claire is walking away from a powerful-looking motorbike, the sort Nate imagines might be difficult to hold up when stationary at a set of traffic lights. 'Just so you know,' Anila says, 'she is a force of nature, no joke. Not that I want to worry you.'

Nate nods. 'I'm not worried.'

When she joins them, Anila conveniently makes her excuses about having to check the gate to the exercise yard is closed properly, before mouthing the words 'Good luck' when Claire isn't looking and leaving them to it.

While Katie and Wayne busy themselves with paper-work, Claire asks, 'Nate, is it?'

'Yes.'

'I heard you were joining us.'

She looks at him closely like someone examining a par-ticularly unusual fossil. 'So, exactly how old are you?'

'Sixty,' Nate replies. 'Sixty-one this year . . . if I am being exact.'

One eyebrow shoots up into the rainbow of stars tat-tooed above her left eye. 'Wow.'

Nate can't tell if she's impressed or dismayed.

'That's old.'

'It's all relative,' he says.

Claire is unfazed.

'Married?'

'Once.'

'So, now, what's your situation . . . Remarried? Single? Girlfriend or boyfriend?'

'Neither . . . of either kind,' Nate says, feeling like someone on one of the quiz shows he's seen too many of lately.

'Are you sure? It's important. I like to know everything about anyone who joins us.'

Claire is wasted at Happy Tails, Nate decides. She should be working for MI5 or interrogating wealthy pop stars about their tax returns.

Claire doesn't lose eye contact with him once. It's an admirable skill.

'Me,' she says, clarifying her position for his benefit, 'I like women . . . and some men. Only a few of them, though.'

Nate nods in agreement. 'I'm not a huge fan of all of them myself to be honest . . .'

To his surprise, Claire's lips lift at the corners just slightly. She looks very different when she does this. He wants to tell her this but isn't sure how she'll take it.

'You're funny,' she says, without a hint of sarcasm. 'Ha-ha funny, not funny weird. Which is good. Funny weird would be a problem.'

'I think so too,' Nate agrees.

'We should get started on the pens,' Claire instructs, as if she's shared too much. 'Grab that bucket and mop from over there. The hose is round the corner. Begin at the first pen in the block.'

'Right.' Nate does as he's told, believing you'd have to be very brave or very stupid to disagree with a woman who looks like she might wrestle bears for a pastime.

At the first run, he stops and looks through the wire mesh of the nearest enclosure and sees two pairs of hard-as-marbles brown eyes. Attached to the two sets of eyes are two stocky bodies and some dangerous-looking teeth. Unable to miss each occupant's impressive jawline, enough to rival even Wayne's square profile complete with chin dimple, Nate wonders how soon he will be required to take his life in his hands and enter their pen. Conveniently, one grinning resident stands under a sign saying 'Stan', and the other is equally close to another identifying him as 'Eric'. Like twins, it's difficult to tell them apart, except Stan does have uneven top teeth that stick out quite a way beyond his bottom set, giving him the look of a dog trying to imper-sonate a horse.

'He was kicked in the head by his owner on the daily,' Claire explains, appearing behind him holding the mop and bucket and making Nate feel like he's somehow been slacking. 'It's left him looking like that,' she adds. 'He's one of our lifers. Gets passed over through no fault of his own. Can't be around other dogs, only Eric, and can't be left alone in the house 'cos he has separation anxiety,' she explains. 'Oh, and he's food possessive, not house trained, and he has medical needs. Arthritis, a sensitive stomach, weak bladder. Also, he farts, dribbles and can be unpredict-able around new people.'

'Sounds like someone I used to work with,' Nate smiles.

Claire has nothing to say to that.

Nate looks back at Stan, who gurns even more threaten-ingly from the other side of the fence.

'So, Nate, no time like the present . . . shall we?' Claire says, suddenly reaching forward and unlocking the gate to the pen, causing two tails to lash enthusiastically in unison. Eric and Stan steam towards her as she squats down on the pee-stained floor. Stepping in, Nate resists the urge to close his eyes. If he's going to be eaten alive it's probably better to know when it's going to happen.

'Come on,' Claire says, without any concern. 'Get properly in.'

She strokes Eric in a certain spot just behind the ear and he closes his eyes in ecstasy.

Nate realises his feet are still refusing to move, despite the instruction to do so from his brain.

'People get the wrong idea about Staffies,' Claire says, still matter-of-fact. 'Visitors go on looks and reputation and, as a result, don't think these two'll make good family dogs when they're actually ideal. If you don't mind the farting. Lots of our dogs have problems. You've got to be willing to put in some effort.'

Nate looks at Stan, who still seems to be staring at him with the same look he imagines a gladiator reserves for their next victim.

'Dogs give you unconditional love,' Claire says, reaching out to Eric. 'No matter what.'

She pulls the dog close, and he acquiesces like a limp ragdoll. He opens a lazy eye to check on her and she buries her face in his short fur.

Nate watches them both, and wonders who is really rescuing who, before taking the plunge and moving further into the pen.

When Stan approaches with all the swagger of a John Wayne impersonator, he follows Claire's lead and strokes him behind the ear until the Staffie's eyes close, and he appears to be in a state of unabashed bliss. Soon, Nate's new friend has rolled over on the concrete floor, with two feet sticking straight up in the air and his tongue lolling out of one side of his mouth.

'You've got the knack!' Claire tells him, looking impressed. 'You're better at this than I thought you were going to be. Did I mention it's bloody hard work and you don't get any pay?'

Nate nods. ' 'I can see the charity needs all the money it can get to keep Happy Tails going.' It can't be easy, he thinks, looking around at all the items that have been donated – bowls, brooms, and he'd seen some bags of food being dropped off from a local company earlier.

Claire gets up, dusts herself down and takes a moment before speaking. 'I think you're going to fit in just fine, Nate,' she says. 'More than fine, in fact.'

Two hours later, he checks each pen a final time, now clean and full of contented residents. The yard is swept, water bowls refilled and evening meals served.

Eric and Stan are already enjoying their fresh-smelling living quarters after a spin around the exercise field, and Nate has made the acquaintance of nine other canine residents: six ex-racing greyhounds flown in from Ireland, a hyperactive collie called Bruce, a timid beagle called Lucy and, finally, an emaciated poodle with unsalvageable, matted fur who had been rescued from one of the most affluent postcodes in Godalming.

'You can never tell,' Wayne says, his jaw clenching and unclenching rhythmically. 'Sometimes the animals just get picked up on the street and sometimes they come from places you wouldn't immediately think of.'

Nate has a feeling his colleague is a man who has seen much of humanity's dark side and isn't easily moved to tears, unlike Katie who has had to collect a handy pack of tissues from her bag in the staffroom. 'Two cars on the driveway and three foreign holidays a year but they couldn't whizz the poor fella down the groomer's,' she says, before blowing her nose like a trumpet. 'People like that should never be allowed to own a pet in the first place.'

The poor animal is now pink and bald but when Nate passes his pen, the latest resident looks as if he is enjoying his first peaceful rest in years, his tired eyes closed in relief.

In the car park, Anila catches him up.

''Claire likes you, which is kind of a miracle. Everyone's a bit surprised,' she says, with the air of someone meeting a snake whisperer for the first time. Behind them lights are being switched off and there is the sound of an alarm being set.

'Thing is,' Anila adds. 'Katie said Claire doesn't usually take to many people. Not straight off anyway. I've been keeping my distance for that very reason.'

Nate looks back at the centre. 'I think she might just be a little misunderstood.'

Anila nods. 'If it weren't for the three of them there wouldn't be a rescue centre.'

When she stifles a yawn, he says, 'Shall I follow you back?'

Anila nods, 'Sure. I'm so tired.'

They drive home in a short convoy of two cars. At Weatherley Gardens they say a weary goodnight before disappearing through their own front doors.

In flat nine, Nate makes a cup of tea he doesn't drink before lying on the sofa, fully clothed. Tiredness envelops him instantly, a pleasant sensation, making each arm and leg feel weightless, and forcing his eyelids to close like shutters against the advancing night.

PEARL

On his next visit, there is no cajoling required to get Connor to step over the threshold, slip off his grass-stained trainers and make himself at home. He washes his hands at the sink and enthusiastically tucks into a slice of chocolate and vanilla marble cake.

'You should so be on *Bake Off*, Pearl,' he says, between mouthfuls. 'You'd win easily, hands down.'

She decides to type 'Bake Off' into the search bar of the computer at the earliest opportunity, intrigued by the title and the fact that it sounds like a race.

'I'm glad you like it. I will make another at the weekend, so that it's ready for us to have on Monday.'

'Oh, no. You don't have to,' he says, shaking his head. 'I don't want to put you out.'

'It's no bother. None whatsoever.'

'OK, then. That'd be great. Thanks.'

'I'm so sorry, again, about your mother.' Pearl thinks back to their last conversation. It would be more than remiss not to mention it. 'It must have been extremely hard for you . . . and when you were only sixteen.'

'I had Molly and Derek. I was lucky.'

'Friends . . . from the *new estate*?'

'Kind of,' he smiles. 'They live in Westdown. Derek lives with his mum, dad, brothers, and sister, and Molly lives with her mum. She's got a son,' he adds. 'And I've known Derek and Molly since the first day at primary. All my life, that's what it feels like. We've always been there for each other, no matter what.'

Pearl contemplates the concept of close friendship. Forty-three years without it feels like an eternity.

'You'll miss them when you leave. I remember you saying you'll be going to university at the end of the summer?'

He shifts in his chair like he's trying to polish it with the seat of his trousers. 'I don't really want to go. It's a problem but I'm not really dealing with it.'

'I see.'

Pearl thinks about offering a cup of tea. It might help. She's always found a cup to have restorative properties in times of need. But then it might be best just to listen.

'If there was another way, I would stay,' he confides. 'If I could, I wouldn't leave at all, not like this.'

'Is it beyond your control?'

'Hmm. Mmm,' he says, keeping his eyes fixed on a point somewhere in the distance, beyond the stone wall, the great oaks and the crows watching from the convenient boughs.

'What would you do?'

'If I could, I'd work outdoors. Landscaping and gardening.'

'You know what you want to do.'

'I really don't mind, just as long as I'm outside. And I'd stay in Westdown too.'

'Near Molly and Derek?'

He nods.

'But you can't . . . stay?'

He shakes his head. 'I don't think so.'

Pearl waits. Still listening.

'Dad has a new partner,' he says. 'There's a lot of changes going on at the house. It's not the same. And I'm not sure there's a place for me there if I'm honest. Not anymore.'

***

In the afternoon, the sun rises high in the sky, and Pearl collects her cleaning tidy from the pantry and begins her timetable of chores for the day several hours later than usual. Outside, Connor is busy sweeping the cut brambles into a huge pile on the patio, ready for burning in a bonfire. His presence is a welcome distraction from the timetable of chores designed to anchor the day, else, she is sure, it will run away from her. For years, with so little to do, it had seemed as if the walls were closing in. But slowly, she discovered a way to live within the confines of the house. Routine, she soon learned, is everything; everything is routine. Without it she's not sure what her life would be like. In place of a job and a family to care for, there is cleaning (on Mondays, Wednesdays, and at the weekend on a Saturday), walking up and down the stairs (a bubbly woman from Benfleet who did an interview on Radio 4 called it 'stair aerobics'), feeding the crows (boiled eggs and a handful of monkey nuts), listening to the radio, watching an hour of television in the evening, and her favourite pastime of all, reading. In addition, there are always the sunsets to watch from the kitchen window (sometimes for hours), ordering food supplies online (also on a Saturday), and Travel Tuesdays, the day of the week reserved for visiting unseen corners of the globe via the stand-alone computer, seeing the highest of glacial mountains, the driest of yellow deserts, and the deepest of blue oceans. Many a captivating hour has been spent discovering fascinating new places, from the comfort of the spare room and without boarding a single aircraft, train, or bus. With just the press of a button, Pearl had discovered, it is possible to spin through the sun-bleached streets of Valletta, and float high over the Amazon rainforest. Travel Tuesdays make for an exciting addition to an otherwise pedestrian week. A day that makes it easier to forget that she cannot walk further than her own front door.

CONNOR

At the window of Matthews Solicitors on the way home, he uses both hands to block out the glare of the sun, and moves as close as possible to the glass. Inside, his father is deep in conversation with a woman who has brought four bags of shopping and two small children with her. They run around the office, while the woman nods and appears to be trying to take in everything that is being said. On the drive over, he'd hoped there might be an opportunity to speak to his father too, but a conversation will have to wait. Again.

Across the road, just inside the automatic doors of the Co-op, he sees Derek, busy marking down bunches of chrysanthemums wilted by the heat.

'All right, Derek?'

'Connor! It's good to see you. How's the job?'

Derek's welcome is as cheery as always; it's the Clayton way, just like Derek's mum Annie and his father Michael, Aaron and Cain, the six-year-old twins, and Derek's sister, Amber. They'd always treated him like one of the family, and even more so in the last two years since the loss of his mum.

On the first day of primary school, he had been struck by the old-fashioned first name of the red-haired boy sitting next to him, whose ambition was to be manager of the local Co-op. In a room full of Callums, Aarons and Joshes, Derek had stood out more than most, especially when the teacher read out the register. It earned him nicknames like 'granddad' and 'old man', but Derek took it all in his relaxed stride. He explained to Connor without any hint of regret that he'd been named after a popular grandfather on his mother's side and had happily learned to live with the consequences ever since. Thirteen years later, Derek applied for a Trainee Deputy Manager job at the local Co-op, and no one was more surprised than the manager when a fresh-faced eighteen-year-old arrived clutching his CV.

'We were expecting somebody older,' the store manager at the time said. 'And with considerably less hair.'

Derek had brushed the comment off with a practised flick of his fiery red fringe. He was used to being mistaken for someone more likely to hold a bus pass than a student railcard and, thanks to a maturity surpassing his years, aced the interview with flying colours.

'It's all good,' Connor says, bringing his focus back to Derek's question. 'The job's better than good, actually. The garden just needs some work to get it back to how it was before . . .' He stops, realising he never really asked why it had become so overgrown in the first place.'

'So, nothing unusual?' Derek raises an inquisitive red eyebrow and lifts his pricing gun into the air before bringing it down on a bunch of lifeless freesias suffocated in cellophane. 'No mantraps, rabid Alsatians, or house cows?' he continues. 'A place all the way up on the moor, in the middle of nowhere like that . . . I thought there'd at least be something under the shed. You know, like a high-tech secret spy bunker or a forgotten underground shelter that nobody's been down to in years. All high-tech and double-o-sevenish.'

'There's flower beds, lawns and trees,' Connor replies. 'That's more or less it.'

Derek is prevented from engaging further in his favourite subject of conspiracy theories by the interruption of the automatic doors whooshing open. They usher in a Gulf Stream of warm air and a girl with hauntingly dark eyes and long ebony legs. She wears white shorts, equally white trainers, and a cropped yellow hoody that comes down as far as her belly button. Balanced expertly on the girl's hip is a robust, eighteen-month-old baby boy, with a balled fist pushed permanently into his mouth. He has a patch of black curls on top of his head, and her dark Afro is swept up on all sides into an artfully balanced bun secured in place by a multi-coloured wrap. Connor catches his breath.

'All right, Con . . . Derek?' she says, with an easy smile; the sort of get-out-of-jail-free dazzler that had once saved them from having to spend a night in the cells for breach of the peace. They'd been singing in the High Street at three in the morning. There had been cider involved. It wouldn't have been so bad, but Derek had also been wearing a traffic cone on his head. Molly's secret weapon had worked like magic. It didn't surprise him when it did. When she smiled the world seemed a better place.

'So, what are you two up to?' she says. 'Spill.'

'Nothing much,' he replies instantly, wishing a wittier, cleverer, more astounding answer had come to his mind in the moment. 'How about you?'

'Getting some stuff for Tommy, then home. You know what it's like. What am I gonna do?' she says, her eyes twinkling under the Co-op's blinding strip lights. 'It's not like I can flag an Uber and take us both shopping for designer clothes. This is Westdown. Eh, Tommy?'

At the mention of his name, Tommy stretches his uncovered toes in Connor's direction with all the poise of a Royal Ballet School professional.

'What are you doing with those?' Connor reaches out and gives them a tickle, earning him the reward of a rumbling gurgle and a thin stream of milky saliva.

Molly catches it expertly with a long, peach, pearlescent fingernail. 'He's teething real bad,' she says, and then, 'I'm just gonna grab some Bonjela, and a couple of other things, and when I get back, Con, I want to hear all about that new job. Full details. Don't leave anything out. To us unemployed, it's a brilliant ray of hope that one day we too might find work of our own, you know, temporary or otherwise.'

Connor watches her walk away down the aisle, while Derek adds a markdown sticker to a packet of Soreen that has somehow found its way onto the shelf next to the fresh flowers.

Over the milk and yoghurt aisle, Molly's voice reaches them still. *Cheese! Semi-skimmed!* The pitch rises at the end of each word, so that even her sing-song identification of a pint of milk sounds exciting. *Marge and Petit-Filous!* Connor knows this is all for Tommy's benefit, to make him feel safe and loved in the absence of a father – Molly's a good mother, despite the looks she gets. She hadn't had the easiest of times, getting pregnant at school, being dumped by Tommy's father next to the war memorial in the centre of town in front of everyone, and having to deal with the fallout as a result. For Connor's part, he thinks she's nothing short of amazing.

'Right, that's all I need. So, let's hear it. I want details.' Molly appears back at the end of the aisle and is walking towards him, all six-foot-one-inch of her moving with style and grace, despite being weighed down by a toddler on one hip and a basket of shopping in her only free hand. 'And like I said, don't miss bits out.'

He realises the expression on his face is best described as goofy. He does his best to alter it to one closer to cool, just as the store manager appears, eyes fixed like a torpedo on Derek and the inactive pricing gun in his hand. 'Clayton! Tills!'

Derek sighs in response, placing his markdown weapon next to the dead flowers. 'Laters.'

And as he heads off towards the customer service desk, Connor tries to sound sophisticated, as he asks, 'So, where shall I begin?'

'At the beginning,' she says, smiling and shifting Tommy back into a more convenient position on her side. 'I'll get Derek to scan these, then you can tell me all about it.'

NATE

At the end of the day, Wayne is nursing a baby gecko in the staffroom. It's no bigger than his little finger. While he coos over the reptile, Katie is making tea. The smell of it reminds Nate of compost.

'Nate, I've made you a coffee,' she says.

He takes it, feeling grateful she hasn't automatically made him a camomile. It's been another busy day at Happy Tails, and he doesn't want to risk falling asleep at the wheel on the way home. A fresh supply of caffeine is most welcome. There is still an ache in his bones, but each day it lessens as he gets used to a new physical role.

Outside, the pens are washed and cleaned, dinner has been served, and the residents of the rescue centre are settling down for the evening. Even Eric and Stan have been cajoled to sleep with an ear rub.

The heat of the day has begun to subside, and it's almost time for him to leave.

'Thanks for stepping in,' Katie says, fishing around in her not-so-secret chocolate drawer for a KitKat and finding it completely empty apart from a tell-tale wrapper. 'We'd have been down to just Wayne and me today otherwise. Claire's been on fourteen days straight. She needed a day off. We should have five on, but there you go. It's hard to get people to work, especially when there's no pay at the end of the month.'

'I'm happy to help,' he says. 'Anytime you need me, just let me know. I don't mind doing more shifts if you're short-staffed.'

He stops short of telling Katie it's lonely on his own in the flat, and how much helping out at Happy Tails means to him. How it's opened his eyes to a new way of working, and proved he still has something to offer an employer. Still a useful member of society.

'I do need someone on Sunday. And a few days next week,' Katie says. 'Would that be OK?'

'No problem.'

'You're a lifesaver.' Katie says, letting out a relieved sigh. 'Oh, and any chance you could drop this in to Anila when you get home?'

She hands over a new Happy Tails polo shirt still in its plastic wrapper. 'Anila's spare one got chewed up in the tumble dryer.'

Nate takes it in both hands. The packaging makes it slippery to hold. 'I'll drop it round when I get back home.'

At the gate, Wayne does the honours with the heavy-duty padlock and a key from a large bunch. He rattles both sides of the gate to make sure they are locked securely before they all leave.

'Thanks again, Nate,' Katie shouts as she heads off to her car. 'Much appreciated.'

'See you tomorrow,' Wayne says. 'Have a good evening.'

Nate is behind Katie and Wayne in getting into his car. If it is a race to leave, he is last. Before he goes, he stands looking at the homemade sign and collection of old timber buildings behind the equally aged wire fence that makes up Happy Tails Rescue Centre.

It's difficult for a charity with dwindling financial support, that much is clear. He hopes the shelter won't have to close due to staff shortages. With the increasing numbers of residents, he can foresee that day might come. But it'll be over Claire's dead body, Katie's and Wayne's too, he's sure. All their hearts are here. And it's easy, Nate realises, to see why.

★★★

At Weatherley Gardens, he knocks on Anila's door. She answers wearing a long-sleeved grey top that reaches down as far as her hips and knuckles, and baggy tracksuit bottoms.

'Oh, hi, Nate, come on in,' she says. 'You look battered,' she adds. 'Busy day?'

He nods. 'Katie advertised some Dogue de Bordeaux puppies on the website, and the phones didn't stop ringing.'

Anila nods. 'It was crazy busy at the vet's today too. Must be something in the air!' she laughs, lightly. 'Summer madness.'

Nate smiles. Anila always puts on a friendly face no matter what sort of day she's had and however hectic it's been.

'Katie asked me to drop this off,' he says, handing over the polo shirt. 'She thought you might need it after your other one was eaten by the tumble dryer.'

Anila takes it. 'Ah, brilliant. I'd have to put my one surviving top in the washing machine after each shift otherwise, and I can't keep doing that. Do you know what I mean?'

Nate nods but doesn't say anything about how he washes his Happy Tails polo shirt by hand every night in the sink and then hangs it over the plastic tray spanning his bath, the one that usually has soap, a flannel, and his shaving kit on it.

Anila puts the packet on the floor and sinks down onto her small sofa.

'What a day! And in this heat too. I'm glad it's cooled down now,' she says, getting back up to push open the windows overlooking the street a little wider. Outside, there is the the usual commotion of the early-evening rush hour: horns sounding, buses and cars passing.

He takes a seat on the chair opposite and asks after Ryan. 'Football. There's a game on down the pub,' Anila explains. 'I said he should go without me. I fancied having a bath and just relaxing. That and a glass of wine,' she adds, reaching for her half-drunk glass on the low table beside the sofa. 'Can I get you one, Nate?'

'I won't,' he says, knowing a glass of wine will send him off to sleep in an instant. Instead, Anila makes him a strong cup of tea.

Still in his Happy Tails uniform, Nate listens to his neighbour recount stories about a couple whose Labrador puppy swallowed ten pieces of their son's Lego, and a woman who brought a seagull into the vet's in a cardboard box. 'She said it had a broken wing, but it flew right out when we opened the lid!' Anila says. 'All around the consulting room. Nearly gave the vet a bloody heart attack!'

'Did you catch it?'

'Just about. I managed to get a hold and wrap him in a towel. He calmed down after that – just his head poking out, the odd squawk. They're bigger than you think, seagulls.'

Nate thinks of the birds he has seen at the beach, wings spread wide, crying plaintively into the sky overhead.

'It must have been far from home?'

'Right,' Anila says. 'I've no idea where she found him. I'm not even sure if it was a him to be honest. Nobody checked. Not sure how you do with a seagull. And we were too busy trying to get him back in the box.'

When she has finished describing her day, Nate tells her about an elderly couple who visited the centre to rehome a dog.

'They're going to take Lucy the beagle. The husband has dementia,' he explains. 'The woman looked so relieved. Their faces lit up when Lucy came trotting out to meet them.'

'That's a great match,' Anila says.

'The woman said it's their diamond anniversary in March,' he adds. 'They looked very happy.'

'I hope Ryan and I stay together that long.'

Nate recalls how the couple had turned to face at each other while they waited in reception for Lucy to be brought out, as if no words were needed between them. A lifetime of connection and the ability to know exactly what the other was thinking. A relationship of companionship and under-standing, based on the years they had shared together.

'And I'd love a dog of my own,' Anila says, reflectively. 'But I work such long hours. It wouldn't be fair.'

'It would be good company,' Nate finds himself saying, the idea having occurred to him several times since joining Happy Tails. 'Someone to come home to.'

Anila nods, a look on her face he can't decipher. 'Nate? I know I've said it before, but have you ever thought about, well . . . getting back out there? My aunty is single and always available. She has a car, a house . . . and all her own teeth. She's someone to come home to. And if not my aunty, there's the usual dating websites and apps . . .'

Nate thinks of his ex-wife and his failed marriage.

'I'm not sure I'd be all that good company.'

'That's not true! You're great company!' Anila is resolute. 'And you're not afraid to get massive spiders in the bath and fix my tap when it's on the blink. There's a lot to be said for that. In fact, a huge amount.'

'That's good of you to say, but I think after Jean—'

'She ran off with a man half her age, Nate. That wasn't down to you. That was Jean having some sort of weird mid-life crisis.'

'He was forty-three.' Nate feels he should make the point.

'Still totally unfair.'

'It's complicated like these things often are,' he says.

'But the way I see it, you marry for life,' Anila continues. 'Not until someone you like the look of better comes along.'

Nate nods. 'I hope I wasn't a bad husband for my part,' he adds. 'We just weren't right for each other. I don't think we ever were, unfortunately.'

Anila sighs, the determined look on her face showing that she will always believe in true love no matter what.

'She didn't deserve you. Plain and simple.'

'I think we grew apart. Or perhaps we never really grew together in the first place.'

Anila yawns and, after a moment of deep reflection, says, 'Am I a hopeless romantic, do you think, Nate?'

'Maybe just a romantic.'

Anila yawns again. 'I like that. Sounds better. That's what I'd do for a living if I didn't work with animals, you know? I'd set up a dating website and do it properly. Take the time to find the right person for every client.'

Momentarily, Nate thinks of the team at Happy Tails and how they all have a person they talk about; Claire has a girlfriend called Melissa, Wayne is married to a police officer called Trudi, and Katie's husband, who was the one who encouraged her to volunteer at Happy Tails in the first place, is a man called Sol.

'So, can I just check, is that a definite no to my mum's older sister?' Anila asks, rallying temporarily. 'Only I could give her a call right now? She's at Bingo but she'll pick up, I know she will.'

'I wouldn't want to interrupt her evening,' Nate says. And then, 'I should probably go and let you get some rest.'

Anila rubs her eyes, and nods. 'OK. I'll just finish my wine and then have an early night. I'll text Ryan and ask him not to make too much noise when he comes in,'

She waves him goodbye at the door, the long-sleeved top pulled over her arms flapping awkwardly like the seagull's injured wing.

Back in flat nine, there's time for Nate to reflect on how he could have said so much more to Anila, how he could have explained that, once, he had been fortunate enough to know the sort of love that changed his life completely and made him feel so incredibly lucky to have found it. He'd experienced it long before meeting Jean, but it had disappeared just like sand slipping through his fingers. It destroyed his heart. But he still has the memories of what it felt like to care so deeply for another that it's impossible not to think of them always, and should he ever tell anyone about it, Nate decides, in that moment and without any doubt, he will tell his good neighbour Anila.

PEARL

At the weekend, Pearl misses Connor's presence, the reassuring sound of the mower in the garden, their conversations in the kitchen over tea and cake.

Fastening the Velcro straps of her sky-blue tabard on both sides, she collects her cleaning tidy from the larder and climbs the stairs to the landing in her slippers. At the top, she makes her way to the room at the end.

The door is closed but when she opens it, she is greeted by the scent of lavender furniture polish. Each of the walls of the large room is lined with mahogany shelves, from floor to ceiling. Ray had done the work, converting it into a library for her to read, somewhere to pass the hours. Even the wall that has a window with a view out over the outhouse has shelving built on both sides and underneath and above the window frame, like a Virginia Creeper diverting its course to avoid the glass panes. Each shelf is full. Fact and fiction side by side. Novels and encyclopaedias. Books on Ancient Egypt alongside those of the Brontë sisters. Each section is divided by colour, ranging from bright red leather to a set of antique sand-coloured tomes, with midnight navy, maroon, and pine-green spines marking out the sections in between. There is one section devoted entirely to languages: French, Italian and Spanish. Over the years she has studied them all and become proficient in each. A way to pass the time.

In the centre, there is an olive-coloured velvet chair, its winged back patterned with studded buttons, and its legs curling into upturned feet on the wooden floor. Beside it sits a low table made of the same mahogany as the shelves, and on its shiny surface is a well-thumbed copy of her favourite novel, *Wuthering Heights*.

With duster in hand, Pearl takes her time gliding her cloth along each shelf, lovingly ensuring each section is restored to its original order, pushing back a thin book that is standing out too far. It is quiet, peaceful and warm. With the shelves gleaming in the sunlight that streams in through the window, Pearl makes a promise to herself that she will return later and close the door on the rest of the house, lose herself in a story for several blissful hours and read until it grows dark. But until then, there is work still to do.

Downstairs, the crows are waiting on the patio. They move awkwardly on land, Pearl has long ago observed, without any innate skill or grace. But they are able to mimic noises as well as a mynah bird and are as loyal as Labradors. While they gaze back at her through the open French doors, she can't help feeling they are too often misunderstood. Like Connor said, they are more amiable than people think. When she had opened these doors to the elements on the day her mother died and sat at the kitchen table weeping, she'd heard the cry echoed back to her. It was as if they felt her loss just as keenly. A 'murder of crows' hardly seems fair. They have proved to be such good companions to her, arriving each day on time and in a line of sorts, ready to receive the hard boiled eggs she throws to them on the patio, and the monkey nuts that follow shortly after.

Pearl walks into the front room and checks the time on the grandfather clock. A few minutes are left before the arrival of the grocery shopping, the simple provisions that will sustain her for the week and the extra ingredients needed to make more cakes. When she listens, there is the sound of heavy footsteps on the path. But through the kitchen window she sees it isn't the grocery-delivery driver arriving but the postman with his light, flowing hair tied in a ponytail, who wears shorts in all weathers, and solid-looking boots.

The post falls through the letterbox like a shoal of brightly coloured fish from a net: a shiny pamphlet from a company selling double-glazing, a leaflet for a garden centre with a 2-for-1 money-off coupon for coffees in a café she'll never visit. There's also a flyer for a new Zumba class in Westdown. The junk mail comes more days than not, together with bills to be paid and censuses to be filled in, items of post she cannot ignore. But sadly, nothing more. Not a letter she has waited for for forty-three years.

On the patio, the crows are waiting. Pearl opens the French doors wider and throws out a handful of monkey nuts from her position just inside the threshold.

'You silly old woman,' she says to herself while they eat. 'Stop waiting. A letter won't come. Too many years have passed for that now.'

1977

It was late autumn. Leaves of burnished gold hung from the oak trees like metal decorations, and the moor had fallen silent as if it were holding its breath.

With Ray in agreeance, Lana telephoned the doctor.

'It's been over a year,' she told the locum on duty. 'My daughter doesn't ever go outside.'

'I'll make sure someone comes out to Highview. We've been rushed off our feet.'

A day later, a young doctor arrived from Westdown. He told Ray and Lana there had been a bout of stomach flu in the town and two of the three resident doctors at the practice had gone down with it. He added that he had a growing backlog of patients to see on his rounds. He examined Pearl by looking in her ears and taking her temperature, before writing out a prescription.

'These will help with the nerves. She must take them morning and night.'

He spoke, Pearl noticed, as if she wasn't in the room.

Lana and Ray left the brown plastic bottle of tablets in the bathroom, and she took them as the label on the front instructed. They numbed her mind and caused her to wet the bed. She stripped the sheets each morning and washed them before Lana hung them out on the line to dry in the chilly air. After two weeks of feeling unlike herself and losing track of time, Pearl put the tablets in her drawer and closed it. The weeks that followed felt even more desperate than before.

There was so little to do in the house. Alone in her room, she curled up in a chair by the window, and prayed. First for courage to go outside and then for a letter from Nate. She looked out at the old black tin post box nailed to the fence. Every day Ray or Lana walked down and collected what there was of the mail. Every day she had waited and hoped for word from Nate. But still nothing had arrived. It didn't make any sense.

Pearl had telephoned his number in Godalming on the day they arrived at Highview. His mother, Mrs Williams, had answered and said he wasn't available to come to the phone. When Pearl asked if she could leave a message for him, Mrs Williams said she thought it was for the best that she didn't. *Not after what happened that summer. He is moving on and I think it's better under the circumstances if you leave him to do that.* Her words had stung like a slap across the face. *Don't call this number again.*

Pearl wept. Lana was furious and Ray paced up and down in the kitchen, his knuckles white with rage.

'She had no right!' he said, barely able to contain his anger. 'Doesn't she understand what happened? Bloody do-gooder!'

'I'm going to call her right back,' Lana said. But Ray was adamant.

'Don't give that woman the satisfaction.'

After the shock, Pearl felt a wave of extreme loss. It had been all that was keeping her going, the hope that Nate would write, telling her about his everyday experiences in Godalming, making her feel that life was normal even if it wasn't. Nate was a good person. It wasn't his fault that they had had to leave. The terrible day was not his doing. He wasn't to blame in any way. He loved her and had said so, holding her hand before she left, and promising her with all his heart that nothing would stop them from being together in the future. What had happened to change his mind so completely? Mrs Williams had told her not to ring again and been firm about that. Maybe Nate had moved on. But she couldn't think of a reason why.

'No good can come from stepping back into the past, Pearl.' Ray had been emphatic. 'That's clear. Mrs Williams has said enough.'

And Lana wholeheartedly agreed.

CONNOR

On Monday morning, the traffic in Westdown is held up by a coach from Germany stopping to let off passengers in the middle of the High Street. Slowing to a halt, Connor waits behind a Land Rover and a line of 4x4s towing caravans, all waiting to pass. Keen to distract his thoughts from an earlier discussion with Yvo about train tickets and leaving dates for York, he looks out of the window at the steady line of day-trippers exiting through the automatic coach doors. A group of six immediately break off and head for the Singing Kettle – a large black A-board is positioned just outside the café promising *The Best Cream Tea in the West*. Others stop first to look at the rotating stands of postcards outside the gift shop. Like all excursion groups, Connor knows, they will be on the clock, with a set amount of time to explore the tourist town and grab a coffee or an ice cream before they are sitting in their coach seats once again and travelling on to another destination.

Passengers delivered, the coach driver indicates, moves out and drives off, trailed by the line of cars and caravans, until he reaches the large pay and display car park at the bottom of the road where he turns in.

Shifting up a gear, Connor follows the Land Rover, passing the coach and heading out of town. The Land Rover chugs up the hill while two black-and-white collies eye him avidly from the back. When the Land Rover turns off, he passes it and carries straight on, over the cattle grid and onto the moor.

On the grass, in patches where the sun hasn't yet reached, there are diamond drops of glittering dew. Steam rises slowly from the ground. Ahead of him, on the verge, is a woman in shorts and a checked shirt, walking with her dog. She lifts her hand in a wave and smiles. Connor recognises her as a woman his mum used to know and waves back. On days like today, the locals walk early, before the holidaymakers get this far. In the winter, it is quiet by comparison, just the dog walkers like his mum's friend and the farmer rounding up his sheep for market.

Arriving at Highview, he sees the gate is hanging more lopsided than before on its one remaining hinge. On the first day he'd arrived, he'd worried about pushing on it too hard and ending up standing on Pearl's doorstep holding it apologetically in both hands. It needs fixing soon or the newly rescued garden will be invaded by sheep. He'll add it to the list of jobs he's forming in his mind which will later be transferred to a handy note on his phone.

Crossing the lawn and skirting the side of the house, he finds the French doors already open.

'Sorry I'm late,' he apologises, seeing Pearl in the kitchen. 'Traffic was crazy in town.'

'Don't apologise,' she says. 'Here it is. I copied it from a recipe on *Bake Off.*'

On the kitchen worktop, there is a new cake.

'It's raspberry and vanilla Battenberg,' Pearl says. 'I made it yesterday while I was listening to *Songs of Praise*.'

'Looks amazing,' he says, noticing his mouth is watering just like it does in the queue at KFC.

He slips off his trainers, leaves them at the door and wonders if he should be eating so much of Pearl's cake. In case she has other visitors due at any time, he decides it's better just to take one slice.

'I went to speak to my dad,' he says, taking a plate. 'At the office in town.'

'And were you able to talk? About going to York and the gardening career?' Pearl's expression is hopeful.

Connor shakes his head. 'There was somebody with him. A client. I'll have to try and catch him another time. It's often like that.'

'A busy man.'

'Always. There never seems to be a good time. If he's not at work, he's in his office at home, or out riding his bike with Yvo.'

He remembers the earlier conversation at home. Train tickets, dates, times. 'Yvo's booking me a train ticket for York . . . we . . . talked about it this morning.'

'And then you'll have a leaving date?'

Connor nods.

Pearl looks sad when she says, 'That's a shame. I am so very sorry.'

Her words are comforting, just like the Battenberg cake.

'I guess it is what it is,' he manages. 'Too late to go back on it all now.'

'And there's nothing to be done?' she asks him.

'Not really. It would need some kind of miracle to happen. Or one of those interventions you see on the TV.'

Pearl nods.

'And your hope of becoming a landscape gardener?'

'I don't see how that can happen now. There's no point avoiding it. Everything's organised for uni.'

She offers him another slice of cake and he takes it, instantly forgetting he'd intended to only have one.

'I hope you'll be able speak to your father.'

'Sometimes I think, even if I did, I wouldn't know where to begin.' As he says the words, he accepts the truth of them. 'It's been such a long time. Two years.'

'You haven't spoken about any of this since your mother died?' she asks.

'No. Not once.'

★★★

As the sun lifts high over the garden, he collects the last of the brambles and some broken fruit cages that are lying on the ground next to the outhouse, with the intention of burning them all on a bonfire. It had been on his mind since he first arrived. Highview, in the middle of the moor, miles from another house is the perfect place. No worries about smoke drifting over a next-door neighbour's fence and all over their washing. No danger of anyone knocking on the door to complain. It's only the crows who might be slightly put out, but then he's sure they've seen it all before, just as he's sure Ray would have no doubt lit a bonfire years before too. In search of a bin to start a fire in, he walks to the bottom of the garden, past the greenhouse with the impressive vine growing out of it. Heavy bunches of black grapes dangle just out of reach between its leafy green branches. On the ground a hose snakes along the path in the sunshine. If he can get it connected up to the outside tap, it'll be useful for watering the newly pruned roses later.

He takes the path round to the outhouse and pushes open the door that is made of the same corrugated iron as the roof. Inside, it is filled with the heady, intoxicating scent of dried grass, mower fuel and old wood. He breathes in the comforting smell and looks around for a metal bin, the sort Ray might have used for bonfires in the past. Along one side of the outhouse is a row of neatly placed spades, forks and a hoe, and a shelf above stacked with boxes of grass seed and bottles of plant feed. There is everything here he could need. It's almost as if Ray knew someone would come to look after the garden again one day.

After some searching, he finds the metal bin for the bonfire at the back, cleaned after all previous fires and ready to use. He lifts it up and carries it out to the garden. He lights the fire and watches the brambles burn, thoughts of university and leaving Westdown filling his mind. Soon he'll be looking at York stone buildings and the inside of a lecture hall. The embers flicker and die. He watches, lost in thought.

For the rest of the afternoon, he clears the chickweed from the front walls and window ledges, before connecting up the hose and giving the roses a good soak. He even manages to squeeze in trimming back the foliage on the vine. When it is five o'clock he goes back in through the open French doors and finds Pearl sweeping the hall floor.

'Thank you for burning the brambles,' she says. 'Good riddance to them.'

'They're definitely gone now.' He looks up at the old oak staircase, its banister shiny from polishing, the large hall with its flagstone floor, the doors leading off into other rooms. It's such a big house. And in need of urgent repair, unfortunately.

'I love this old house, but it needs so much looking after,' Pearl says, as if she's reading his mind. 'Since Ray got sick and then my mother passed, I . . .'

Her voice dies away between them, and a thought strikes him. It must be so isolating living up on the moor, especially when the roads are flooded or iced over, and no one can get up to Highview.

'Would you like to see the sitting room?' she asks him.

Despite having somewhere to be, he agrees without hesitation.

In the large room, there's an open fireplace, scrubbed clean and empty as if a fire hasn't been lit in years. A faded gold sofa has a Pearl-shaped dip in the middle and crocheted covers over both arms. There's a solid-looking, mahogany coffee table in the centre of the room and a television on a pine display stand in the corner. It's the sort of mismatched collection of furniture styles that would have Yvo running for the nearest IKEA. But it feels comfortable, like a front room should. There is an old television and a VHS recorder, and alongside on the floor is a tower of boxed tapes.

'That's all the series of *Detective Donnelly*,' Pearl says. 'I watch it of an evening. It's an oldie but a goodie. Except when a tape jams in the machine.' She smiles at him. 'Then it's just a blur.'

'Thanks for listening to me today.' He thinks about offering to make another cup of tea. Staying a little longer. Perhaps next time.

'Thank you for all your help in the garden,' she replies. 'And it's been my pleasure. Very much so.'

'I'll be back tomorrow, then. Goodnight, Pearl.'

'Goodnight Connor. Drive safe.'

NATE

'If you've finished filling the water bowls for the night, there's a new resident just been brought in who could really do with a bath,' Claire says. 'He's a stray. I've called him Frank. He was tied to the gate when Wayne opened up, can you believe it? Didn't even have a microchip, so we've got no way of knowing if he belonged to anyone. Not that the owners deserve to get him back after leaving him like that. Anything could have happened to him; he could have been attacked by another animal or some drunken idiot.'

At the end of the pens is a space that reminds Nate of the walk-in showers at the swimming pool when he was a child. Open on all sides, with a floor sloping to a drain in the centre. The tiles are tiny squares of navy, blue and white. Attached to one wall are two shower heads on extendable silver hoses, ready for use, and in the corner there is a row of dog shampoos of all kinds: mild, sensitive, de-flea, and one for dogs with especially long coats.

'I'll just fetch him,' Claire says, sounding calmer now. She disappears out of the door, leaving Nate to slip on one of the plastic aprons conveniently hanging by the entrance.

When she leads Frank in, Nate's first impression is that he's so painfully thin it's difficult to tell exactly what breed he is. Heartbreakingly, the dog is completely emaciated. He looks like a Labrador judging by his height and golden fur, what can be seen of it under the thick mud and grease, but it's impossible to be sure. At the sight of Nate, Frank whimpers, a pitiful sound that's uncomfortable to hear.

'Come on, boy.' Nate bends down low and extends a hand to greet him.

Inch by inch, Frank moves forward, shaking all the time. With gentle encouragement from Claire, he is soon standing close to Nate. Not touching but close.

'That's it,' Nate says, wondering how anyone could treat an animal so badly.

Not wanting to spook him, he slowly turns on one of the shower heads and tests the water to get it to the right temperature, then very carefully, Claire leads Frank into the shower. Together, she and Nate rinse off as much dirt from the dog's coat as they can. They watch the grimy water disappear down the drain before filling their palms with sweet-smelling shampoo.

With hands covered in soap bubbles, and Frank seeming to warm to the pampering, Nate and Claire get to work restoring his former good looks. As they work, they talk about the dogs at the centre, and Nate catches Claire up on who has been successfully rehomed. She seems relieved when he mentions Stan and Eric have still to find new owners.

'I'd have them in a heartbeat, farting and all, if I could,' she says, rinsing Frank's coat after the wash. 'But the property owner doesn't allow pets in our flat. When Melissa and I get a place of our own, we'll rehome as many as we can,' she says, sounding determined. 'But until then there's nothing we can do.'

'What does Melissa do for a living?' Nate asks.

'She's a care worker,' Claire replies. Works nights quite often, so we don't get much time together. We've been talking about getting engaged, making it official, you know? Maybe even a night out at a club to celebrate.'

Nate nods, realising he has no idea what a night in a club involves these days. It must have changed in the last four decades, there might even be an upper age limit.

Claire has a faraway look in her eyes. 'Dancing . . . drinking . . . maybe a kebab afterwards. I'll get Katie to put a notice up about it in the staffroom,' she adds. 'It's overdue. We all need a bloody good night out, and we've been wanting to do it for a long time. Plus, it'll be good for everyone to let loose and relax.'

Frank wags his tail and Nate says, 'Congratulations. I'm really pleased for you both.'

'Thanks,' she says, stroking Frank's head. 'I'll warn you now though, Melissa's a maniac on a night out, from what I can remember anyway. It's been that long. We've not had the money for stuff like that, or the time. Anyway, she will insist that everyone gets up on the dancefloor. No excuses.'

Nate makes a mental note to wear his trainers when the time comes and nothing too restrictive in the clothing department. Smart but definitely casual. It's been so long since he's been required to think about getting dressed for anything other than work or bed, he's not sure what will fit the bill. Trying to recall the days of disco, he remembers the last time he went anywhere even remotely close to a dance-floor, flares were in fashion and glitter balls were mandatory.

With Frank waiting patiently between them, Claire switches off the shower. The dog looks up adoringly at

Nate who gives him a rub behind the ear. Alone at Weatherley Gardens, the idea of offering a dog a home has grown
on him. He's checked the details in his deeds and spoken
with the company who maintain the gardens around the
flats. There is nothing in the paperwork to say dogs are not
allowed. No covenants or restrictions. There is even a dog
bin next to the garages.

'He's a handsome boy, isn't he?' Claire says, running a towel
over Frank's sopping back. 'And I'd say definitely a Lab.'

Nate agrees. 'Hard to imagine anyone giving him up.'

'Probably the usual story. You know, they bought a puppy
because it looked like the one off the Andrex advert, then
realised they didn't have the time to look after him when he
got bigger.' Claire's eyes darken momentarily in anger. 'Still,
someone will get a great dog,' she says, wiping a streak of
shampoo from her arm. 'That's the way you've got to look
at it. And Frank will get the home he truly deserves. We'll
make sure of that. He's an absolute star,' she says, smiling
now.

Frank confirms the point by standing stock-still as they
dry him with the blower, like he's giving his best side for the
judges at Crufts.

'There, you're done,' Claire says finally. 'Now, let's get
you settled in your pen and you can have a good rest. Catch
up on all the sleep you didn't get last night.'

Back in the office, Nate looks up Frank's details on the
computer. He's been vet checked and his age is estimated
at four years old. No health problems or injuries to report.

Nate lets out a sigh of relief. At least Frank won't have
to be operated on or take medication for the rest of his life

for joint problems, or because of the unhealthy way he's been kept. And judging by his wagging tail after they'd finished giving him a wash, he's already beginning to forget how badly he's been treated by mankind before arriving at Happy Tails' door. It is a miracle really, Nate decides. A miracle of good nature triumphing over shameful neglect.

Now all Frank needs is a new home.

PEARL

Tomorrow it is Tuesday, and she will travel to Istanbul, to take in the spectacle of the famous Spice Bazaar, marvel at the Topkapi Palace, and enjoy a leisurely cruise along the Bosphorus Strait. Meanwhile on Dartmoor, an amber sun sinks in a rose and lavender sky. It almost takes her breath away. Pearl is sure there are no finer sunsets anywhere in the world. Not even in Istanbul.

Tonight, she makes herself a simple meal of scrambled eggs on toast, eaten at the kitchen table. When she has finished, she washes up her one plate, knife, fork and saucepan. Then she will watch television. It is always this way. Part of a routine. Keeping the loneliness and silence at bay.

In the front room, she bends down in front of the television and selects a tape from the tall pile alongside it. Episode ten of *Detective Donnelly*, series two. There's something about the way the Scottish crime fighter always gets his man that helps her sleep soundly at night, in the hope and belief that real-life police investigators up and down the country are doing the same. Keeping dangerous criminals off the streets. Art imitating life. Within seconds, the familiar titles appear on the screen. Taking her usual position on the sofa, she settles against a cushion and allows herself to be swept away to the backstreets of Glasgow. A gang of art thieves are planning a raid on a new exhibition;

they are gathered around a table, each focused on drawings of the premises in question. She knows the script off by heart, has watched it so many times, but still the drama draws her in. When Detective Donnelly apprehends the gang of thieves, Pearl feels a comforting sense of security. It is exactly as life should be. Right proved to be stronger than wrong. Justice seen to be done, as the gang members are cuffed and hauled off to prison in a police van. The tape pauses and the picture judders before being released back into life. The final scene is of the gallery owner having his priceless paintings returned to him. Pearl pauses a moment to take in the scene, before pressing a button on the VHS to eject the tape. She puts it carefully back in its case. Laying it on the pile, she thinks of the one episode of the series that she never watches. It is very different from the others.

It is the first episode of the last series. A tape that remains in its plastic box, never to be watched. These days it would come with a warning. *Contains scenes viewers may find disturbing.* A helpline at the end for those who have been affected by viewing it. Pearl finds it impossible to watch. Its content is too close for any comfort to be had, regardless of Detective Donnelly's prowess at removing the deceitful from the streets. Pearl chooses not to put it in the machine and let it play on her television screen. It stays in its plastic box. Unseen. If it didn't, Pearl knows, she would lie wide-awake and troubled in her bed, and sleep would evade her until long after the foxes cry into the night.

CONNOR

Pearl's kitchen has become as comfortable a place to be as any he has ever known, and the routine they have settled into has become equally as relaxed. The simplest of things. Cake, a cup of tea, and conversation. The conversation that helps him more than Connor can say.

At the table, with a slice of zesty lemon cake in hand, he finds himself going back to the day after the funeral.

'Dad was upstairs taking all of Mum's clothes out of the wardrobe and putting them in bin bags. It was like he was clearing her out of the house,' he says, feeling anger rise up out of nowhere. 'He didn't tell me he was going to do it, and by the time I got home her things were all gone.' He stops and takes a breath. 'I wanted to have at least one thing, but I didn't get the chance. I wanted to go down to the charity shop the next day and buy everything back.'

'Did you?' Pearl asks. 'Go to the shop, I mean?'

He shakes his head. 'But now, when I think about it, I wish I had. The house felt empty after that . . . different.'

'And afterwards? What happened then?' she asks, gently.

'We didn't talk about any of it. Not about the clothes or the funeral . . . or Mum being gone and the house feeling empty. I wanted to. We were just like two people sharing a house but never speaking.'

After a moment, she says, 'I wonder, do you think your father struggled to cope after your mother passed away?'

'He loved her . . . before she died. More than anything.' Connor feels tears pushing at the corners of his eyes at the remembrance of how simple things used to be.

'Of course. She sounds like an incredible woman.'

'But then. . . after the funeral. . . he just, sort of carried on as normal.'

Connor recalls how, after the funeral, he had thought his father's behaviour insensitive because he didn't discuss anything. At the time, it had seemed unreasonable for him to be behaving this way, as if nothing had happened.

'I thought he was shutting me out, but I guess it could have been his way of dealing with things,' says Connor, feeling his earlier anger subside.

'We're all different,' Pearl replies.

He sighs, feeling lighter. 'I guess we are.'

'Do you mind if I say something?'

He shakes his head. 'No, of course not.' Connor takes another bite of cake.

'Do you think your father knew all the time that he needed to say something to you but couldn't find the right words?'

'He didn't talk at all. Just went back to work.'

'Keeping to his old routine?'

Connor nods.

'As if nothing had changed? As if your mother was still alive?'

Yes, I think so.' He stops to think about how his feelings towards his father are changing. 'He went to work, stayed up late in his office at home . . . and avoided talking about it to anyone.'

'Anything rather than face the truth?'

'Anything but that.'

'Like it was a way to escape from it all,' Pearl says. 'More cake?'

'Thanks.'

'It would be good to have that conversation from two years ago.'

'It would,' he says. 'I just need the right opportunity.'

★★★

After another cup of tea, he leaves Pearl in the kitchen and walks down to investigate the site of a disused vegetable patch at the bottom of the garden, all the while running over their conversation in his mind. Donald Matthews, town solicitor, doesn't feel so distant as a father anymore. He's been dealing with his wife's passing, while at the same time Connor has been trying to come to terms with losing his mum. Two people doing what they can, getting by one day at a time. They've both been trying, but in separate ways. He takes a deep breath and lets it out slowly as his shoulders lower. It's been good to get a new perspective on things.

At the far end of the garden, before the post-and-rail fence that separates Pearl's garden from the open moorland, he finds the space that he will work on until it is time to go home. It is a sizeable rectangle of loose, cultivated soil. Bending down, he lifts a small clod of mud from the top of the plot. It has a few shoots of grass sprouting out of it but breaks apart easily. The soil here is richer, better fed, and has obviously been used for growing crops before. It won't take long to restore it, with a bit of digging over and new planting.

With the sun beating down pleasantly on his back, he stands picturing how it could be laid out. A line of new bamboo canes standing tall, fledgling green beans curling around each one. Another row for raspberries and black-berries, their distinctive maroon and black fruit on the stems, alongside neat ranks of carefully spaced vegetables in the ground: carrots, potatoes, swede. And jam-jar lids full of beer to divert any slugs that might be looking to eat the first new shoots. All he needs are the seeds. He will stop off at the DIY store in town to buy them. It will give Pearl a harvest she can cultivate long after he has left for York.

Connor imagines the rectangle of soft soil at his feet in years to come, with the addition of leafy spinach, curly heads of broccoli, and rainbow chard. There's plenty of room to add in new varieties and extra fruit, like sweet strawberries for making jam to put in Victoria sponges. A space Pearl can use as she would like to, growing food to keep the grocery bills down each week and fresh, organic ingredients for her cakes. Focused now on making this a reality, he picks up the spade lying alongside and pushes it into the deep, dark earth.

PEARL

She watches him from the landing window with a pile of clean tea towels occupying her hands. Pearl remembers the day Ray dug over that patch for the first time. She had watched from the same window and seen him working steadily in the sunshine until it was done.

Now, from her vantage point, she can see the broken panes on top of the greenhouse and the vine that grows through them. Dark green leaves, woody stems and glossy black fruit. Under the sun the grapes ripen in big, shiny bunches, ready for picking. They are a specific kind that makes the most delicious wine, rich and full bodied. Ray had made his own from the fruit for years, and he and Lana had drunk it by the glassful, sitting at the kitchen table, talking and laughing. It had been good to see them this way. There hadn't been a great deal of happiness at Highview. The past had put a curse on them all. But there were days when it was like old times, when Lana and Ray danced, drank, and sang. It reminded Pearl of the parties they'd held at the house in Godalming. An expensive house, up in The Heights. Ray had always had good fortune; a successful haulage business left to him by his parents, and the deliverance of the entire proceeds of their estate on their deaths. He hadn't needed to worry about money as a result and had bought Highview without the need for a loan. It was fortunate. For him and for Pearl. Without his money, what would she have done?

Below, Connor is digging over the loose soil under the sun, stopping only occasionally, and then just to wipe his forehead. She imagines him in the days to come, carefully planting each row, pressing tiny seeds into the soft soil, restoring the vegetable plot just as he has the garden, taking pride in his work.

And then it occurs to her. How long will it be before he asks her if she'd like to come outside, to smell the roses and enjoy the garden? It is only to be expected that he will. They are becoming friends. It would make her the happiest woman alive to do so – to help Connor with the vegetable patch and turn her face up to the sun. Pearl hopes he won't think of her any differently when she tells him why she can't. It will be hard to explain but she will try as best she can, because his opinion of her, Pearl realises, matters more with each passing day.

NATE

Nate is talking to a middle-aged couple who are interested in adopting an ex-racing greyhound. Tonight is the night of Claire's engagement party and the sense of bubbling excitement in the Happy Tails reception area is almost palpable.

'Is it true they don't need as much exercise as you think?' the man asks.

'That's right, not a long walk at all. Do you own any small furry animals?'

'No.'

'That's good.'

'It is?'

'Yes, greyhounds have a strong prey drive, unfortunately. Any pet rabbit or gerbil might come in for some unwanted attention.'

'Could we think about it?'

'Of course. Come back and see us any time.'

As soon as the couple have left, Anila looks up from the rehoming form she is completing.

'Right, so tonight, I'll drive because I've got work tomorrow morning so it's no drama. I won't be drinking, just dancing! Like it's 1999! Oh yeah!'

She waves her arms in the air and spins around on her rotating office chair like someone testing the up and down system still works.

'I can't wait.' Katie beams at them both from where she's busy pinning a photograph of a chihuahua under the 'New Arrival' sign on the noticeboard. 'Sol's got the kids and I've bought a new dress. Wayne, is Trudi coming?'

'She's on nights,' he says, unable to hide his disappointment. 'But I'll be there.'

'Good, 'cos we're going to make this a night to remember,' Claire promises. She looks so happy, Nate notices, like a bride on her wedding day. It warms his heart to see her smiling, this young woman who gives her all to Happy Tails for no financial reward, regardless of the fact that she cannot afford a home where she can keep a dog of her own.

When it's time for them to leave, the dust in the car park reaches unprecedented levels as Claire wheelspins on her motorbike in her haste to be off, and Katie does the same in her people carrier, although Nate is sure it is unintentional in her case. It must be the prospect of a rare night while Sol looks after the kids getting to her. Nate feels a tingle of anticipation himself.

At Weatherley Gardens, he waits in his flat, dressed in his best trousers and a shirt Anila gave him for Christmas. It had been unexpected. She'd also invited him round for Christmas dinner at Ryan's parents'. He'd declined and she'd Facetimed him instead just as he'd finished his microwave turkey meal for one and the Queen's speech was starting.

Now, in the full-length mirror in his bedroom, he checks his appearance. The pale blue shirt is well made and simple. Just the way he likes his clothes. No bells and whistles. Nothing fancy, nothing from a shop aimed at teenagers, like he's attempting to look years younger. Just Nate.

When Anila arrives, she looks impressed by the effort he has made. 'Nice,' she says. 'That colour looks really good on you.'

Not used to compliments, he isn't sure what to say. He is completely out of his comfort zone, wildly so, getting dressed up in the evening and going to a club. Usually, it's a a repeat on TV, and an early night. For a moment, he questions what he is doing.

But Anila is looking eager to get the night started, just as she did at work. 'Shall we go? Ryan's going to meet us there. I'll get the first round in.'

The drive across town takes longer than either of them expected due to roadworks and a new contra-flow system, and when they arrive, the bar is heated to the temperature of the sun and playing music that makes Nate's heart jump erratically.

Ryan joins them ten minutes later, while they are trying unsuccessfully to order a drink and are still several bobbing heads back from the bar.

'Nate!' he shouts over the music, waving his hand to get their attention. 'Don't worry, mate, I'll get these.'

At six foot four and with a pair of shoulders built for battering through a rugby scrum, Ryan reaches over the line of people jostling at the bar with ease and immediately secures the attention of the bartender. Nate feels himself being engulfed by the crowd of thirsty customers pushing forward from behind, who are all considerably more used to the process than he is. When he comes out the other side, he is back where he started originally. Anila emerges from the ruck shortly afterwards looking dishevelled but smiling.

'Drinks are on their way,' she says, happily. 'I've got a mocktail.'

'I can't let Ryan spend all his hard-earned wages. I owe you both so much as it is,' Nate says, thinking of Anila knocking on his door, the leaflet for Happy Tails in her hand, and her friendly encouragement of him to get out of the flat. If it hadn't been for her thinking of him in the way that she did, he'd be watching *Midsomer Murders* in his pyjamas right now.

'You don't owe us anything, Nate,' Anila shouts over the music, her face glowing in the heat. 'We're just glad to have you living next door to us! Drinks!' she gasps, as Ryan appears carrying a tray full of pints and two of Anila's non-alcoholic mojitos. 'I'm thirsty already and all I've done is get in the queue for the bar!'

Soon they are all making the most of cold drinks and marvelling at Claire and Melissa confidently taking centre-stage on the dancefloor. With equal enthusiasm, Anila shimmies her way forwards towards them, leaving her two empty glasses behind, and soon after, Katie arrives and joins the throng without even stopping to get a drink. Her need to join in overriding any thoughts of a gin and tonic.

The music shifts up a gear in tempo and volume, and Nate can't help swaying to the infectious beat. It reminds him of when he first moved into the flat. The quiet was the most deafening sound he'd ever heard. He'd unpacked a box of CDs, put one on to drown out the quiet, closed his eyes and made the most of the confined space between the sofa and the coffee table to move to the music. It had helped but he felt incredibly alone.

'Nate?' Ryan is standing in front of him, offering him another pint. 'You thinking of getting up there?'

Nate points to his pint. 'Maybe, after this,' he nods.

Ryan smiles. 'Here, I've got us four each, saves going back to the bar. So, let's get started!'

Over the rim of his plastic pint glass, Nate spots Wayne walking in. His quiet colleague looks uncomfortable without a small reptile in his hand but soon relaxes when he sees them both, and even more so when Nate engages him in conversation about chameleons. Within seconds, Wayne is looking much more like his usual self.

'You know, it's not going to be long before we'll all be dragged out there,' Ryan says to them both, pointing to the mass of moving bodies on the floor. 'We're sitting ducks here, lads. They won't take no for an answer.'

Wayne looks uncomfortable again, but Nate feels he has nothing to lose, an unusual but liberating emotion that is helped along by the power of beer. When the moment comes, he heads out onto the floor and is immediately swamped in an enormous hug by Claire. Melissa does the same. Introductions over, Nate, Claire, Melissa, Anila and Katie dance the night away. Nate doesn't feel so out of touch as he dances, albeit a little unsteadily. The DJ even plays tracks he's sure are from years ago, until Claire lets him know they are remixes, sampled from the songs he remembers. Nate enjoys them just the same, singing along to the words and even appreciating the subtle reworking of the bygone chart-toppers.

Two hours later, everyone agrees it's time to call it a night. They all have work to go to in the morning. Outside, the difference in temperature feels like winter has come early.

'You were right,' Nate tells Claire. 'It was a night to remember. A great night to remember.'

Her face is covered in a sheen of perspiration, and she looks more carefree than he's ever seen her.

'Forget going to the gym for a workout,' Anila adds. 'I just need to go out dancing once a week. I've been doing it all wrong!'

'I really don't know why we don't do this more often,' Katie says, her breath carrying on the cold night air. 'Why do we only save having a good time for the odd occasion?'

'You've got a point,' Melissa agrees. 'We *should* abso-bloody-lutely do it more often. Maybe once a month, make it a regular date. And there's the wedding bash to look forward to when we get everything organised. We'll make that a special one too.'

'I'm so happy for you.' Anila smiles, as if suddenly reminded of why they are all here, and hugs Claire and Melissa at the same time. 'You two are made for each other. Can I be bridesmaid?'

'Of course,' Melissa says. 'Why not. We'd love it.'

Katie waves her hand at an oncoming taxi. 'Anyone going my way?'

'We'll jump in with you if that's OK?' Melissa says. 'We're that side of town as well.'

And as they tumble into the waiting vehicle, Nate, Anila and Ryan stand back on the pavement and wave them off, before walking back to Anila's car in the pay and display car park.

In the relative warmth of her small hatchback, Nate listens while Anila, powered by a dozen, sugar-loaded, non-alcoholic mojitos, talks about love stories, and how Claire and Melissa are a perfect match.

Nate watches the dashboard swim in front of his eyes.

'Is the wing mirror moving?' he asks.

Anila laughs. 'Nate, am I going to have to carry you up the stairs?'

He closes his eyes, feeling like he's floating above a seventies disco dancefloor, flashing with spinning lights and full of people enthusiastically doing the Funky Chicken. 'I think you might,' he replies, happily.

PEARL

The next morning breaks with a brief shower of rain. Pearl watches the crows tapping at the freshly mown lawns with their clawed feet, hoping to encourage worms to the surface for a pre-breakfast appetiser. There isn't a moment to lose. The birds will have to wait for their boiled eggs and monkey nuts today.

When Connor appears at the French doors, he is carrying a plastic bag full of groceries.

'There's a Jamaican ginger cake, tea, milk, and a bag of sugar,' he says, listing each item individually as he removes various packets and puts them on the side. 'Derek let me use his staff discount in the Co-op, so I went all out.'

Pearl can't remember the last time someone bought groceries for her. It's a good feeling. For a moment, she almost forgets what she must do. Instead, her thoughts are waylaid by thinking about a slice of spicy ginger cake, a cup of hot tea, and finding out if Connor managed to start a conversation with his father the previous evening.

'Tea?'

'That'd be great.'

She switches on the kettle and lets it come to the boil like a tiny watery volcano.

Connor digs around in the plastic bag some more and removes a handful of seed packets from the bottom.

'I picked up these from the DIY store on the way. Thought we could go down and have a look at the vegetable patch afterwards, if you fancy it? Plan where we're going to put the veggies and the fruits?'

Hearing the words, Pearl feels her heart begin to race, knowing the time has come for her to explain; it can't be put off a moment longer. Just as she'd envisaged it would while she had stood watching him the day before from the upstairs window. The thought of taking one step onto the patio, let alone all the way down to the newly dug over vegetable patch, causes The Fear to rise immediately, robbing her of breath.

'Pearl?'

Words catch in the back of her throat before she can say them aloud.

'Is everything OK?' Connor's young face is full of concern.

'I should have mentioned something so much earlier than this, I realise that now,' she begins. 'It was wrong of me not to.'

'Wrong of you . . . ?'

'To not tell the truth,' she admits. 'It's so difficult, you see, to find the right words to explain.'

And then he is there, by her side.

'Pearl, it's OK. Whatever it is.' His voice is steady as his hand reaches out and lands very gently on her arm. His presence is reassuring, undemanding. Not something to step away from or avoid. Like she listens to him, he is listening to her now.

'I'm so sorry. I should just say it, shouldn't I?'

He nods.

'I'm sorry but I can't go down the garden to the vegetable patch.'

Tears of sadness start to push from her eyes, forcing her to search for the tissue up her sleeve.

'I don't understand,' he says, looking confused.

She lifts one hand, lays it gently on his and gives it a comforting squeeze, for her own benefit as much as his.

'Well, I can't go outside, unfortunately,' she says. 'Although, it sounds odd to say, I know. Not even out onto the patio. In fact, I haven't walked through the front door for over forty-three years.' The words come a little easier now she has started speaking. 'It seems like forever.'

'Not once?' he asks, shocked but not repelled, she is grateful to see.

'Not successfully. I tried but I didn't get far.'

'Has it always been like this?'

Pearl smiles as she remembers happier times. 'Not always, no. When I was a girl it was different. I didn't mind walking to the shops or going to the cinema. When I was young I went outside without thinking. I didn't stop at the doorway and just look out; I walked through it and kept going. I remember the places I used to go, like Oxford Street at Christmas time with all the lights and the crowds, or the sea at Brighton and eating fish and chips on the pier.' For a moment, she recalls the sights and smells: the brush of people in the crowd passing by, the taste of salted chips and the tang of vinegar on her lips. 'Sometimes, at night, I dream that I'm walking down the front path and out onto the open moor, leaving the house behind and taking a trip back to the places I used to go. I can feel the ground beneath my feet, the wind blowing in my hair. It seems very real. But then when I wake,' she sighs, feeling the reality of her situation creeping back, 'I realise it was just a dream and nothing more.'

'Shall we have that tea?' Connor says gently. 'I'll put the kettle on again and get the cups.'

'Yes, tea would help.'

Brew poured, she can see he is thinking hard about what she has said. 'Can't we just *step* outside a bit, though?' he asks. 'Slowly, I mean. And we could do it together. One foot in front of the other and then, if we took it slowly, we'd be down to the end of the gate.' He stops, a new thought evidently coming to him. 'We could get in the car and go anywhere from there. Even London or Brighton. If the Fiesta will make it.'

Pearl feels her heart racing at the thought of it.

'Or take a drive into Westdown?' he tries. 'We could go to the café or the gift shop. Walk along the High Street?'

His words are coming faster now, his breath running out at the end of each sentence.

'A few steps . . . and then we get in the car. It's not far into town.'

'I would like that. To see Westdown. And London and Brighton. Very much.'

'Let's go.' he says, brightly, getting up.

He holds out his hand to her, like someone politely requesting a dance, but The Fear pushes her back in the chair. How to explain?

'I've lived like this for such a long time now, I really only know the inside of this house.'

'But we can try . . .'

She feels her heart might break at the sight of him, looking determined and lost at the same time.

'I wish with all my heart that we could.' Pearl feels a familiar feeling in her chest. A tightness. A physical pain. The hurt of all the years. 'I am so sorry, more than I can say, but I know that I can't go out the door and walk along the path, and I don't think I ever will.'

CONNOR

He searches furiously for everything he can find on the internet as quickly as his fingers will type and his eyes can scan the words on the screen. Stories appear about people who stay in their homes and never leave. According to the information available, the term used for it is 'agoraphobia'.

Extreme or irrational fear of entering open or crowded places, of leaving one's own home, or of being in places from which escape is difficult.

And a shocking statistic. As many as one-and-a-half million-people experience it in the UK alone. Teachers, soldiers, lorry drivers, celebrities, a man who lived alone inside a run-down house on a Scottish island for five years, a woman in America who walked out of her job as a high-flying marketing executive twelve years ago and hasn't set foot on the street outside her New York apartment since. There are message boards filled with stories and he stops to wonder how many more people in the world are living in the same way as Pearl.

Sitting on his bed in Fern Crescent with his laptop open in front of him, he scrolls down a page dense with information. There is the story of a teenager, nineteen, a soldier who fought in Afghanistan. His name is Tom, and he has PTSD.

He first had a panic attack in his local branch of Tesco. He ran all the way home, leaving his car in the car park, and hasn't been able to face going out since. There is the story of a woman in India. The photograph that accompanies it is of a dark room and a sari-clad, middle-aged woman sitting serenely in the corner; relatives surround her, parents, a husband and six children.

While he reads, a text arrives from Molly.

Got yr msg. Meet me park xx

And one from Derek.

On way.

He texts back.

Leaving now.

Hurrying downstairs, Connor slips on his trainers, grabs his car keys from the hall table and heads out of the door.

★★★

'It's not right,' Molly says, adjusting her position on the edge of the playground's roundabout, while holding Tommy expertly on her lap. 'Why isn't someone doing something? You know . . . helping.'

Connor adjusts his position on the swing, arms wrapped around the thick metal chains to either side of him. '*I'd* like to help if I can.'

'And I do too, definitely,' Molly says defiantly, getting off the roundabout and coming to stand next to him. She shifts Tommy onto her hip and touches Connor's shoulder. 'And Derek will – won't you, Derek?'

'Sure,' he says. And then, 'Forty-three years?'

Connor nods, trying not to think about the feel of Molly's hand through his T-shirt. 'It's a long time.'

'Some would call it a lifetime,' Derek muses.

'Good job we're here now then, talking about it,' Molly says, getting back on the roundabout. 'Because someone has to.'

Westdown Park has been their go-to meeting place for as long as they can all remember. And at this time of night, they are unlikely to be disturbed. No laser-like glances from protective parents watching over their small kids and wary at the presence of teenagers. The place is quiet and empty this evening save for the four of them.

'If I could just work out where to start,' Connor finds himself saying, all the while worrying that what's needed might be completely beyond three teenagers and a toddler in a park. He looks out at the recreation ground beyond the swings. One of the goalposts on the grass is listing to one side and there are irregular gaps in the chalky outline of the football pitch as if someone didn't have enough paint to do all of it. At the far end of the field is a shelter, covered in fluorescent graffiti – shifting shapes of orange, green and yellow, with a silver lining of spray paint. In front of the shelter is a bin, filled to the top with crisp packets, equally fluorescent plastic bottles, and a broken skate helmet. On the patchy grass around it is a smattering of used tissues and aerosol spray-paint cans. It's a long way off the picture-perfect High Street with its pastel-coloured shop fronts, and Britain in Bloom-winning flower displays.

'But then maybe Pearl's the one with the right idea,' Derek says. 'I mean, perhaps there is a secret a bunker under the house after all, filled with survivalist equipment and supplies – you know, tinned food, weapons, the antidote to all known human diseases? Come the zombie apocalypse, Pearl Winter could be the last woman standing.'

Molly smiles. 'Mate, I love you as a friend, you know that, but you do say the weirdest stuff.'

Derek shrugs his shoulders nonchalantly. 'Always good to have a fresh look on life though, right? Otherwise, how boring would it be?'

Molly nods. ''Course, wouldn't have it any other way.' And then, looking at Connor, she asks, 'Did Pearl say if anything caused this? Why she ended up this way?'

He shakes his head.

Molly pulls Tommy close and begins a slow turn on the roundabout, her long legs reaching straight down to the ground, allowing her to push off with her feet. 'So, what do we do now?'

Connor gives it some careful thought. 'I really don't know.'

'What about Red Bull vodka shots . . . several of them?' Molly replies, almost immediately. ''Cos I feel like I can do pretty much anything after five of those. It's not a bad shout, if you think about it.'

'It's not.' He smiles at Molly. 'But I'm not sure Pearl's much of a big drinker, not really. Not unless you count tea.'

'Right,' his friend says with a small sigh. 'Scrub the vodka shots then.'

A woman running alongside the park in Spandex work-out gear stares at the group of teenagers as she passes. Molly stares back unblinking until the runner looks away.

'We get a lot of those types at Jingle Tots,' she says, appearing distracted. 'It's packed with Alpha-mum types who won't ever admit they bottle fed their babies, got their roots dyed when they were pregnant, or pulled on a pair of Spanx when they were pregnant.' Tommy reaches out and clings on to her T-shirt. She caresses his tiny hand. 'Don't let the Yummy Mummy outfit fool you,' she concludes phil-osophically. 'It's just camouflage.'

Derek and Connor look from the woman's retreating form back to Molly. 'You get all that from Jingle Tots?'

Molly nods. 'The town hall on a Thursday morn-ing is full of them, all desperately vying for Mum of the Year award. Secretly of course,' she says. 'Then there's the second-time-arounders with new toddlers in tow and kids our age still at home. They're a bit more relaxed about the whole thing. Last week there was this woman in her early forties called Lou who offered me a carrot stick after class. Think she thought I was somebody's kid and Tommy was my brother. I didn't know whether to be offended or grateful.'

'But you took it, right?' Derek asks.

'Course, I love carrot sticks.' Molly smiles at them both, before taking her phone out of her short shorts and checking the time. 'And speaking of which, it's dinner and bath time for this one so I should probably go. I'm sorry I couldn't think of anything better for helping Pearl, Con, but I won't stop trying, I promise. I will come up with something less crap in the end.'

'To be fair, my mind's a blank,' Derek echoes.

Connor nods and sighs heavily. 'Mine too.'

Tommy sucks his hand, already looking forward to his own carrot sticks.

'I'll text you later,' she says. 'Night boys.'

'Night, Molly.'

As she walks away towards the park entrance, her voice carries back to them by the swings. 'We'll think of a plan, don't worry, we'll sort it.'

Connor gets off his swing and thinks about what to do. It's an uphill climb. More like scaling Everest, if he's being truthful. Pearl hasn't left the house in double the years he's been on the planet. And there's nothing so far to suggest he can change that.

Derek gets off his swing too and leaves it moving back and forth like a piece of equipment possessed by a supernatural power.

'What are you doing tomorrow night?' he asks.

'Nothing.'

'Fancy dinner at ours? Save you having to third-wheel it with your dad and Yvo? Mum's doing a spag Bol.'

'Maybe she could give us some advice.' Connor says, feeling marginally less hopeless.

'Don't see why not. It's worth a shot.'

'Tomorrow night then,' he hears himself saying as he falls in beside Derek and they leave the empty park, graffitied hut and overflowing bins behind.

PEARL

Lying in bed in the early evening, she thinks about what will happen now. The blanket is folded neatly on her dressing-table stool. The air is still heavy with warmth. Just a double sheet over her does a more than adequate job on these balmy summer evenings.

Fading light edges the heavy curtains like a halo, a hint of the glorious sunset to be witnessed outside. She had had every intention of spending an hour cleaning the kitchen floor and giving the front-room carpet a good Hoover, but after Connor had left, an overwhelming feeling of tiredness had descended and there seemed little point in fighting it. The emotion of the day had taken its toll.

'Don't worry, Pearl, we'll do this together,' he'd promised before leaving, and for a moment she'd allowed herself to believe that they might.

Feeling herself slip away into an easy slumber, she allows a final thought to take shape and grow in her mind. It is one she hasn't considered for so many years. The idea of it seems impossible until now. Pearl catches her breath. What if? One foot in front of the other. Just a few steps. Simply that and she could be standing outside.

1989

It was a year of new beginnings for people all over the world. Ray bought a bigger television and on it Pearl watched the fall of the Berlin Wall and the first democratic elections in Brazil in decades. The images reminded her that times were changing, even though life on the moor stayed exactly the same.

In early December, a woman called Sandra visited High-view at Lana's invitation.

'The doctor said she might be able to help,' her mother said. 'It's a new type of treatment.'

The woman asked Pearl to sit back and relax on the sofa, close her eyes, and take three deep breaths. She guided Pearl's imagination, asked her to go back to a time when she felt safe. Pearl remembered life before the summer of 1976. Sandra asked her to remember only the good feelings in as much detail as possible, to amplify the experience, picture where she was and what she was doing, to store it up and use it whenever she wanted to go outside. But when she opened the door, all Pearl could see was a never-ending space ahead of her, just grass and sky and nowhere to hide. She heard the blood whooshing in her ears and felt the violent beat of her heart. The sound in her ears drowned out Sandra's encouraging words and chased away any courage she believed she had garnered from their sessions.

At twenty-nine years of age, she considered how many years lay ahead of her and the vastly different future that could be hers if she could make it out of the door. She persevered with the technique Sandra had suggested but some memories from the past were stronger than others, always breaking through and hijacking her thoughts. More than ever before, it seemed an impossible feat for her to walk just a few steps out onto the path. With each failed attempt, The Fear only grew stronger.

Sandra recommended Lana speak to a friend of hers who might be able to help.

A week later, a fashionable young lady called Dee arrived. She had long shiny chestnut hair and was wearing a woollen maxi-coat and high-heeled leather boots. Pearl realised her own shoes and clothing were old-fashioned and lacking in attractiveness compared to Dee's. She'd been wearing outdated outfits borrowed from her mother's wardrobe for as long as she could remember and had been making do with cutting her own hair with the kitchen scissors for years. Pearl listened to Dee and considered this young woman's life: a career, the opportunity to earn money, buy clothes in a boutique, visit a hairdresser, and go to parties. They were the same age, Dee said. Twenty-nine. In that moment, Pearl felt the inescapable sorrow of living a life only on the inside, a life that seemed empty in comparison to that of another woman her own age.

Dee was a professional. She asked Pearl to sit with The Fear, let it do its worst, and then move on. Buoyed by the advice, Pearl opened the front door one morning and stepped outside. When Lana and Ray woke they found her collapsed on the path halfway to the gate.

They carried her back inside and laid her in bed. For three weeks, Pearl didn't leave her room, let alone the house. The Fear had won again, and hope began to fade of anyone or anything ever being able to change that.

CONNOR

The idea of a spag Bol becomes more enticing the closer he gets to Derek's house. His friend lives in Chestnut Close, a road where the white bungalows on either side have neat green squares of garden at the front and clusters of weather-beaten gnomes gathered round the door: a few pushing wheelbarrows exactly nowhere and others fishing in tiny concrete ponds. Annie and Michael's front lawn looks noticeably different from the rest – it has bikes, scooters and a broken skateboard scattered across it, and a concrete mixer and an exploding bag of cement monopolising the driveway.

After letting himself in, he finds everyone in the kitchen. Derek and brothers, Aaron and Cain, and elder sister, Amber, jockey for position around the table, keen to get the seat with the most elbow room. Clad in her navy Willows Residential Nursing Home uniform, Annie is busy ladling spoonfuls of Bolognese pasta from a heavy-looking sauce-pan onto plates, with the steady motion of a robot building cars on a Japanese production line. Derek's dad, Michael, is at the sink, busy washing the day's dust and plaster picked up on the building site from his hands, while Sausage the sausage dog sleeps soundly under the table.

'Come in, love, grab a seat,' Annie says warmly, looking up from her saucepan and server. 'I'll get you a plate.'

Connor realised a long time ago that Annie, a hard-working woman very rarely off her feet or without a tea towel in her hand, would rather run the London Marathon dressed in a chicken costume than see anyone go hungry at her table. With a plate of spaghetti in front of him, he reflects on how glad he is to be here at the Clayton family table and not sitting awkwardly with Yvo and his dad in the newly lime-green dining room at Fern Crescent. Two evenings ago the three of them had eaten a Chinese takeaway together and not spoken a word the entire time. He'd ended up making an excuse, going to his room and staring blankly at the chicken-pox walls.

At the table, he is flanked by Aaron and Cain, busy tucking into their food.

'All right, boys?' he asks.

'Yep,' Aaron says in a confident voice in between mouthfuls. 'Just gonna have tea, real quick, then go back out and play.'

Cain nods in agreement. 'Playyyyyyy,' he adds, for clarification. 'Gotta pump up the paddling pool. It's got a puncture. Just happened. Not sure how. Dad's gonna fix it.'

'I think I've got a couple of tyre-repair patches in the garage ought to do it,' Michael chimes in from his seat at the end of the table. 'Soon that's all there's going to be left of that pool. Patches!' he says, shaking his head good-naturedly and causing a tiny flurry of brick dust to fall from his greying hair onto his shoulders, like snow being blown down from a winter roof.

'Here, let me get that,' Annie says, reaching over and using her tea towel to remove it. She takes a moment to look lovingly at her husband, and he winks in return.

'Mum! Dad!' Derek gasps. 'Get a room!'

Annie laughs and deftly flicks the tea towel in his direction. He swerves to avoid it, almost falling off his chair.

On the other side of the table, Amber reaches for her glass of water and ignores the fact that Derek is now putting a considerable amount of ketchup on his spaghetti. 'Hey, Connor, Derek was saying you've got a job for the summer?' Amber, he notices, is wearing make-up *and* a dress, both of which he has never seen her do before. The only concession to the regular Amber he can see is her favourite faded denim jacket with the hole in the top pocket.

'It's gardening, so all good,' he replies, still surprised to see her looking so different from usual. 'You going out?'

Amber nods. 'Pub.'

'It's a date,' Derek says, adding one final dollop of ketchup to the spaghetti on his plate. 'With her new man.'

'He's not my new man,' she intones, raising her eyebrows in mock despair. 'He's just a mate. Nothing more. And it's an innocent drink at the Traveller's. I'll probably be home by ten.'

'Right,' Derek laughs. 'Just a drink.'

'You'll still need to line your stomach, no matter who you're meeting, George Clooney or not,' Annie chips in.

'Who the hell is George Clooney?' Amber asks.

'Someone your mum thinks might one day walk into The Willows and sweep her off her feet,' Michael says.

'In my dreams,' Annie sighs. 'Here, have some more Bolognese.'

'Mum! The zip on this dress'll never hold if I do.' Amber pats the sides of her outfit like someone looking for a lost wallet. 'Can you imagine if it busts open in the pub!'

'You'll be fine,' Annie says. 'Besides, you've got a jacket. Just keep it on. No one will ever know if the zip fails. Do you want some ice cream for afters?'

'Is that someone at the door?' Amber replies. 'Yep, it is!'

At the sound, Sausage wakes up and starts barking as if his life depends on it, just as Amber stands and gives Annie a quick hug.

'I'm out of here,' she tells Annie. 'I don't know what time I'll be back, *but* it won't be late, and, *yes*, I'll be good and not drink too much.'

'Fine.' Annie nods. 'Just give Dad a ring if you need picking up. I'll still be on shift at two tomorrow morning, let alone ten o'clock tonight.'

'Don't worry, I will,' Amber replies. ''Bye,' she says, hurrying out of the kitchen like someone responding to a starting pistol being let off.

'So, ice cream?' Annie asks breezily, looking slightly bereft now one of her own has left the fold. 'I've got Neapolitan or Mint Choc Chip?'

There is a resounding and unanimous request for Mint Choc Chip.

Aaron and Cain bolt down their bowlfuls of dessert, beating Connor and Derek by a millisecond as if it was a photo finish, and run out to the garden with Michael following dutifully to fix the lining with a remaining patch and fill the paddling pool they love to jump in. Through the open window, the sounds of the hose running water into the blue plastic and their delighted screams carry through to the kitchen.

'Those boys,' Annie says. 'Thank God we've got good neighbours. Connor, you OK, love?'

'Sorry, I was just thinking about work.' It's only now that he realises he has fallen silent, distracted by the idea of talking to Annie about Pearl and how to start. With just the three of them left at the table, now is as good a time as any.

'Can I ask you a question, Annie? It's kind of a medical one.'

'Of course.' She says and gives him a reassuring nod. 'Fire away.'

Derek looks at Connor who continues, 'It's just – I wanted to ask you about Pearl, the lady I work for.'

'Is there something wrong?' Annie's face is serious now. Connor knows he must get to the point but it's hard to put it into words.

Derek leans forward and rests his elbows on the table, narrowly avoiding a blob of Bolognese. 'The thing is, Mum, Pearl doesn't go outside. Like ever. And she hasn't for forty-three years.'

Connor takes a breath. 'Me, Derek and Molly, we want to help if we can, only we don't really know where to begin . . .'

Annie listens carefully while he speaks and takes a moment to mull it over. 'It's a difficult situation and that is a very long time to be inside. Poor Pearl.' Connor knows Annie is used to delivering the worst news to a relative at Willows Residential Home. The hardest part of the job, she always says. 'Does Pearl have anyone at home, Connor?'

'No one,' he says. 'She lives alone up on the moor.'

'That must be so hard at times.'

'It is, I think, but I don't want to call Social Services or anything,' he says, feeling that would betray Pearl's trust in him completely. 'And I'm not really sure what else is out there. Do you think there's somebody who could come round, like a professional?'

Annie smiles sadly. 'Do you know, love, I wish I could say there's an army of qualified, trained people available right now to treat each and every person who's experiencing problems like Pearl is, but the truth of it is that mental health services are stretched to the limit and overloaded. I couldn't say for sure how quickly she might get to see someone. The waiting list is long unfortunately.'

'Can anything be done?' Derek asks. 'Other than us trying to think of something?'

Annie nods. 'I hope so. But it's worth remembering, all those years ago . . . was it forty-three, you said?' she asks, and Connor nods. 'Well, there wasn't very much done about it back then, so Pearl might have not got the help when she needed it. I think problems like that were nearly always put down to nerves. I don't know if it was even given a name. Patients were prescribed sleeping pills and tranquillisers. It was a sort of one solution fits all. Which wasn't always helpful. And those tablets were strong, and addictive. Real knock-out jobs. It's a wonder people got through their day.'

Connor thinks about Pearl when she first came to Highview, younger than he is now, without access to anything more than strong medication and no real understanding of the unfamiliar anxieties she was experiencing.

'What can we do?' he asks.

Annie picks up the tea towel again as if holding it helps her. 'You know, I think the best thing you *can* do for Pearl right now is to let her know you'll be there for her as a friend. Don't give up if it seems like nothing is changing.

Just keep trying different things. In my experience, letting someone know they're not alone and understanding what they're going through goes a long way,' she says. 'It really does.'

'Thanks, Annie.'

'I don't think I've done much,' she says in return. 'I'd like to stay and chat some more, but I'll be late for my shift if I don't get a move on.'

She checks her watch. 'Try not to worry too much,' she says, and he accepts he must look defeated in her eyes. 'I'll have a word with the staff at work and see if anyone can add anything that might be useful, and I'll talk to the doctor who visits from the surgery.'

'Thanks again, Annie.'

'I'm happy to help,' she replies, slinging an old leather handbag over her shoulder. 'You take care, love. And, Derek, can you make sure those two get in the bath before they go to bed?'

As if on cue, there is a delighted squeal from outside in the back garden.

When she disappears out of the door, Connor listens to the sound of Annie's people carrier starting up on the driveway, recalling one key fact he's not yet told anyone. He really should have done, he knows, because when he'd read the messages posted on the forums, it had become clear that Pearl's story was different in one respect from all the others. He'd found there wasn't anyone in the world who'd lived inside for longer. Not in any city, country, or continent. Thinking about how much he wishes he wasn't leaving in a matter of weeks, Connor counts the reasons why. It's not just because he doesn't want to study law, or to live in York, or to leave behind everyone he's ever known. It's much more than that now. It's about helping Pearl to go back outside and live like she used to all those years ago when she walked down Oxford Street under the Christmas lights and ate fish and chips on Brighton pier.

PEARL

'Have you got anything that isn't slippers, maybe?'

Connor has arrived early, before the first cup of tea even, and is standing looking at the moccasins on her feet.

'Yes, I've just remembered!'

Thinking of her mother's shoes, Pearl walks quickly into the hall and opens the understairs cupboard. After digging about in the cobwebs, she spots a pair, takes them out and checks the bottom of each for grip. When she studies the soles more closely, she notices there is still a slither of mud on either side. A reminder of her mother's last walk around the garden before she became ill.

'I feel like I'm going on an expedition,' Pearl calls through to Connor from the hallway, in an attempt to keep the nerves that threaten to sabotage her at bay.

'I'd better just give these a try out.' The first thing she notices is the tight feel of the firm leather around her feet. For years, she has only worn indoor footwear. There had seemed little point in putting on anything else.

Acclimatised to the alien feel of proper shoes, and after two cups of fortifying tea and a slice of coffee and walnut cake, she joins Connor at the French doors and together they look at the garden and the rolling moor beyond.

'Ready?' he asks, and she is so grateful he is by her side.

'I am now.'

A lorry rumbles past on the road, belching fumes. The smell of petrol reaches them seconds later.

Pearl waits for the smell and the sound to subside.

'What do I do?' She hears the tremor in her voice.

Connor offers his hand and she gladly takes it.

'One step,' he says. 'And we can stop at any time.'

When he'd rung the night before, she'd been encouraged by his youthful enthusiasm and belief that anything in the world is possible if you just give it a try. There was an added urgency to his tone that had reminded her of the fact that it was only a matter of weeks before he must leave. He had said he wished they had more but that he would do all he could to help in the time they had left.

Three unruly-looking crows with beaks the colour of ash fly down from the trees, almost colliding with a new bird feeder Connor has speared into the ground. They stand waiting on the lawn like spectators.

Onwards and upwards. It's better not to look down, she reminds herself. A tightrope walker once said that, she's sure. If you do it only serves to unsettle the nerves. Looking straight ahead, Pearl fills her lungs and reminds herself she is not making this journey alone.

Gripping the handle, she eases the door open a little further and feels the reassuring solidity of the flagstone floor below her feet. Then the aluminium threshold of the French doors, sticking up and catching on the sole of her mother's shoe. Beyond that is a step down onto the patio. As she traverses the threshold, it feels as if she is being asked to cross a mine shaft, with the ever-present risk of plummeting into the watery darkness below.

'That's it. Here we go,' Connor says, but she's concentrating so hard, his voice sounds like it's coming from a long way away.

The Fear arrives again. Raging at her for even thinking she can do this. How dare she? She attempts to steady her breathing, but it's picked up an erratic rhythm all its own and isn't responding to her attempts to keep it under control.

She steps back into the kitchen quickly, and away from the threshold. Just like the times before. History repeating itself over again. She is stuck. Stuck inside. Imprisoned by fear. A fear that will never weaken. Why did she think it would?

'Pearl?'

'I'm sorry, Connor,' is all she can say. 'I'm letting you down, I know.'

'We could take a break . . . try again in half an hour?'

'I'm sorry, no. I need to stay in the house.'

As she turns, Pearl sees the crows lift into the sky, their feathers as dark as coal. They know just as she does there is nothing more to see here. Not today.

31st December 1999

'Happy New Year!' Pearl watched the fireworks erupt on the screen and listened to the commentator on the television welcoming in the New Millennium.

From the sitting-room window, they stood and watched rockets streak across the inky sky in the distance, like shooting stars. It seemed there wasn't a square foot of land anywhere that didn't have fireworks exploding over it in scintillating patterns of shimmering lights, not even on the moor. The whole world was lit up and everywhere people were celebrating.

Faces shone from the television screen in the front room – happy, radiant faces. People flocked to Trafalgar Square, and the Queen was ferried up the Thames in order to open the Millennium Dome.

'Dance with me, Pearl!' Ray called above the noise of explosions and cheering from the set. 'It's a new century!'

They waltzed around the sitting room while Lana clapped enthusiastically. It was the most at peace Pearl had seen her mother since they'd come here. For those few snatched moments, they rejoiced in the promise of a new future, one that began with a party the entire world was invited to.

They stopped dancing briefly to watch the festivities unfolding on television. Pearl took in the sight as the camera operator panned to the thousands of people lining the

streets of London, the brightly dressed entertainers inter-
spersed with the crowds, all cheering and clapping. When
the Queen joined thousands more inside the Dome, Pearl
couldn't help thinking she looked like a woman who would
rather be at home having a nice cup of tea than performing
an opening ceremony on such a wintry night. When the
drapery covering the inside of the Dome fell away to reveal
its pure white carapace, it looked like the inside of an enormous golf ball.

Lana and Ray drank whisky and sang 'Auld Lang Syne',
spurred on by a band of bagpipe players and an all-male
choir. When the bottle was empty and her mother and Ray
waltzed in silence, Pearl retreated to her bedroom and left
them to it.

Lying in the dark, fully clothed in jeans and a wool
jumper, she allowed herself to contemplate her fortieth
year. The time had passed so quickly, days turning into
weeks, weeks into years, slipping away, one after the other,
with no major life events to mark the passing decades in
between. No work to go to, no foreign travel from which
she might return with stories of her time in Bali or Prague.
A life devoid of the comfort of a partner or children of her
own.

She thought about how a letter from Nate had never
come. He was married, she was certain, with a family. A
wife and children. She wished him well. Whatever the reason for his not writing to her, she didn't hold it against him.
He had always been a good person and no doubt still was.
She trusted wholeheartedly that he hadn't changed at all in
that regard.

Pearl turned on her side, flicked on the bedside light and traced the daisy-print pattern on the wallpaper with her fingertip.

From downstairs, she could hear the television still, but suspected Ray had fallen into a stupor and her mother had retired to bed.

Outside, she sensed the crows had retreated further into the embrace of the giant oaks. It must have seemed like they were under fire from a hundred shotguns. Rockets screaming and sparks whirling through the sky. How long would it take for the birds to return? To trust the world hadn't gone mad? To believe the sky would no longer crack and fizz and be pierced by a hundred lights?

In cities all over the world, crowds joined together, drinks were raised, spilled and drunk. Pearl lay listening to the sound of broadcast cheering, the chorus of thousands of good wishes for a brighter future. She decided to make a wish of her own: that wherever Nate might be living, he knew only happiness and love.

'Happy New Year, Nate,' she said, before closing her eyes on the old century. 'Wherever you might be.'

NATE

Along the quiet country lane leading away from the rescue centre, Nate walks Frank and Anila leads a greyhound called Tiny, who is so tall his head reaches her waist. The ex-racing star bobs along rhythmically by her side.

Bringing up the rear, Katie and Wayne's voices carry on the late-afternoon air as they lead a skittish lurcher and an overweight pug.

Anila and Nate walk on towards a bridleway, the one where they let the dogs have a longer lead and allow them the freedom to explore. There are squirrels, rabbits and birds here, a tempting trio of live targets for the greyhound to chase if he wasn't tethered to Anila via a long line. It's clear that she has her work cut out for her, keeping Tiny in check. A thrush darts out from under a bush and Nate feels Frank pull urgently too. 'Steady, boy,' he soothes. 'It's nothing for you.'

The remnants of the day's sunshine filter through the branches of the nearby trees, casting shadowy impressions of them on the ground.

'I think I've still got a hangover even after three days,' Nate says, feeling tired and wishing now, with the benefit of hindsight, he'd done more dancing and less drinking at Claire's engagement party.

'Whereas I have a head as clear as a bell.' Anila smiles smugly.

'I'll be having soft drinks the next time,' Nate points out. 'And I'll do all the driving.'

'You're on!' Anila says. 'Or Ryan can do it.'

They'd all agreed at the staff meeting that another work get-together should be planned. In fact, it had been the first item on the agenda.

Katie had suggested a meal at the new Mexican restaurant in town and there had been a brief show of hands before it was written up in the diary and booked the same day.

Nate has been looking forward to it ever since. It has also served to temporarily take his mind off an unexpected phone call from his ex-wife until now.

'Jean wants to sell the house,' he says, realising it's a sudden announcement and not one he'd been expecting to make. 'She's moving to Wales to be near her sister.'

'How do you know?' Anila asks. 'Did someone tell you?'

'No, she phoned me this morning. Just before I left for work. I was surprised to get a call after five years of no contact. She's not shown any interest in getting in touch before now.'

Anila takes a moment to hold Tiny back on the lead while another squirrel with a death-wish bounces across the path in front of them. 'But that's a good thing, right? Her finally selling the house?'

'It is,' Nate agrees. 'She wants to meet up in town and talk about the arrangements.'

'Can't you do it over the phone?'

'I don't mind meeting. I think it's time we talked face to face.'

'Well, at least you'll get half of the money from the house.'

Nate shakes his head. 'I'll be giving it all to Jean. Along with our joint savings.'

'What?'

'I said that I would.'

Anila sighs heavily and shakes her head. 'You're a better person than I am, Nate, you really are. I know what I'd do in your place. I'd take what's rightfully mine.'

★★★

On the way back to the centre, Wayne and Katie catch them up.

'Car!' Wayne shouts as a silver people carrier slows behind them. Katie moves over and beckons it forward. It passes by carefully, the driver lifting his hand in thanks.

'You two up for a slightly longer walk?' she asks, out of breath from the exertion. 'I need to cheer this one up and show him what he's been missing. Never got walked before apparently, poor thing. Tied up in the backyard. Is it any wonder he looks like he does?'

'I'm happy to keep going,' Anila agrees.

''Course,' Nate adds.

'Good,' Katie says. 'Let's see if it does the trick and puts a spring back in the step of Victor Meldrew here.'

They all turn down a lane that will give them a longer loop back to the centre. Nate is glad of the extra time outside. It feels good to take in the fresh air and the last of the day's sun. It gives him the opportunity to think as well. Jean had sounded odd on the telephone. Not the way she did five years ago. Then she had been full of confidence, her self-esteem boosted by the amorous attentions of a younger man. As they set off on the long return stretch of the road, he wonders what has made his ex-wife want to move after all these years. He wonders if she'll be going alone. She'd not given him a great deal of detail on the phone. Nothing to explain the reason for a life-changing decision and no indication of whether or not she'd be accompanied by the man she left Nate for so suddenly five years earlier.

CONNOR

The next day, the news he had hoped he could somehow magically avoid all summer, reaches him as soon as he wakes up, courtesy of the ever-present newsfeed on his phone. 15 August.

Results Day – What It Means for Millions of Our Teenagers!

Feeling annoyed, Connor pushes his legs with force into a pair of non-muddy jeans. There are so many other, more important, things to be doing instead of driving to college today. Going to Highview and helping Pearl to walk further across the patio for one. The garden at the back of Fern Crescent could do with some weeding too, and the flowers need replacing on his mum's grave. With little motivation, Connor pulls on a fresh T-shirt and only after he has put it on, he remembers to spray deodorant under both arms.

In the lounge, Yvo and Donald are waiting. Yvo is holding a drinks bottle with what looks like green slime inside it.

'I made you a smoothie,' she says, passing it to him. 'Enjoy.'

'Thanks,' he replies, taking it but unable to think of anything else to say in reply. It might be filled with poison. Or, worse, kale.

'So, results.' Donald steps forward as if it's impossible for Connor to hear him from the other side of the coffee table. 'It's the big day!'

Connor looks at his father, wondering if they'll ever really be able to talk about the important stuff.

He watches as his father rocks back and forth on his heels like someone about to shout, 'March!'

But instead, Donald says, 'So no Cs, remember. Just As!' As if he has any control over that now. Feeling for his car keys in his jeans pocket, Connor realises he must be the only eighteen-year-old in the country hoping to fail their A-levels today. It would be tricky to be seen looking delighted if he does. He'd have to work on that for the sake of those around him. But as yet it's still an unknown.

Yvo steps forward so she's in line with Donald, close by his side. 'It's important. This day. Your future. You must do well.' Her eyes are unblinking as she speaks, her accent as strong as the day she arrived. He sees there is a splat of pink paint on her cycling shorts, the exact colour of a dead salmon.

'It would be good to see you do well,' Donald announces. 'York requires the best. Nothing less.'

Connor can't remember when his father's idea of a successful future had morphed into the reality he is now living. Sometime just after Mum died or was it before?

'And if I don't do well? What happens then?' He feels it's worth asking the question even if his tone has come out more confrontational than he'd hoped. 'It's been a difficult couple of years,' he adds.

Donald, he notices, has the good grace to look away, to the old bookcase in the corner where a framed photograph of his wife used to stand, the photograph that is now consigned to a cardboard box somewhere in the garage.

'Dad?'

'Yes, it's been . . .' His father's voice falters, and he appears unable to find the right word. His face is flushed, he looks tired. More so than before. 'Difficult,' Donald finishes.

'You will do well,' Yvo fills in. 'You have your father's brain, Connor. So clever.' She smiles and takes his father's hand in hers.

Connor feels his stomach flip again at the thought of getting straight As. He'd happily take an out-and-out fail for every subject and breathe a sigh of relief. 'I've got to go,' he says.

'We will wave off from the window,' Yvo says. 'Break your leg.'

'Good luck,' Donald adds, his voice softening in a way Connor hasn't heard in a very long time.

'Thanks, Dad.'

And then Donald says, 'Remember – top marks,' and the moment is gone.

★★★

Derek is waiting for him outside the Co-op, and Molly is there for added moral support for them both. When Connor pulls up and gets out, he notices her looking at him intently.

'Con, look at you!' she says, raising her voice and scaring a couple of Japanese tourists photographing the town's memorial. 'Damn! Pearl's cakes and all that digging have shaped you right up,' she adds. 'Definitely noticeable.'

Connor feels his cheeks reddening; he's hot, really hot, and not just because of the bright sun beaming down on the streets of Westdown.

'Thanks. Must be the cake, you're right.'

Molly delivers one of her kilowatt smiles. 'Looks really good on you.'

'Hello? Person needing to get back to work ASAP,' Derek interjects. 'If you two have quite finished?'

'Give over,' Molly laughs. 'I was just saying.'

Derek shakes his head. 'I'll never make Deputy Assistant Manager if I'm not reliable and I said I'd be back in an hour and a half.'

'Shall we get this over with, then?' Connor asks him, and Derek nods.

'Let's do it.'

Molly waves them off. 'Mum's got Tommy today so I might get a bus and go into Exeter. Good luck.' She smiles at Connor. 'Or whatever.'

Molly has never tried to hide the fact she doesn't want him to leave Westdown. 'And break up our gang? No way. We've known each other too long,' she is always saying. She leans in at the car window, the sweet smell of her perfume tickling his nostrils and making him want to sneeze. 'So actually, I hope you do really, really badly.'

'Me too,' he says, before starting the engine and heading off to the college he had been content to leave behind at the start of the summer holidays.

PEARL

She is standing in the front room staring at the TV. It's not usually on at this time of day, but today is an exception. There is footage of teenagers in highly emotional states. Talk of A-Levels and GCSEs. Grade boundaries and expectations. Mixed in with the students are reporters brandishing boom mics, and there are an assortment of parents, some of whom also appear to be highly charged. The pupils answer reporters questions about how they are feeling. Pearl thinks it is quite obvious from their faces if they are confident of doing well or not.

She turns off the television, goes into the kitchen and switches on the radio. The newsreader is talking about exam results. There seems to be no escape from the topic. She listens to a man who presents a TV programme all about cars who says he left school with very few qualifications and has succeeded in becoming a multi-millionaire. He advises every young student to stay calm and not panic.

Unable to settle, Pearl retires to the reading room and selects a book from the biography section. It's about an astronaut and is full of plenty of breathtaking *previously unreleased images* taken from the International Space Station as it orbits the earth. She studies each one and feels slightly light-headed at the high-altitude views. Sunrise looks different from the heavens, she notices. A pure white luminescent curve poised high above the earth.

At eleven o'clock, Pearl climbs the stairs and then cleans them as she descends, brushing the faded carpet and polishing the wooden banister until it shines.

Just as she is considering making herself a cheese and pickle sandwich for lunch, the phone rings. When she answers it, there is the sound of young voices all talking simultaneously in the background. And then Connor's.

'Pearl?'

'Connor?'

'I'm here. It's quite busy. Lots of people.'

She imagines him holding the phone close to his ear and pressing a hand over the other so he might hear more clearly.

'Are you and Derek all right?' she asks. 'I saw it all on the news. The exam results and the students. Have you been in?' she adds, reluctantly. 'Have you heard?'

'I have.' His reply sounds as disheartened as she imagined it might. He is clever, of this she is in no doubt. More than able to pass exams with flying colours. But Connor has other priorities: working outside, seeing a garden grow, following in his mother's footsteps not his father's this time.

'Is it bad news?'

'I've passed.' He sounds momentarily lost in the sea of students around him.

'Oh, Connor, I'm so sorry,' she says. 'Does that mean you have the grades for university?'

'Every single one I need,' he says in a hollow voice.

'I'm so sorry,' she says again.

'My dad won't be.'

There is a brief pause during which someone calls his name. A girl. A fellow student. She sounds happy.

'I'd better go.'

'I am so sorry, really I am.'

'Thanks, Pearl . . . for understanding.' There's a pause and then he says,' 'I'll see you tomorrow.'

After he says goodbye, she puts the receiver down in its cradle and contemplates the course Connor must now follow. With things the way they are, time is undoubtedly running out. It would seem to her he is no more able to avoid an unwanted move to York and three years at university than she is capable of flying to the moon.

January 2010

Pearl woke to the sound of something heavy slipping very slowly from the roof. It dropped and landed soggily outside. Bleary-eyed, she swung her feet from under the covers and searched out her slippers with her toes. The room was bright even though she sensed it wasn't quite morning. Pulling back the curtains, she was greeted with a vision of the garden covered in snow. It lay all around like a thick white blanket. Imprinted in the crisp, icy surface were the tracks of an animal; Pearl pictured a fox. The tell-tale marks showed its circuitous route. A flash of colour diverted her attention. Red on pure white. A robin on the frozen fence. His eyes searched the snow for food. The moorland glistened in the distance and the hills looked like ice-capped mountains from a faraway land. Pearl moved closer until her face was almost touching the window. Each pane was etched with a delicate decoration of frost. Her breath made a misty patch on the surface, which she decided not to clear with her fingers for fear of them being instantly frozen to the glass.

The winter worsened. Overnight temperatures of minus twenty-one degrees were recorded in the Scottish Highlands. The man presenting the evening news said the country was in the grip of the Big Freeze. Lorries were stuck on motorways, schools were closed, and two people were killed when a bus overturned on a minor road in Cornwall. Ray developed a cough that kept him awake at night. He promised to visit the doctor and get it listened to once the weather improved. Lana fell ill at the same time with a chest infection. Pearl stayed away from the window and the cold, wrapped herself in blankets, sat in bed and drank hot tea to keep her warm. The wind whistled through gaps in the windows and stole through the cracks in the walls. The flagstone floor in the hallway and kitchen was as cold as the icy roads, she was sure. Lana lit a fire in the grate and kept it going. Ray chopped logs outside, which only served to make him cough more, increasingly so until he was leaving a stain of blood on his handkerchief.

Pearl stayed in her room to avoid catching a chill. She couldn't go to hospital. Not for any reason. The thought made her retreat to bed and lie as still as possible for long hours of the day. The previous summer she had slipped on the stairs and twisted her ankle. The relief that it wasn't broken was the greatest she'd ever known. If she couldn't step out of the door, how could she visit an Accident and Emergency unit miles away?

Eventually, the harsh winter broke, the snow and ice melted, and the moor was flooded as a result. Great lakes of water lay on the grass, and the Fire Brigade worked day and night to unblock drains stuffed with sodden leaves and debris that had been washed down from higher ground. Pearl watched them from her window, clearing the roadways for vehicles to get through. When the road was usable again, Ray visited the surgery in Westdown to get a diagnosis. It was the smoking, the doctor said. Blood when he coughed was a worrying sign.

Ray slept fitfully and grew paler, diminishing in size before Pearl's eyes. He became increasingly angry, recalling how as a young man he'd been told smoking cigarettes was good for clearing the lungs, not harmful to them. It was even encouraged in advertisements endorsed by doctors and dentists alike. That didn't seem fair. He told Pearl he hated being half the man he once was and no longer being able to do what formerly he did with ease. She sat with him in the front room when he became too weak to move, while Lana tried to come to terms with the fact that his lungs were eaten alive with disease. When he passed, Lana went to the funeral while Pearl sat alone in the kitchen and cried, wishing she had been able to accompany her mother to the service. The Fear had robbed her of the moment, a chance to say a last goodbye to the man who had been the only father she'd ever cared about.

Lana never fully recovered from Ray's death or the chest infection she'd fallen ill with that winter. It returned each year along with the change in the weather, and in 2016 it removed her from the world altogether.

CONNOR

When the call comes from Annie it's a Saturday. On his way back from St Stephen's, he pulls over and answers his phone. The churchyard had been busy with people decorating the wooden gate and archway with flower garlands in preparation for an afternoon wedding. Life going on as normal.

'I think we might have found someone . . . someone who might be able to help. Finally!' Annie says jubilantly on the other end, instantly reminding him of their conversation in her kitchen the night they all ate spaghetti Bolognese and Amber wore make-up for a date in the pub. 'His name is Jim. Can you come to The Willows? He's here right now.'

'I'll drive over now. I'm just at the church.'

'Great! I'll let them know at reception to expect you.'

On the way, he tries to imagine what Jim will look like and what he might say. Is this man a doctor, a nurse, or a resident? Help from someone knowledgeable would be welcome right now. Time seems somehow to have accelerated towards his leaving date, reminding Connor how little of it is left. Passing through the town and out the other side, he soon arrives at the former stately home that used to belong to a family, and which is now home to twenty elderly residents enjoying their twilight years in the comfort of rooms with high ceilings and thick carpets.

In the smart entrance area, he waits while people dressed in the same navy uniform as Annie's walk past, acknowledging his presence with a friendly nod or a smile. When she appears, Annie herself looks delighted to see him. 'Hello, love. Some good news at last, eh?' she says. 'Come on, it's this way. I'll take you to him.'

In the seclusion of the visitors' lounge, she explains: 'He was talking to one of the nurses. They had quite a chat, the other nurse said. She also said I might want to talk to him so I asked if he wouldn't mind and he said, no problem. You see, he's been in the same situation as Pearl. It was just Meals on Wheels that was keeping him going after his wife died. That and a woman from across the street who was concerned for him because she never saw him out. But then something quite amazing happened.' She beams at Connor. 'Anyway, he knows you're coming. It's just this way.'

They pass a room with a TV humming quietly in the corner and three residents, a man and two women, blissfully unaware they are missing *Countdown* because they are fast asleep in their chairs. In the next room, a young woman is standing in front of four residents demonstrating how to stick pieces of patterned paper on the surface of a small box.

'It's called découpage apparently,' Annie says, hurrying on. 'Next week it's indoor crazy golf.'

At two sets of enormous, green-painted doors with panes of toughened glass, she stops and turns around. 'I should say, he's actually called Mr Hayward, but we just call him Jim.'

'Thanks, Annie,' Connor says. 'I keep saying that.'

'My pleasure, love,' she says. 'Don't worry about it. I'll be keeping my fingers crossed that he can pass on some words of wisdom that might help. Give me a shout if you need me. I'll just be in the residents' lounge.'

When Annie leaves, he turns around and immediately scans the garden for a sign of anyone waiting.

The area at the back of the nursing home opens out into an expansive lawn, and in the middle of this is a giant yew tree. There is only one person visible, sitting on a bench beneath it, his head covered in snowy-white hair that just shows over the back of the seat.

When Connor reaches him, Jim's eyes are closed, and he isn't moving.

For a moment, Connor thinks about going back indoors and leaving him to his afternoon nap. But Annie said he was expecting a visit, so a visit it is.

'Hello, Jim?' He keeps his voice low for fear of startling the elderly man.

And then more loudly, 'Mr Hayward?'

First one rheumy eye opens and then the other. Jim stretches his spindly limbs and taps his hearing aid. There's the hiss of a response from the cream gadget in his ear. 'You must be Connor,' he says.

'I'm sorry to disturb you.' Connor tries to pinpoint how old Jim is. Mid-eighties at a guess. 'I just got here.'

'No bother, lad,' Jim replies, turning up his hearing aid. 'I was having a nap to pass the time.'

'If it's OK, I wondered if I could ask you a couple of questions.'

'Ask away.' Jim shuffles himself along the bench. 'Don't you want to sit down? Take the weight off your feet?'

The backrest has a gold plaque on it and engraved on this is an inscription.

For Winnie who liked nothing more than to rest here a while.

Jim taps his ear again and looks up.

'Did you say something?' he asks, tilting his head. 'Did I miss the question?'

Connor smiles. Jim seems nice. 'No, I didn't ask anything. Not yet, anyway.'

'Ah, good.'

Connor takes in the sight of the garden around them. It's well looked after and manicured. A quiet space. 'It's very peaceful here.'

'It is,' Jim says. 'Beautiful, in fact. I'm glad I can enjoy it now.'

'And before?' Connor asks, glad the elderly man is taking the lead about the matter in hand. 'When you couldn't go out, I mean?

Jim nods. 'Annie said you wanted to talk about that.'

'Is it OK?'

'She said you were trying to help someone.'

'I am. Her name is Pearl, and she hasn't been outside for a very long time.'

'Then I'll tell you everything I can.'

Jim clears his throat with a small cough. He shakes his head in dismay, remembering. 'After my Lizzie died I sort of shut meself off from the world. Then after a while, I got used to just being inside the house and not going out. Outside looked frightening to me. It's a bugger of a thing, to be honest. Not to be underestimated. It sort of catches hold of you, and then there you are, never going anywhere but inside the house.' Jim moves his lips like someone chewing a boiled sweet. 'And I worried all the time, too, about what would happen if I had to leave one day – you know, if I fell or did my hip in. They'd never have got me out, not without strapping me down or giving me a sedative to knock me out. It was a grim time, I don't mind saying now. I did nothing for fear of injuring myself or needing help. I barely existed, lad, if I'm being truthful. Just sat inside all day until bedtime.'

'Can I ask what changed that?' Connor says, feeling sudden admiration for Jim. He has been through so much. Just like Pearl.

'You need a reason . . . to go outside. That's the thing,' Jim says, turning to him, watery eyes half closed against the sun. 'Something to make it worth facing the fear head on. A goal to get you through taking that first step. It's tough. You have to tell yourself you'll be OK, and you need other people to tell you that too, for when you're having a difficult day. That helps more than it sounds like it would.'

Jim swallows hard.

'It was one of the hardest times of my life. And if it hadn't been for my daughter getting back in touch after a couple of years, then I'd probably never have done anything about it.'

'Your daughter?'

Jim nods. 'We'd not spoken, and when my wife died she stayed away, some stupid argument we'd both let go too far.' He sighs deeply. 'Anyway, she brought my granddaughter and two of my great-grandchildren with her to the house and the little ones wanted to go outside. You know kids – they just wanted to run around, not sit inside with a stuffy old pensioner. At first, I sat and watched them playing out in my garden. I didn't go and join them, even when they shouted to me. I couldn't, you see. Then one day my daughter came round and asked me why I did that, and even though I felt embarrassed to admit it, I went right ahead and told her.'

'Did it change anything?'

Jim nods. 'It did.'

'People kept coming round after that. More family and friends. At all hours of the day and night! I couldn't get rid of them!' he laughs. 'So, I thought: Sod it, they'll never leave me alone if I don't do this and go out. Then, after I'd taken the first step, I walked a bit further every day. Down the street, round to the social club. Took time and a lot of patience. I think perseverance is the main thing. You have to keep going and not give up even when you want to.'

Jim stops, looking like he's walking those steps all over again, and takes several deep breaths before carrying on.

'Now, I go out with my great-grandkids and my daughter. To the park, the zoo – you name it, we visit it. I sleep like a baby in the evening on those days. I'm exhausted!' He smiles again, then leans forward and fiddles with his hearing aid. 'Is that OK, lad?'

'More than OK, Jim.'

'Are you sure?'

'I am, only . . .'

'Yes?'

'What if it's been a really long time that someone's been inside – like decades?'

Jim takes another deep breath, his withered frame lifting like a light sail in the wind. 'I think it's always best if you can get help at the beginning, before things become too bad, you know?' He stops and shakes his head at a memory. 'But it's hard. And that many years . . . it's bound to make it even more so. I'm sorry, lad. That's probably not what you want to hear.'

'It's OK, I'm grateful for everything you've said,' Connor says.

'Just remember. Don't give up.'

Connor nods his agreement.

'That's the idea, lad. Perseverance. And remember, what frightens the life out of one person might not even register for another. It's all about understanding. You never know what folk have been through.'

'Thanks . . . for talking to me.'

Jim nods. 'Here we go. Looks like we've got company.'

A ginger cat appears on the lawn and stares indignantly at them both. Jim's lined face breaks into a wide smile. 'That's George. Well, it might be Bob or John for all I know, but I call him George.'

Connor wonders if George is another reason Jim sits outside.

'Nice cat.'

'He is,' agrees Jim. 'But he's not mine. He just wanders about the place like he owns it and joins me sometimes on this bench if he deems fit.'

Connor nods, sensing he might be sitting in George's favourite spot. 'I'll leave you to it then.'

'Good luck, lad. I'll be keeping everything crossed for you and . . .'

'Pearl.'

'Pearl,' he repeats. 'That's a name you don't hear very often. It's a special name. I hope she can find the reason she needs. I really do.'

As he walks to the door that will take him past the activities room and into the residents' lounge, Connor turns back to look at Jim. He isn't alone on the bench anymore. The space where Connor had sat is now occupied by a large ginger cat licking his paws in the shade of the giant yew tree.

NATE

The Harvest Café and Bar is filling up with early-evening diners. Ambient lighting, an unobtrusive jazz soundtrack and the smell of freshly brewed coffee all make for a relaxed and welcoming atmosphere. Overhead, brushed-metal pendant lights hang from the ceiling on industrial-looking chains, and a long, wooden trestle table and matching chairs dominate the centre of the room.

Nate takes a seat at a similarly rustic table for two by the window and a young woman with pink hair and a T-shirt with the slogan YOUR HARVEST HOST approaches him, holding an iPad.

'Can I help you?' She smiles.

'Just a white coffee, please.'

'No problem. I'll be right back with that for you,' she says.

As the waitress walks away, Nate looks around at the busy restaurant, feeling a sense of relief that he booked a table with a view of the street. At least he will know when Jean arrives and see at once if she is bringing her younger male companion along to join them.

Ten minutes later, he sees her crossing the road and heading towards him. She looks older, and her bobbed hair is now grey all over, not just at the roots.

Nate is sure her impression of him will be the same, an aged version of the man she last saw five years ago. With huge relief, he notes she has come alone.

A couple in their early twenties stand to one side at the door to let Jean pass. She nods a curt thank you, before looking around and then circumnavigating the tables to get to him.

He stands up as she approaches.

'Hello, Jean.'

'Nate.'

'Can I get you a coffee?' he asks, sitting down as she takes her seat.

'I'm quite tight on time. But a coffee, yes. Espresso, please,' she says, lowering her eyes immediately and retrieving a thick document from her handbag.

Nate manages to get the attention of the waitress to put in the order.

'I need you to sign these,' Jean says, without any preamble. She slides the document across the table. 'If you could get it back to me soon, I'd be grateful.'

The paper looks official. Wordy and detailed.

'So, you're leaving? For Wales?'

'I am.' Jean's tone is clipped. 'As soon as possible.'

The young woman brings the extra coffee and Nate is glad. He has the feeling he has done something wrong already and the girl's arrival is a welcome distraction.

'And . . .?' he continues, struggling to remember the name of the man from the charity shop with whom Jean ran off. 'Erm . . .'

'Brian.'

'Yes, that's it, Brian. Will he be going too? Have you got plans?'

Jean shakes her head, her bare lips suddenly pursed. He notices she isn't wearing any lipstick. Last time he saw her they had been painted a bold, show-stopping red; the sort a famous actress might wear on an equally vibrant red carpet on the opening night of a star-studded premiere. It wasn't like Jean at all.

'No,' she says in answer to his question about the young man she worked alongside who had prompted her to change the colour of her lipstick to something more noticeable, not to mention take up a daily high energy aerobics class which caused her to severely strain a muscle in her back and have to pay for the services of an osteopath immediately after. 'We're not together anymore. He's moved out. It's over.'

'I'm sorry to hear that.' When the words leave his mouth, Nate knows that he means them wholeheartedly. Jean appears significantly distressed and deflated by the whole experience.

He looks at his ex-wife. She averts her eyes and focuses on the pavement outside. He follows her gaze, and sees the shoppers with their bags of groceries, the smartly dressed office workers on their way home, a young couple walking past hand in hand and looking very much in love.

'Jean, would you like to talk about it?'

She falls silent, as if the words she says next are set to define her for the rest of her life.

'It turns out Brian wasn't who I thought he was. He was a very clever man in some respects. I didn't see it coming at all.'

The young couple outside stop to read the menu stuck to the Harvest Café window just above Nate and Jean's heads. The couple steal a quick kiss before walking away.

'It turned out to be nothing more than a sham.' Jean looks dangerously close to tears. 'He was just looking for someone to buy him expensive gifts. Several of them,' she clarifies.' A car and a watch, some designer shoes, and a set of luggage that cost over five hundred pounds. I should have realised. I feel so ridiculous . . . all the signs were there, and I had no idea.'

'Brian was a conman?'

She looks back at him and nods. 'A prolific one.'

Nate tries to take it all in. The last time he saw his wife, she'd been standing in the porch of their home in a new dress and uncharacteristically high shoes while he walked away with a suitcase, about to move into his flat at Weatherley Gardens. Their parting hadn't been acrimonious, despite the situation. Their marriage had been over years before. Jean's adultery had simply marked a line in the sand and brought it to a sudden but ultimately predictable end.

'It gets worse,' she adds. 'I wasn't the first, not by a long shot. A woman who lives in Crawley phoned me towards the end and said Brian wasn't actually Brian at all. She told me his real name is Clive. He'd been seeing her at the same time and had taken her money too. She'd found my number on his phone and plucked up the courage to call, thinking I was the other woman. Actually, one of several other women she'd found contact numbers for on his phone.'

'Jean, that's terrible,' he says, wondering exactly how many middle-aged women Brian targeted in his quest to fund his flamboyant lifestyle.

'Almost everything is gone,' she says, dropping her voice to a level that is almost inaudible. 'I've just got the house left. It's why I need to sell so I can start again. I'll look for somewhere so I can be near my sister. I'm sorry, but I have no other choice.'

'Jean. . .' Nate begins. 'I don't know what to s-'

'Will you sign the documents? It's all I need,' she asks, her eyes desperate and pleading.

'Yes, of course.'

'Thank you,' Jean says, breathing a sigh of relief. 'I don't know what I would have done if you'd said no.'

★★★

Back in his flat in Weatherley Gardens, Nate drops the thick document onto his bedside table.

He'd taken no pleasure in hearing Jean's news. Before they parted ways outside the Harvest Café, she had suggested they meet up one final time.

'We still have things to discuss, before I go,' she said. 'Not about the house or money, but about the past. I think it would do us both good. Clear the air.'

And Nate had agreed. He had always known the day would come when they would have to address the elephant in the room. The unspoken reason their marriage had never been fuelled by any love or passion and had died many years before he actually walked away. They can't pretend the elephant in the room doesn't exist. After all, it is so large, unavoidable, and impossible to ignore.

PEARL

The feeling of taking the first step outside, when it comes, is overwhelming. Not to a marathon runner or the hikers who conquer the moor, but to a woman in an old pair of her mother's shoes it is everything. Connor had explained about Jim, his self-isolation, and the success he had had leaving his house, just when he'd give up hope. It had come as a much-needed boost.

The crows on the grass shuffle about in anticipation of the main event, their feathers lifting and lowering in a slight breeze. If she didn't know better, it looks like they are forming a finishing line of sorts and encouraging her to aim for it with every ounce of courage she can muster. Determined not to let Connor down again, she thinks of Jim stepping out of his house, and puts her right foot forward and down onto the step.

In a voice that is no more than a whisper, she says: 'One . . .'

The crows jostle. A robin lands alongside and they chase it away. While they flutter their wings excitedly, Pearl tries to slide the other foot over the threshold, but it feels unnaturally heavy, like it's made of lead, and so difficult to move.

'Two . . .' It is rooted to the spot, but she tugs it free and down onto the patio, swaying unsteadily from the effort. She rights herself.

'Three . . .' Connor says, close beside her.

Pearl hears her own ragged breathing and feels the familiar unpleasant sensations that remind her she might pass out and fall at any moment, like a toppled monument, crashing onto the rough stone and breaking into pieces that roll away and can never be put back together again.

But Connor is holding her hand. She concentrates on the fact that he's standing alongside her, willing her on.

'Is it better if you take a rest now,' he says, 'for a minute?'

He waits patiently for her answer and Pearl realises she needn't rush. 'Yes, just a minute. Then I'll try again.'

'Don't worry,' he smiles. 'There's another twelve hours of daylight before it starts to get dark.'

And she laughs, feeling instantly better.

'Let's try again.'

She closes her eyes, intent on stepping a proper distance away from the house that has been her home, refuge, and confinement. She slides a foot further over the patio. Taps it gingerly just to make sure. One more step. Then another. Breathe, she reminds herself, don't forget to breathe. Forget the past. Just think of the future A different future. Life can change. Hadn't Jim proved that, even after the devastating loss of his wife he'd found his way?

'One step, then another,' she says. 'And another.'

'Pearl, you're doing it!' Connor's voice sounds distant. Then suddenly closer.

'Pearl, you're properly out! You're actually standing in the garden!'

When she opens her eyes, he is looking at her with admiration and amazement on his face, as if he can't quite believe it himself.

She feels the caress of warm sun on her outstretched hands, hears the gentle rustle of the leaves in the oak trees and smells the air, the grass, the earth, and the many roses in their beds. Her senses heightened and her heart pumping, she takes it all in.

'I'm out!' she says, feeling the sheer shock and joy of it all at the same time. With another deep breath, she immediately turns her face to the sky. 'The world is so large without a ceiling to it.' Her senses feel more alive than ever before. The smell of flowers and fresh air, the feel of the solid stone beneath her feet, the sun slowly warming the skin on her hands and face. If she walks a little further and bends down, she can touch the grass. Another day. Hopefully soon. It will be a new goal.

The crows, sensing this might be the end of today's performance, fly away to the oak trees and disappear behind their canopy of leaves.

'You did it!' Connor beams, his eyes shining bright. 'What happens now?'

The enormity of it is difficult to comprehend. After all these years of looking at the same wallpapered walls and flagstone floor inside.

'I think I need a drink! Shall we have a drink?'

'Definitely,' he laughs. 'Something stronger than tea, though?'

'I think I've got some ginger beer in the larder,' she says, still feeling giddy. 'I bought the sort with alcohol in it, by mistake. Will that do, do you think, as a celebration?'

'Sounds ideal,' he smiles again.

Pearl feels her heart swell. 'Thank you, Connor, what else can I say?'

'That we'll do it again tomorrow? And maybe go further this time.'

'Tomorrow . . . we will,' she agrees warmly. They retrace the monumental half a dozen steps back to the French doors and inside.

They drink glasses of ginger beer full to the brim, and by the end of the third glass, her cheeks are rosy thanks to the sun and the alcohol, and her heart is filled with joy. Feeling encouraged by the morning's achievements, she makes a note to order more in the next delivery. As many as ten bottles, Pearl decides, in the gentle hope that there will be further call to drink to their achievements, more progress made across the patio, all the way to the other side of the garden and even beyond.

★★★

They walk much further the next day, talking about Jim, his daughter, his granddaughter and great-grandchildren as they go, to the end of the patio and onto the lawn, far enough to touch the new bird feeder that is providing a morning snack for a starling.

When they eventually stop, they are more than halfway down the lawn, next to the boundary post-and-rail fence. Over it Pearl can see unexplored moorland stretching away before her. One day . . .

Target reached for the morning, they turn their backs on the sunshine and head inside.

Back in the kitchen, she says, 'Let's do something different this afternoon. No cleaning or gardening. We could just
sit down and relax.'

'Sounds good to me,' Connor agrees, switching the kettle
on to boil while reaching up for the cups and saucers for
tea.

He looks relieved by the suggestion. No doubt he has a
lot to think about. If only he had had the time to speak to
his father before the train tickets are bought for York. The
final stage before it is too late.

'I was thinking we could watch a programme on the TV.'

Connor fills the teapot and leaves it to rest. 'Sure. I'll
bring this in, shall I?'

In the living room, Pearl hunts down just the VHS tape
she has in mind.

'Tea and brioche coming right up!' he calls from the
kitchen, and Pearl wonders what it will be like at Highview
when he isn't in the garden, mowing and digging, or talking
to her at the table. That will be a sad day when it comes.

When he comes in, she asks, 'Ready?'

'As I'll ever be,' he laughs. 'I'm guessing we're watching
Detective Donnelly?'

'We are.' Pearl feels the tape in her hand.

'From the eighties?'

'The very same.'

'On VHS?'

'Yes. Hopefully, it won't stick halfway through,' she says.
'It's so annoying when it does that.'

Pearl switches on the television. It's antiquated by modern standards, with a humpback and a remote control the

size of a shoe, but it works. The tape she has selected is the Christmas special from 1985, filmed on location in the Canary Islands. She lets the machine swallow it whole and settles down to watch the episode she has specifically chosen for Connor because it is action-packed. Beside her, Connor eats a brioche while focused on the screen, his whole face lit up and interest engaged as soon as the credits roll.

Half an hour in, he agrees with her that there is something quite heroic about the moustachioed Scottish crime fighter who consistently outsmarts even the most experienced of criminals. There is no denying Detective Donnelly is to be admired, Connor admits, especially the way he takes down deadly enemies while at the same time surfing the emotional tidal wave of a failed marriage and a boss who won't promote him, no matter how high his strike rate. Added to that is his ability to drive any form of motor vehicle or transport, including a speedboat across the azure waters off the Tenerife coastline while in pursuit of an arch criminal in a thick Aran jumper and very tight trousers.

After Detective Donnelly has wrestled a man twice his size to the ground back on dry land, and apprehended an entire criminal organisation single-handed, Pearl and Connor remain seated while they watch the closing credits.

'Another?' he says, in the room she has shaded from the sun by half-closing the heavy curtains.

'I'd like that very much.'

'I'll get it.'

Connor reboots the old VHS machine with a new tape. This time it's episode one, the very first episode of *Detective Donnelly* ever made.

'I could end up bingeing on these,' he smiles. 'I think I'm hooked.'

'Bingeing?' she asks.

'You watch them back-to-back, one after the other,' he says, and Pearl realises she can't imagine a better way to spend an afternoon.

The title sequence rolls with a close-up shot of Detective Donnelly staring enigmatically down the camera lens, and the pilot episode bursts onto the screen in a blaze of bullets, lights and outdated clothing. Pearl tries not to think about the future, hard as that is, a future when Connor isn't here at Highview. Determined to put it to the back of her mind, she focuses on the screen. Just for now, they have several action-packed episodes of an eighties crime-fighting classic to enjoy.

NATE

Jean telephones his mobile. She asks if he will meet her this evening and apologises for the short notice.

Thirty minutes later, Nate drives the familiar road to a house he used to call home. It hasn't changed at all, not in any way. Built only two years before they were married, they'd been delighted at the time by its dark wooden window frames and front door, its single garage and driveway that was long enough for two cars. It was a world away in design from his mother's two-up, two-down in Victoria Street, but a short enough distance in actual miles for Mrs Williams to continue to visit the newlyweds in order to give them the benefit of her puritanical advice.

He is sure she hadn't targeted Jean directly; strict guidance was meted out to anyone his mother met whether they liked it or not. Nevertheless, his wife hadn't taken kindly to being told she would be expected to take on duties in her spare time at the church, as well as being questioned on how soon it would be before they could expect to hear the pitter patter of tiny feet. Jean wasn't a maternal woman and never had been. Nate knew this. It hadn't been a secret.

He remembers how his new wife wouldn't settle until his mother's visits were over.

'She's always poking her nose in,' Jean had said, standing at the window of their front room and pulling back the net curtains to make sure Nate's father hadn't driven away and left his wife still standing on the driveway. 'I'm worried she's going to insist on moving in just so she can make sure we're living according to her holy law. Not God's, just hers!'

But the circumstance when Nate's mother might have moved in with them never arose. Mrs Williams passed away a year later. A heart attack. She had collapsed in the centre of Godalming, while returning from a prayer meeting, and the road had been cordoned off while the ambulance staff tried to resuscitate her and the police contained a small crowd. She would no longer control her son's life from that day, Jean had pointed out, and Nate accepted his wife's words in the positive spirit he is sure Jean meant them to be taken.

On his way to the house now, he is reminded of those visits of years ago. It is hard to forget the defining moments that occur in a property. It's as if the memories are hidden deep in the woodchip wallpaper and soaked forever in the plaster behind.

Carrying the legal document, he knocks on the door.

When Jean opens it, she says, 'I'm sorry to bring you back here. I wanted to talk and thought it might be better done behind closed doors rather than overheard by total strangers.'

'I understand,' he says.

Jean steps to one side, allowing him to pass. 'Everything is packed. I don't actually have anywhere for us to sit.'

Inside, the house is empty of furniture. Each room has an island of boxes in the centre and patches of carpet to the sides that are lighter than the rest, where a couch, a dresser or sideboard has stood for years protecting the hundred-per-cent wool twist beneath. They are still good carpets. They had paid extra. Nate notices a faint purple stain under the harsh light of the bare bulb overhead. The stain on the carpet was caused by a glass of red wine being accidentally tipped over on the night of the New Millennium. Their neighbours had come round. There had been a small gathering. He remembers how he and Jean had slept in separate beds that night, like they had begun to as a matter of course. He in the spare, she in the main. When he woke up in the morning, Jean was on her hands and knees scrubbing at the carpet, but the stain had always remained.

Without anywhere to sit, Nate allows his arms to hang at his sides and flexes his knees just a little to avoid the backache that is sure to come from standing in one place for too long. This won't be a brief discussion, he is sure of that, but before they get straight into it, he begins by returning the completed paperwork.

'It's all completed,' he says, laying the documents on top of a packing box. 'I understand it's just a formality, but I wanted to make sure there wouldn't be anything to cause an issue.'

'I'm grateful, I really am,' she says, as if keen to let him know how much. 'It's been an extremely stressful time.'

'I wouldn't ever have tried to make this difficult for you, Jean, please know that,' Nate replies, sincerely. 'I'm sorry if you worried that I would.'

'And you really *don't* want anything?' she asks. 'From the sale of the house?'

He shakes his head, not wanting to make this more complicated. 'I have a pension. It will see me through.'

They'd struggled when they first got married, using an upturned wooden crate as a makeshift table, and barely surviving on his low wages at the insurance company. Now, they have nothing again. Somehow, life has come full circle.

Jean looks up. There are unexpected tears in her eyes. 'I gave him every penny I had, Nate. All the savings, and I took out a loan. I was a fool and ended up in trouble financially. I was blinded by . . .' she stops, before admitting '. . . infatuation. I really thought he cared.'

'Jean, I am sorry.'

She nods. 'Given the circumstances, you could have made this extremely hard for me.'

'I wouldn't do that.'

'I know,' she smiles, sadly, and then, 'Nate, about our marriage . . .'

He nods.

'There's so much to say before I go,' she says.

He watches as she looks around at the home they once shared, the packing boxes marooned in the centre of the room.

'I was getting older, wasn't I, when we met?' she begins. 'I couldn't believe you would look at me twice. I thought it was too good to be true. Turned out it was.'

Jean stops and chooses her words more carefully before she resumes. 'I don't say that to be mean, honestly. It's just – I hoped we might be like other couples.'

Nate knows that what Jean is saying is more than fair, but it doesn't make for easy listening. They should have called a halt to the wedding before the church service with more flowers than people, and the wedding breakfast at the local town hall. They should have stopped it before it gained a momentum all of its own, culminating in them finding themselves standing in front of a vicar and saying 'I do.'

'I thought we could love each other, Nate, if I'm honest. I thought we could grow into it. Marriage. You and me. And I realise I was the one who pushed us towards an unworkable situation.'

'I could have said no,' he says. 'I wouldn't want you to think I walked into it with my eyes closed, or under duress. That wasn't what happened.'

'I know, but it was clear to me that you were still in love with someone else.'

Nate nods. 'Jean, I am so sorry.'

'You have no reason to be,' she says simply. 'Look at me – running off with a man almost half my age who clearly didn't care for me and losing all our money. I have to acknowledge what I did.'

She pauses and Nate waits.

'I knew you loved Pearl. I knew you loved her before we met.'

At the mention of that name, Nate closes his eyes. It hurts still, the memory. Even with the passing of time, he doubts the recollection of events will ever leave him.

'We were young,' he says. 'It was a long time ago.'

'But you loved each other,' Jean says, softly. 'And if life had turned out differently you would have stayed together and been married. But it didn't. What happened to her . . . it was so very wrong. I still remember that day, what people said, and how she left with her mother and the man who ran the haulage company in town.'

'Ray.'

'Yes, that was his name,' Jean says. 'I felt for them all. Most of all for Pearl,' she adds, earnestly. 'Such a beautiful girl.'

'I let her down.'

'I don't think she would see it like that.'

'She left and I lost her.'

'Perhaps,' Jean says. 'But you weren't to blame for her leaving.'

'Thank you for saying that.'

'It's all right,' Jean replies, her voice softening. 'We just weren't meant to be together, Nate. I know that now. And we're both too long in the tooth to dwell on it further, aren't we? It's time to move on.'

Nate nods, wishing they had talked like this years before now.

When he leaves her at the door of the house he used to call home, Jean waves him goodbye. They'd never been the sort of couple to hug each other and he notices neither of them feels the need to begin now.

'Take care, Jean,' he says.

'And you, Nate.'

'Please give my best to your sister.'

'I will. And good luck with whatever you choose to do now.'

He realises he hasn't told her about Happy Tails.

'I work with animals,' he says. 'Dogs mainly. It's a rescue centre.'

Jean smiles. 'I'm glad. You always did like them; it was just your mother who didn't.'

★★★

Anila texts him when he is back in Weatherley Gardens, standing in the bathroom cleaning his teeth.

> *Hope you're OK. Found new dating site. S.O.S. Singles Over Sixty? I could make you a profile?*

The text is followed by a trio of emojis: a smiling face, a pair of hands clasped in prayer, and two fingers crossed for good luck.

He decides to go round and see Anila after his shift has ended the next day. He owes her an explanation, the reason he cannot take her aunty out for dinner or sign up to the matchmaking site for older people that she has spent precious free time researching for him online. The conversation with Jean is spurring him on. Better to be straightforward and upfront about what happened in the past, and how he still thinks of Pearl even now. He had gone into one relationship, believing he could forget all about her. But he hadn't been able to do it.

As sleep takes him, he tumbles into the past. Memories of Pearl stirred up by Jean's words and the conversation that evening. Back to a time long before dating websites and algorithms determined a match. Back before Singles Over Sixty existed and when meeting the person you knew you wanted to spend the rest of your life with was simply down to old-fashioned good luck.

1974

It was early evening. His mother was preoccupied with a new cleaning rota for the church and his father had yet to return from work.

'I need some cigarettes. Can you go and pick me some up from the shop?' Mrs Williams shook an empty packet. 'Don't be spending this on anything else.'

Nate took the money she gave him, left Victoria Street and headed into town. He was in no hurry to return home, so he took his time. After buying a bag of chips at the fish and chip shop for his dinner, he threw away the newspaper they came in and made his way along Bridge Street. It was cold, even colder than usual for November. Wishing he'd not left in such a hurry and had remembered to put on a coat, he continued towards the shop at the end of the road, remembering his mother's request. Perhaps he'd go home straight away after, return to the house on Victoria Street, in the hope that his father had come home and started a fire in the grate. He had no idea how his life was about to change, walking through town that chilly night in the direction of the corner shop and without a coat.

The book was lying on the pavement. Up ahead, she was walking away, her conker-brown shoulder-length hair swinging from side to side. It glistened under the stream of golden light from the streetlamp. When he picked up the novel she'd dropped, the words on the hard cover swam like fishes in a pond, as difficult to read as he'd known they would be. He'd escaped the word 'dunce' in class, and other similar criticisms only because he'd managed to keep the problem of not being able to read as well as others could strictly to himself. When the teacher asked for pupils to speak lines aloud in class, he'd always kept his head down and avoided being chosen. In lessons, he just about got by.

His teacher went to church and was part of the same flower-arranging group as his mother. When parents' evening came around, they talked in front of him about tulips and the New Testament. Nate's poor ability to recognise words wasn't even mentioned. There were too many more interesting matters relating to the church for them to discuss. And in a packed class of often rowdy pupils, he succeeded in being overlooked.

With the book in his hand, he called out to the girl, realising she had already made good headway up the road ahead of him.

'Excuse me! Hello?'

She carried on walking.

'I think you dropped this!'

When she stopped and turned, he realised he had seen her before. She was in the year below him at school, but their paths had never crossed. It had been unlikely they ever would. Pearl Winter lived in a big house on The Heights and carried so many books in her bag that she hadn't noticed when one fell out. He lived in Victoria Street and struggled to decipher the simple title of the one he held in his hands.

'Sorry, I think this is yours,' he said, jogging towards her and offering it to her. 'It's not damaged or anything.'

'Thank you.' She took it and pushed it back into her gaping bag, looking embarrassed. 'It's *Wuthering Heights*. Have you read it?'

Nate shook his head.

'It's good.'

He realised he'd have to take her word for that.

Up close, under the lamplight, he noticed her eyes were the brightest blue. 'Is something wrong?' She smiled at him then. 'Have I got something on my face?' With one hand, she patted both cheeks self-consciously. 'Is it a bit of cottage pie?'

He laughed. 'No, no cottage pie. I was just . . .'

'Just what?' she said, bemused.

'You live up at The Heights?' Nate asked, more for something to say than any other reason.

'We do now, but we haven't always,' Pearl replied, openly. 'We used to live in a flat above the dry cleaner's in town. Until my mother met Ray. It's his house, not ours. How did you know?'

'I've seen you at school. Somebody said you lived up there.'

'I didn't realise it was that interesting.'

'Does it have a pool and a garden big enough to play cricket in?'

Pearl smiled again. 'It does. Although I wouldn't want to swim in that pool. Not today. It'll be freezing.'

She rubbed her arms up and down the sleeves of her woollen coat and her breath floated on the misty air. 'I'd better be getting back.'

'I'll walk with you if you like?' he said, surprising them both.

'Really? Are you sure?'

He nodded, forgetting the errand for his mother. 'If that's all right?'

While they walked along Bridge Street, out of town and up the hill towards The Heights, Nate asked Pearl all about what it was like to live in a great big house, and she said it was the same as living in any other size of house, only with more space for storing stuff.

Nate liked this answer. It made him feel like there wasn't such a difference between them after all.

CONNOR

Arriving at Highview, he feels it, the same determination as the day before. Time is running out; it also feels like it's speeded up. When he walks around the side of the house to the French doors he finds her waiting, feet already laced into her mother's old shoes.

'All ready?'

But Pearl doesn't look the same today. She is slower, and sadder. Not anything like the Pearl who walked confidently across the patio the day before.

From the French doors, each step is as careful as her first. He keeps close, and where the mottled stone of the patio ends and the neat grass begins, they stop for a breather. Three crows fly down from the trees and land at their feet. He watches as Pearl bends down and strokes each one. To his amazement, they let her. Her relationship with the birds always surprises him, like a falconer and his hawk at a display he watched at the Westdown Fete one summer. It was the last display of the day, when everyone had had their fill of ice creams, cake competitions and Morris dancing. The bird had performed dips and fly-pasts to the falconer's call and received the reward of a dead mouse at the end. Everyone clapped, and the falconer took a bow, while the bird did an extra soaring fly past that clearly hadn't been part of the act. That was the best part – seeing the bird wild and free.

When Connor looks back at Pearl, she is looking straight at him.

'There's something I need to show you,' she says, anxiously. 'Could we go inside? I don't think I can leave it any longer.'

'No more steps?'

'Not today . . . unfortunately.'

He follows her in and takes each threadbare step on the stairs up to the landing. As usual the house is tidy and clutter-free. Not like Fern Crescent, where every room has DIY equipment and pots of paint lying around.

Off the landing, there are three bedrooms and a spare room. The door to the spare room is open wide, so much so that he can see the stand-alone computer in the corner. It reminds him of the type his father used to have in the work office some years ago.

The door to the second room is closed.

'This was Ray and Lana's bedroom . . . before,' Pearl explains, her face suddenly flushing red. He wonders if it's just the heat of the day, or the short walk across the garden under the burning sun. She steps forward and with a small shove, pushes the door open. 'It's something of a problem,' she says, and as he follows her in, the scale of the situation becomes clear.

The floorspace is completely covered, every space taken up by cereal boxes, tin cans, plastic milk bottles and glass jars. Looking more closely, he sees that all the tins and plastic containers are washed, just as clean as the teacups and kitchen worktops downstairs. Years of recyclable waste in vast quantities, either lined up, stacked, folded, concertinaed, or crushed.

Pearl looks ashamed. It is painful to see. 'I've been storing it since Lana passed away,' she says. 'I'm so embarrassed by it.

But I didn't know what else to do with it. Thankfully, Ray had a waste-disposal unit installed in the kitchen sink. I don't know what I would have done if he hadn't, all those potato peelings and bones, there would have been nowhere for them to go.'

While he takes it all in, Pearl explains, 'The men stopped coming to collect the waste, you see, after Lana died. I suppose they thought, as there was never a bin left outside, there was no need to stop and collect. Now, I'm almost out of room and I don't know quite what to do.'

'Don't worry, we can shift it,' he says, mentally calculating exactly how many trips to the recycling centre it will take to clear the room. 'Honestly, it's not that bad.' Had he believed in superstitions, Connor knows he'd be crossing his fingers behind his back right now.

He sees the wave of relief wash over Pearl's face. 'It's been such a worry. I've been meaning to say, but then I hoped somehow I wouldn't have to . . . '

He smiles encouragingly, keen to let her know that she'll have her room back in no time. 'I'll sort it,' he says, looking back at the mountainous piles of recyclable waste leaning against each wall. 'I'll get a van. Derek's dad's got one. Then we'll come over and shift it.' Pearl nods gratefully. 'Getting to the end of the path . . . well, it was just too far,' she says, as her words fall on the empty packets and plastic bottles surrounding them.

★★★

In the car on his way home, Connor tries to chase the image from his mind of Pearl's embarrassed face and the bedroom filled to the brim with recycling. There is more to this than he thought. Who will deal with trips to the dump for her when he's gone? Who will stop the weeds taking over and the grass growing three foot high again? Who will drink tea and eat cake and be there so Pearl isn't always alone?

He drives over the moor, rumbles over the cattle grid and heads into town.

In Westdown, the streets are emptier now the coaches and day-trippers have gone home. All the gift shops and cafés are closed up for the day, quiet behind their dark windows before another busy day's trading begins again tomorrow.

Outside L'Epoque, tiny fairy lights twinkle, looped under the edge of the thick, thatched roof, just above a straight line of blue, white, and red bunting. Inside, the walls are painted white and covered in giant pieces of artwork. All very avant-garde. There's a light coming from the Co-op too. A beacon of hope.

Getting his mobile out of his pocket, he sends a message to those people he knows will do whatever they can to help, before going in search of his best friend. He already knows what Derek will say when asked, and Annie and Michael and Molly too when they get his text. They'll say yes, of course they'll make sure Pearl isn't alone when he leaves. They'll look after the garden and make sure she has someone to call in on her for a chat and lend a hand with the recycling. Because that's the sort of people they are. Derek appears from behind the cereal aisle and makes his way over, just as Annie and Molly message back.

Yes! When? I'm off on Wednesday and Michael will have the van. No problem at all. A.
Yes! Can't wait 2 meet Pearl! M xx

PEARL

Annie and Michael are the first to arrive the following week with Connor.

Fortunately, she has had plenty of time to search for extra cups and saucers in the dresser, crockery that hasn't been used in several years. Connor let her know the idea in advance. It has also given her plenty of time to prepare an apricot frangipane tart.

Over a cup of tea and a slice, Annie tells Pearl about her work at The Willows.

'I wanted to be a nurse from when I was a little girl, now I come to think about it. So, when I left school, I trained and then worked in the local hospital. A couple of years ago, I fancied a change and made the move. The residents have some stories to tell.' She smiles. 'Sometimes things you just aren't expecting at all. Last week we had to break up a game of strip poker in the TV room. Two slightly chilly gentlemen and two ladies, all in their nineties and down to their undies and playing for Murray Mints!'

Pearl warms to Annie instantly.

'I'll just go and have a look at that wonky gate,' Michael says, finishing his tea. He lets himself out of the front door, with Connor following.

It's clear to Pearl that Annie's husband is a man of few words but a whizz at fixing anything and everything.

He's already offered to fix a support to another section of falling-down fence, so that it stands upright once again, and put an end to the leaky tap in the upstairs bathroom.

'Always just give us a ring if there's anything you need,' Annie says.

'I will, thank you.' Pearl nods in relief. 'The house hasn't been touched in years. It's a little rundown, I'm afraid.'

'But so beautiful. And with such a wonderful view,' Annie replies. 'Michael can always pop round if you have any problems.'

While Michael and Connor work outside, Pearl shows Annie upstairs to the reading room.

At first, Annie is speechless.

'It's a library!' she says after a moment of looking around and taking in the number of shelves and volume of books. 'I wasn't expecting that.'

'Please help yourself to any you'd like,' Pearl offers. 'There are some in a box behind the door too. I've completely run out of room.'

Annie takes a novel from the nearest shelf. She flips it over and reads the blurb on the back, before telling Pearl, 'Do you know, I'd be lost without a good book. A read before bed helps me nod off no matter what sort of day I've had or what's playing on my mind. Ten pages and I'm out for the count. And if I had a spare room, I'd do it just like this.'

Pearl remembers the many weeks it took Ray to build all the shelves. 'My mother's partner did all the work himself.'

'He did a wonderful job,' Annie says, appraising each row. 'What a peaceful space to escape to!'

Pearl smiles. Annie is easy company. She wonders if they might be friends.

'I could stay here all day,' Annie tells her when it's time for them to leave. 'And thank you for the book,' she says, waving her borrowed novel in the air. 'I'll bring it back as soon as I've finished.'

'Come whenever you like.' Pearl hears her own words and hopes Annie will know she means them.

Downstairs, Pearl thanks Michael, and he says that he'll be back in ten days or so to fix the roof.

'It won't take me long,' he guarantees. 'Just need to make it watertight. There are some slates missing, just up in the corner there. I'll aim to get it done before the weather changes.'

'I'm very grateful, thank you, Michael.'

'It's no problem at all,' he says. 'As long as it stays dry until then we'll be fine.'

***

In the afternoon, it is the turn of Molly and Derek to arrive. Pearl watches from the open front door as Connor unstraps Tommy from his car seat in the back of the Fiesta and Molly carries her son up the path, with Derek bringing up the rear.

'Pearl!' Molly waves from the path and Pearl waves back. She is struck by the girl's beauty first and her apparent boundless energy second. She is wearing jeans with rips in them like Connor's, and a tiny strip of a camisole top the colour of mangoes. Her trainers are pure white, unlike Connor's grass-stained ones, and her slim arms are wrapped around the toddler, who is dressed in light blue shorts, T-shirt and matching sandals.

When Molly reaches the door, she says, 'This is Tommy. Say hello, Tommy, go on.'

Tommy buries his head in his mother's smooth shoulder and peeks back at Pearl with deep brown eyes.

'I'm Derek,' the young man with them volunteers, leaning forward with hand outstretched. 'I work at the Co-op.'

The boy's friendly manner and wild red hair make him easy to recognise as Michael and Annie's son.

'Would you like to come in?' she says. 'I can get us all something to eat and drink.'

Pearl leads the way through to the kitchen.

'Ladies first,' Derek says, waiting for Molly to pass.

'I'm no lady,' she laughs. 'But OK.'

Seemingly mesmerised by the garden, Molly immediately crosses to the open French doors.

'It's stunning,' she says. 'I love your garden.'

'It didn't look like that before,' Pearl says. 'Before, the grass was up to the window and you couldn't see the roses round the patio for all the brambles. Now, it looks like it used to years ago.'

Molly smiles at Connor. 'Boy's got skills.'

Connor blushes profusely.

Derek looks out at the garden and the moor beyond. 'It'd be a great place to set up a time-lapse camera. You know for spotting the Dartmoor Beast when he wanders by.'

'Derek!' Molly laughs. 'There is no such thing.'

'You never know,' he says. 'There's been sightings all over.'

Molly smiles at Pearl. 'Derek's convinced Elvis lives in Okehampton and works in the mobile phone shop at the end of the High Street opposite the pub.'

'I used to love his music, Elvis,' Pearl remembers Lana's old records. She'd had so many from the fifties and sixties. 'Wouldn't it be great if he did.'

'It's always a possibility,' Derek adds. 'He's a dead ringer, and he has a coat with loads of tassels on it.'

When Pearl offers a cold drink, everyone gratefully accepts. As they sit, drink and talk, she marvels at the relaxed manner of the young people in her home, the language of friends and close companions. Tommy contentedly plays with his feet, and Pearl finds it almost impossible to divert her gaze from his endearing expressions, delighted one minute to despairing the next, each feeling he has so instantaneous and heartfelt before changing again in a split second. From happiness to heartbreak in a moment but always returning to the task of studying his toes sticking out from the end of his sandals. It had never occurred to Pearl that one day this house would welcome a child. It had never been a possibility. It wasn't meant to be. For years she'd thought about how it could have been. And now, sitting so close to Tommy, she feels the ache of never having had a family of her own, of missing out so completely on the bond between mother and child.

'Would you like to hold him?' Molly asks.

When Pearl looks up, she realises she must have been staring.

'I warn you though, he weighs a ton. He is as heavy *as!*'

Pearl can see how close he is to his young mother, nestled in, safe and sound. She hopes he won't cry so she has to pass him back straight away, but he allows himself to be lifted into her arms and shifted on her lap with ease. Tommy's face breaks into a grin and he pushes his fingers together into a steeple shape. 'Aren't you a good boy?' she says.

Molly watches them both. 'He looks as happy as anything. He won't want to move now.'

Pearl looks down at the child, playing with his own toes. The feel of him, his skin so soft. When he reaches out a hand, his fingers stretched wide as if he's trying to catch the air, Pearl gently takes it in hers and something inside her breaks. The warmth of his fingers now curling tightly around hers, almost brings her to tears. The feeling is so strong.

When it's time to carefully hand Tommy back to Molly, Connor offers to show his friends around outside. Pearl watches from the French doors, noting the look of admiration on Molly and Derek's faces and the way Connor's lights up as he talks about the work he's done. He has inherited his mother's gift. There is no doubt.

While Derek and Connor push a delighted sandal-less Tommy around in the empty wheelbarrow, Molly joins Pearl inside, and together they pour out some more glasses of lemonade.

'I love this,' she tells Pearl. 'It tastes a bit like a cocktail . . . but without tequila or rum.'

'Would you like me to show you how to make the strawberry version?' Pearl finds herself asking. 'It's very easy.'

'Yeah, thanks, I'd love that. Then I could make some for me and mum. She'd feel proper special if she came home to a glass of strawberry lemonade if I did it all fancy with a chilled glass and an umbrella in it. She's working down the caravan park today, cleaning on a double shift.'

'Then I'll get the ingredients we need.'

Pearl retrieves strawberries and lemons from the fridge and a bag of sugar from the cupboard next to the sink. Together they talk and make a fresh batch of lemonade, this time with a twist, and with Molly giving each step her undivided attention.

'And now,' she asks finally, 'do I just put it in the fridge?'

'That's right,' Pearl says. 'It won't take long to cool. And I'll put everything in a bag so you can make it at home.'

'I feel like this could be my new favourite drink.' Molly concludes. 'You know, even without the tequila or rum.'

While Connor and Derek enjoy their refilled glasses of lemonade out on the patio, Molly changes Tommy in the bathroom and feeds him a packed lunch of chopped apple, cubes of cheese and breadsticks for afters. Pearl watches, noting how long it takes, and how careful Molly is, never urging her son to hurry at any stage. Tommy's eyes begin to droop heavily shortly afterwards, and she carries him back to the car and puts him in his car seat. It is time to leave. The afternoon has flown by.

'I've had such a good time,' Molly says at the door. 'Thanks for having us.'

'Come whenever you like,' Pearl smiles. 'I'm always here, after all.'

Molly face clouds over as she says, 'I don't want Connor to go, Pearl.'

For a moment, the girl looks so innocent and so much younger than her eighteen years.

'I don't either.'

'I think a lot of him.'

'I know.'

'I mean, more than a lot.' Molly sighs.

'Will you tell him, how you feel?' Pearl asks.

The young girl looks out to the moor and shakes her head. 'I don't think I can. It'll make it harder for him when he has to go if I do.'

'I hope he can speak to his father.'

'That would be cool, wouldn't it? I wish they understood each other better. I wish they could get back to how they used to be.'

'I wish that too.'

When Derek and Connor come around the house from the back, Pearl watches them jostle each other down the path before they climb into the car, Derek and Connor in the front, and Molly holding Tommy's hand in the back. The three friends wave back at her as they go.

'See you tomorrow,' Connor promises.

''Bye, Pearl!' Derek and Molly call in unison.

And then they are driving away.

In the kitchen, there are plates and glasses to wash, more than just two for a change. It feels good to have clearing up to do after a full day. It's been a long time since Highview has been filled with so much life and invited so many new people in, although they don't feel like strangers. Annie, Michael, Derek, Molly and Tommy too. Nothing like strangers at all.

Pearl runs a bowl of soapy water, takes her time to clean each of the plates and give the glasses an extra rinse. Leaving them to dry on the draining board, she crosses to the French doors. Lying on the grass is a small light blue sandal. Past the patio and in the middle of the lawn, it lies like a line in the sand. A new target to reach tomorrow.

NATE

In his flat in Weatherley Gardens, Nate tells Anila about the record number of applications that have come in for Frank after Claire posted his picture on the website.

'It almost crashed the system,' he says, trying to avoid a feeling that insists on making itself known. Without having to think too much about it, he recognises it as an impending sense of loss. Finding Frank a new home means saying goodbye to the Labrador and letting him go. 'I did think about asking Claire if I could put my name in the hat, perhaps put in an application myself, but I wouldn't want to deny him the chance of going home with a family.'

Sitting across from him on the sofa, Anila shakes her head. 'Nate, just go for it. You'd be a brilliant owner, and Frank's a lovely dog. Let Claire know. Get her to put your name down.'

'I'll definitely think about it.'

'Is that what you wanted to talk to me about?' she asks. 'Frank?'

Nate realises he's stalling.

'It isn't Frank.'

Anila waits.

'I talked to Jean.'

'How did it go?'

'It made me realise I should explain a few things.'

'Explain?' Anila asks.

'About why I won't be joining a dating website,' he says.

'OK.' Anila looks confused.

'I'm not making much sense, sorry.'

'I just don't want you to be alone, Nate.'

He smiles. 'I know, and I'm very grateful for everything you've done, but there's something I should explain about the past.'

'Why, what happened?'

'It's like a story . . . I suppose that's the best way to describe it.'

'A romantic story?'

'It is.'

'A true romance?'

Nate nods.

'It happened a long time ago.'

Anila looks momentarily confused. 'Do you mean, you and Jean? Because no offence, Nate, but that didn't really work out so well.'

Nate shakes his head. 'It's about someone I loved before I knew Jean.'

'Plot twist!' Anila announces, pulling a cushion round in front of her and hugging it tight. 'Look, I've got goose bumps!'

For a moment, Nate wonders if he can do it. Then, he looks at Anila and is reminded of the reason he should.

'This is my story,' he begins. 'And it's about Pearl.'

1974

Nate had asked if she would help him and to his genuine surprise she'd agreed.

They'd cut down the alleyway, into the small court-yard at the back of Victoria Street where clean washing whipped back and forth on the line in the wind, like loose sails on a ship.

Mrs Williams was by the sink when they went into the house, tapping ash from her cigarette into the plughole. She looked surprised to see her son and annoyed that he had brought someone home.

'I thought you were in town?' she said, looking from her son to Pearl. 'And who's this?'

Nate realised he had no choice but to explain. 'This is Pearl. Pearl Winter.'

His mother stared as if trying to put the name and the face together and clearly unimpressed by what she saw. 'Lana Winter's daughter?' she asked.

Pearl nodded.

Nate shifted uneasily.

'I've seen the woman in town . . . but not at church,' his mother continued. '*Never* at church,' she said again, disapprovingly.

He watched as Pearl's face fell.

'Pearl's here to help me,' Nate said, keen to avoid any unpleasantness.

'What do you mean, *help*?'

'With some . . . stuff from school,' he said. 'We're going to my room.' He motioned to the hallway and stairs.

'Ha!' His mother's forced laugh was cheerless. 'Not in my house, you won't.' She looked from one to the other with an expression that said she didn't trust them not to be jumping each other's bones as soon as the bedroom door closed behind them.

Pearl looked down at the floor, he noticed, to avoid his mother's accusing gaze.

Nate had begun to find his mother's views vastly different from his own. She was a fiercely God-fearing woman who considered dancing around the front room to music the work of the devil. She favoured a fervent approach to religion, the more evangelical the better, but when she wasn't at church, or praying at the sink, she seemed to like nothing more than gossiping about others to a neighbour over the back fence. Which seemed at odds with all Christian values to him.

'I'm sorry,' he said to Pearl.

'It's all right,' she whispered in return. 'We could always go to the library instead.'

'Yes, the library,' Mrs Williams said, looking warningly at Nate. 'You can't get up to much there . . .' she drew heavily on a freshly lit cigarette and closed one eye to the smoke '. . . I'm sure.'

In the courtyard, the sheets continued to billow in the wind. His mother's words rang in his ears. *Never at church.* Nate didn't know what to say for the best.

He vowed never to take Pearl back to his home again and subject her to his mother's unnecessary interrogation.

'Sorry. I didn't know she was going to be in,' he tried to assure Pearl, before adding, 'Take no notice. Please.'

'Don't be sorry,' she said. 'It's not your fault.'

He realised then that he liked Pearl for lots of reasons but for her kindness most of all. It made him feel like he could say anything to her without looking stupid. She listened to him without any judgement.

When they arrived at the library, he breathed in the unfamiliar smell, not having spent any time in the building before. It was modern and airy: a shiny wooden floor, bookcases filled to the brim along the walls, and an upstairs level with a seating area for study. In front of them was the long reception desk that curled in a semi-circle. There was a woman standing behind this talking in a hushed voice to a library user, below a sign that read: QUIET PLEASE.

He began to have second thoughts. He could take a job in the factory. You didn't need to read so well for that.

'Shall we find a book to start with?'

He pointed to the sign. 'It says no talking.'

'Don't worry,' she smiled. 'We'll go upstairs and sit at the back where we won't disturb anyone. I go up there all the time. Nobody seems to mind.'

On the next floor, at the back, the farthest point from the stairs, were two free chairs and a table. With Pearl's help, he found a thick book about aircraft, the sort of planes that had been used in the Second World War.

'Will this be all right?' he asked.

'It's perfect,' she said. 'Come on, why don't we start on the first page?'

He was relieved they were alone. No one to hear him struggling to read each sentence and tripping over every line, while all the words merged into one and seemed to move of their own accord. They sat at the empty table, and he turned over the front cover. There were several library stamps on the inside page and then another with a title and the date when the book was published. After this they were into the text.

Pearl sat close to him, ready to offer her assistance when and where it was required.

'"In 1936 . . ."' Nate began, and then stopped.

'Any words that you can't read,' Pearl said, 'I'll say them if you want me to, until you recognise them again.'

He focused on one syllable at a time, and each time he was lost she said any word he was unable to read, until he knew more in a short space of time than he had learned in a year of trying alone.

Within an hour they had read to the end of the first five pages. He found it difficult at first, but then it became easier.

When they stopped for a break, he said, 'You should be a teacher, Pearl. You make it seem easy. Even for me.'

'I do think about doing that. It would be a good career,' she confided. 'I could go to university or teacher training college and find an infant school to work in afterwards. I'd like that.'

'They'd be lucky to have you.'

She looked at him and he smiled, feeling so incredibly glad she'd dropped her copy of *Wuthering Heights* in the street that night and he'd been the one to pick it up. 'Don't let anyone stop you.'

Nate knew Pearl was teased at school. Some of the others saw her as fair game for taunting, just because she carried a bag full of books and turned up on time for lessons. She wasn't part of anyone's gang. She didn't worry about having the latest style coat or hair that fell a certain way. An oddity. Not exactly fitting in anywhere. But Nate didn't see her like that, he realised, as she sat patiently by his side in the library. He didn't see her like that at all.

PEARL

They aim to make it as far as Tommy's sandal first, which lies halfway down the lawn on its side in the grass. It is Saturday but Connor isn't taking a day off. Not today. Today they are just two friends standing side by side hoping to walk to the end of the garden.

Beneath her feet, the ground feels unstable compared to the patio, her mother's shoes sinking into the soft turf. One step forward, then another.

'Almost there.' Connor says, as he walks slowly alongside her. 'It's not much further now.'

His voice calms her just as it always does. She takes a deep breath, moves forward and takes another step and then another, until she's made it halfway down the lawn and is bending down and collecting Tommy's footwear off the dewy grass.

The sun is shining down on them. She feels it on her arms again. The crows sit on the fence watching, like bathers in deckchairs watching a Punch and Judy show. As before, they look fascinated by her leaving the house and walking down the lawn towards them.

'Shall we push on to the vegetable patch?' she says.

'Let's do it.'

It has been a week like no other. The day after Annie and Michael arrived, Michael returned with the van and, together with Connor, removed all the recycling from upstairs. Afterwards, the room looked spacious and sounded echoey. She spent the next day cleaning it from top to bottom and wondering what purpose it might fulfil. Derek had telephoned with a kind offer to pick up groceries for her at the Co-op using his staff discount, and Annie had popped in for a cuppa and a chat as she promised, changing her book for a new one as she'd read it at lightning speed. She explained about a weight-loss group she had joined in Westdown. There were regular meetings in the town hall and a weekly weigh-in which, she said, was the worst and the best part. Worst if you put on weight, best if you had reason to break open a bottle of wine.

Pearl smiles at the thought of this conversation.

Connor disappears to take a call from Molly and when he comes back into the kitchen he looks like someone who's just discovered a ten pound note in the pocket of an old jacket.

'Molly's only gone and got herself some work at the hairdresser's in town!' he says.

'Today?'

Connor nods. 'Cherry the owner used to employ her as a Saturday girl and now they're short-staffed because the girl who helps out there has fallen off her horse and broken her arm. They need someone to come in straight away. Molly says it's only temporary, but she doesn't care, it might end up being regular shifts.'

Pearl thinks of Molly chatting to the customers with practised ease while she washes hair and takes bookings on the telephone.

'There's just one problem,' he says. 'Her mum's working all day at the caravan park, and Annie's at The Willows, so there's no one to have Tommy.'

'Well, we can look after him.' Pearl offers.

Connor pauses. 'Are you sure?' he asks eagerly. 'Is that OK? I can pick him up. Molly's waiting in town.'

'Of course,' Pearl says, thinking she might need to get her cleaning tidy out and give the front room a quick going-over. Her routine has slipped in the last few days but not in any way she regrets at all. 'I'll just make sure we are completely ready.'

Connor nods. 'Molly'll be stoked. I'll ring her from the car.'

While he disappears off down the path, Pearl hoovers the floor in the front room and checks the room for any obvious hazards to a small child. There is a sharp-looking paper knife in the coffee-table drawer that she removes, before pushing the piece of furniture further to one side of the room, not wanting Tommy accidentally bumping his head on its solid wood corners. After plumping the cushions and doing a final check of the spotless room, she makes a cup of tea and waits.

Connor arrives forty-five minutes later, and Pearl opens the door as he pulls up next to the gate. He leaves the car door open while he unclips Tommy from his car seat, collects a large holdall from the back and closes the rear door with his foot.

'Molly says she's packed everything we might need – food, nappies, toys,' he says, walking up the path and seeming to struggle under the weight of it. 'It's all here.'

It's only as she follows Connor and Tommy into the front room that Pearl realises she doesn't have the first idea how to look after a child.

After a few minutes, it turns out that the simplest of items are the most fascinating to a toddler. Sitting on the floor in the front room, with all the windows flung open wide to let in fresh air, Tommy is only interested in her snake draught excluder that has black crosses of thread for eyes, that and the frayed edges of her hearth rug.

'He's growing so much bigger,' Connor says, watching him closely. 'I remember when he was first born. He came really early and was tiny.'

Pearl sighs. 'It must have been a difficult time for Molly . . . and her family.'

Connor nods solemnly. 'Especially as there's only Molly and her mum. Molly's dad left home when she was a baby.'

Pearl thinks of her own father, leaving before she had a chance to really know him. A man who couldn't live with the responsibility of another human being weighing on him, even when it was his own daughter.

'Molly hasn't had it easy,' Connor sighs. 'Her mum, Caitlin, works long hours, and they just about get by. And Carl's no help at all,' he adds.

'Carl?'

'Tommy's father,' Connor adds. 'Lives up in Bristol somewhere. When Tommy was born, he just disappeared. Didn't want anything to do with them. He comes back every now and then, but he doesn't give Molly any money to help out and couldn't really care less if they're getting by.'

Pearl is reminded once again of her own father, the arguments between her parents, and then moving into the flat above the dry cleaner's shop. The days her own mother struggled to make ends meet.

'But Molly's doing OK. Her mum helps out with child-care so Molly can do things like other teenagers do,' Connor says. 'And if she gets this job, she'll get paid.'

Tommy wriggles around on the rug, trying to lift himself from a seated position.

'I'll just go and get his bag from the hall,' Connor says. 'Luckily, Molly changed him before I left so we should be all right for now.'

'If not, we'll manage,' Pearl reassures him.

When Connor disappears, Tommy's face creases into a frown, followed by tears. His mouth gapes and his eyes squeeze shut, which only serves to force even more tears out onto his round cheeks. Pearl starts to sing 'Humpty Dumpty'. Then when it looks like he might get properly upset, she offers him the snake draught excluder again. Tommy takes it gratefully and promptly shoves its soft felt tail into his mouth.

Connor comes back in with the bag. 'What have you got there?'

Tommy takes the draught excluder out of his mouth and studies it like he's never seen it before in his life while Pearl checks the time on the grandfather clock.

'I wonder if he's ready for his afternoon snack.'

In the kitchen, she carefully chops up a pear and small pieces of cheese from Tommy's Tupperware lunch box while Connor gives the lawns a mow. Watching through the window, she holds Tommy's juice cup carefully at an angle so he can wrap his small hands around it and drink without having to lift it himself. He smiles up at her and she feels an undeniable tug on her heart. She pulls him to her, and he lifts his little arms in the air. When she holds him, he leans in, and she forgets the ache in her back that comes from cleaning the house and brushing the threadbare carpet on the stairs by hand. As the sun fills the garden with warm light, she holds Tommy in her arms at the open French doors. The crows arrive in the hope of extra food, and he giggles at the sight of them. Pearl points to the robin on the bird feeder out on the lawn, the fence dividing the garden from the moor, and a bird of prey circling in the sky overhead. He follows her moving finger and stares intently, taking in each detail. When she stops, he lifts a chubby hand to her face, and she holds it gently in hers. She hopes the moment will last, and it does.

Eventually Tommy's eyelids begin to droop. Connor carries him to the car and straps him into his seat. Molly's first shift at the hairdresser's is over. Pearl watches them both go, still feeling the touch of the baby's hand on her cheek.

★★★

In the spare room, she folds away sheets that have dried on the indoor airer. She pushes the coffee table back into the centre of the front room and puts the draft excluder back in its place by the door.

Shortly afterwards, the telephone rings.

'Pearl, you are an absolute legend!' It's Molly's excited voice she is so glad to hear. 'I couldn't have done it if you hadn't looked after Tommy for me. You've helped me out and I wanted to do something for you, and I was wondering . . . '

Pearl waits, unsure if Molly is taking a breath or has been cut off.

' . . . well, if you wanted me to, I could do you a restyle. Not that there's anything wrong with your hair the way it is, I was just—'

'There is everything wrong with it!' Pearl laughs, reflexively touching the roughly cut strands on her head. 'It's a complete mess.'

'Then I'm your woman,' Molly says. 'It's going to be just like that scene out of Pretty Woman.'

'It is?' Pearl asks.

'Definitely,' Molly replies, full of confidence now she has been given the opportunity to work once again. It makes Pearl smile - this beautiful young girl getting the break she so deserves to have. 'Pearl,' Molly adds then, 'Get ready.'

'I'm ready,' Pearl laughs. 'More than ready in fact.'

'Good,' Molly laughs back. 'Cos Pearl, I'm going to do the best glow up ever!'

CONNOR

The text message arrives at 6.50 p.m. just as he is dropping Molly and Tommy off in Westdown.

Table booked at L'Epoque for 7pm.

'Why am I so sure that's not good news?' Molly says, leaning over his shoulder from the back seat and reading the message he is staring at on his phone. 'What's going on?'

'It'll be something to do with Uni,' he says, just before the recollection of a previous conversation hits. 'It's the celebration meal for me doing well in my exams. I remember Dad saying something about it when I got my results.'

'What are you going to do?'

'Try and get out of it.'

'Or go and tell them how bloody miserable you are and how you don't want to go?'

'In a restaurant? With Yvo and everyone else around?'

'I know. But better to have that conversation now than later when you're stuck in York wishing you were doing anything else rather than sitting in your room in that shared house.'

'You've met my dad, right?'

Molly nods. 'I know, but time's running out. Please, for your sake, Con, just tell him you don't want to go. I hate seeing you like this.' She is so close they are almost touching. 'I care, Con. More than just-' She stops. Outside, he sees Caitlin, Molly's mum, getting dropped off in a taxi after work. She smiles broadly and waves. He waves back. 'Just know, whatever you do, I'm here,' Molly says, as Caitlin walks over to the car to help lift Tommy out. 'Please don't forget that.'

After a chat with Caitlin and carrying Tommy's bag into the house, he drives home, grabs a quick shower and a fresh set of clothes and heads back out.

Arriving at L'Epoque, he can see all the tables at the front are fully occupied. The staff are wearing their usual black uniforms and white aprons. There are the usual giant, brightly coloured canvases on the white-washed walls, and a polished wooden floor.

At the back of the restaurant, he sees his father and Yvo waiting. As he walks closer, his father says, 'Ah, Connor. There you are. I'm sorry we couldn't do this before but at least we're here now. Straight As and a university place confirmed.' Donald beams proudly. 'That *is* something to celebrate.'

Yvo looks up from the menu and smiles. 'I like this restaurant. French food is best,' she says. 'I am hungry like a horse. Shall we order? Now we are all persons here?'

His father summons a waitress and orders *pot au feu* while Yvo orders the minute steak. Connor thinks about asking for a glass of water and a salad. For once, his appetite is non-existent. He feels his gut twist into an anxious knot at the sight of all the difficult to pronounce, cream-laden, overly-priced dishes on the menu and at the thought of spending a whole evening talking about how best to make the most out of his time at university.

'You are away . . . in Connor land.' Yvo says. 'What would you like?'

'Right, yes, ordering. I'll just have the onion soup, please.' He recognises the waitress from school. She was in his English class.

'No problem,' she says, nodding and collecting the menus before leaving them to it.

When the food arrives, they eat while his father talks about academic league tables and the medieval architecture of York.

'Mmm.' Connor says. 'Because that's what every first-year Uni student is thinking about during Freshers Week.'

Yvo stops eating, a piece of steak hovering on her fork between the plate and her open mouth. 'You don't like the architecture?'

He sighs, wondering if there is any point continuing this conversation.

'It is good. Such a wonderful place,' she says for him.

'And you're looking forward to making new friends,' his father says, more of a statement than a question.

'I have friends, Dad. Here.'

'But these will be new ones.'

Connor thinks about the people he's happy spending time with already.

'And there will be so many work opportunities after you've got your degree. A place with a firm in London would be a good start, and from there you can work your way up . . . sky's the limit!'

Connor rubs a hand over his eyes. They feel sore and itchy under the restaurant's low-level lighting.

'The train ticket . . . it has arrived,' Yvo announces with perfect timing. 'I ordered it already. You are welcome.' She smiles at him.

'I didn't say anything about a ticket,' he interjects. 'I didn't want one . . . not yet.'

'But it needed to be booked,' Donald follows up. 'So Yvo went ahead. We thought an earlier date than the official start would be best. Give you plenty of time to settle in, get the lie of the land.'

'What do you mean, earlier?'

Unless Connor's not mistaken, the other diners have quietened, lowered their knives, forks, and spoons, and are now listening in.

'I've still got so much to do here. Important things. I can't leave sooner than Freshers Week, I really can't.'

'The ticket's been purchased for the week before.'

'Then I'll get another one!'

'But it's all paid for,' Donald says, pushing his plate forward.

'I'll pay you back.'

'There's no need.'

'I can't go to York early.'

Donald wipes his mouth with one of the restaurant's thick, white napkins. 'It's all arranged.'

Connor turns away from his full bowl of soup, just as Yvo finishes the last mouthful her steak.

'You'll soon settle in,' his father adds with forced jollity. 'It's for the best.'

Connor thinks about saying it now. He wouldn't need to shout it. He could let the words come out, steadily and with all the emotion behind them that he feels. One simple sentence to explain why he doesn't want to go.

'But York,' he begins, 'it's not—'

'Not to be missed, that's exactly it!' His father nods. 'Such a wonderful city, and in just over a week you'll be there and able to experience it all for yourself.'

PEARL

As the month draws to a close, the radio news bulletins are dominated with stories about the upcoming bank holiday weekend, with the prediction of tailbacks of stationary traffic, and a sudden spike in temperatures across the UK.

'And we'll have regular updates from our reporter on a bridge on the M5,' the presenter of the morning show says. 'On the hour, every hour.'

Pearl pictures the lone newshound on the flyover. A man or woman with a microphone and a perspiring brow.

'And now for the all-important weather forecast,' the presenter says. 'Alan, how's it looking?'

'Thanks, Sally. Well, it's hot,' he says. 'Really hot.'

From her position at the French doors, Pearl looks out at the garden. He is right. The crows are refusing to leave the shady spot in the leaves of the giant oaks. Not even for an extra handful of monkey nuts.

'So, unless you have to travel,' the weatherman is saying, 'I'd say, stay at home at the weekend and enjoy the sunshine.'

'Thanks, Alan, I might do just that,' Sally replies enthusiastically.

The bulletin is followed by strains of 'Summer Holiday' by Cliff Richard, and then the sound of the doorbell ringing.

When Pearl answers it, the postman with the long, blond ponytail is standing on the step, holding a handful of mail.

He is wearing headphones and humming along to the tune playing exclusively for him.

'Sorry, I couldn't get it through the letterbox,' he says, pulling out his headphones from both ears. 'Too thick. I think it's the brochure that's done it,' he adds.

'Thank you, for ringing the doorbell, I'm grateful.'

'No problem. It's hot, isn't it?'

'It's supposed to be even hotter at the weekend.'

'I'm off for five days, so I'm hoping to make the most of it.'

'I hope you have a nice break.'

'Thanks, you too,' he says, before plugging his earphones back in and heading away to his red van parked on the road.

Pearl realises it's the most conversation they've ever had. Life is certainly changing.

She closes the door and examines the post. There are two official looking brown envelopes and the brochure; it is thick with a shiny cover: *Adult Education Courses (Over 18s).*

Pearl leaves the bills on the kitchen table and carries the college brochure to the plastic box Connor has left for her in the pantry, the one now assigned for all recycling.

Annie has said in future she will come over and help put the rubbish out for collection or get Derek to do it if she is at The Willows.

Dropping the college booklet into the box, Pearl doesn't give its contents another thought, distracted by the sight of the tall, thin calendar with pictures of waterways of the British Isles at the top that hangs on her wall and used to be empty but is now filling up with entries for the days ahead.

Looking after Tommy for the afternoon.

Annie – coffee 2pm.

Michael fixing roof.
Birthday (60th)!.

In just a few days it will be that time of year again. Usually, the occasion isn't marked with celebration or ceremony. It is just another day spent cleaning, feeding the crows, or walking the stairs. In the past, it had often been a solitary affair spent in her room, with a gathering around the kitchen table for a meal later on. Ray and Lana always bought her books wrapped in brown paper, which she read eagerly and finished quickly. There was only ever one birthday card, filled in in Lana's neat writing. Never any more than that. The last time the day was marked was after Ray passed. Her mother had gone out and bought her a pendant. When Pearl opened it there was a picture of them all inside, taken years before, standing by the French doors, with the moor and the sun's rays behind them. Pearl noticed she was smiling in the picture.

Lana had opened the last of Ray's homemade wine. The glass bottle was dusty, and her mother took some time trying to find it in the pantry.

They drank and talked. That was the best birthday Pearl can remember having.

With an idea taking shape in her mind, she climbs the stairs to the spare room, sits in the chair at the desk and presses the button that brings the computer whirring into life. By the closed window, a thousand glittery dust motes dance in the light. Outside, the sun sits high in the sky. She taps the keys to take her to the grocery-delivery website. It appears, a brightly coloured screen, filled with facts about 'Buy One Get One Free's and exclusive offers, and a message reminding her to sign in. After doing so, she fills her virtual basket with ingredients – shallots, white wine, fresh pasta, as well as eggs, flour, butter, and the best cooking chocolate money can buy, enough to make a cake fit for a special occasion. She thinks of her usual meals that are simple by necessity – eggs on toast, a little bread and jam, sometimes a pork chop with potatoes. The thought of cooking for other people doesn't daunt her, not like it would have done once. In the preceding days and weeks, she has felt her confidence grow. With each step out into the garden, more so. A party to bring laughter and happiness to Highview is long overdue. It is time to eat, drink and be merry, because there is so much to be grateful for at last. It is time to fill the house with good friends. To raise a glass to Molly and her new job at Cherry's Hair Salon, and to thank Connor, Annie, Derek and Michael for all they have done. Pearl adds more ingredients to prepare the special menu she has in mind.

It's only when she has finished the online shop that she thinks of it, consigned to the waste pile. The brochure. *Adult courses for those over eighteen ...*

Rushing downstairs, and almost tripping on her slippers, Pearl retrieves it from the bed of ripped paper in the plastic recycling box, her heart beating fast and not just, she realises, from the exertion and exhilaration of coming downstairs at record speed.

Turning to the index, she runs a finger down the page to the section she is hoping to find.

It is there, in all its printed glory, just as she prayed it might be. Very carefully she stows the booklet safely away in the dresser, as if it's the most precious piece of literature ever to be printed.

NATE

According to Claire, who knows better than anyone, the bank holiday weekend they are experiencing is busier than it has been ever before.

She takes control and suggests Nate goes on reception to welcome prospective new owners to the centre before showing them down to the pens so they can meet the Happy Tails residents. Katie is also assigned to the front of house, while Anila is posted down at the pens to direct lost visitors and those looking for the loo. Wayne is in his element, having just finished rehoming two corn snakes to a couple who already own thirty of a similar size in vivariums lining all four walls in the front room of their home.

'The car park's almost full,' Claire says, staring at the mass of people and cars outside. 'You'd think people would be busy shopping or going to the beach, on a bank holiday weekend. I would,' she adds. 'Not sweating their way round the local animal rescue centre. It's good, don't get me wrong,' she qualifies. 'I want every single dog, snake and gerbil here to find loving owners and a forever home, but I don't know what it is about a sunny weekend that brings people out. Why not come on a miserable, wet Wednesday instead?'

'That'll come soon enough,' Wayne says, finishing up his paperwork. 'Rain's on its way, they said on the news.

It's always the way at the end of August. Make the most of it while it's here because come Wednesday it's going to be chucking it down. Trust me.'

'I must remember not to put my washing out then,' Katie says, as another family pulls up in the car park and heads towards reception with a look of barely-concealed excitement. 'I always get it wrong and end up with laundry that's wetter than when I first put it out.'

'Sod's law we won't see a soul then.' Claire sighs.

'You can guarantee it,' Wayne replies.

Nate wonders about the truth of weather reports. It's so hot, it's hard to imagine ever seeing rain again.

★★★

At lunchtime, Anila catches up with him in the staffroom.

'All I've been talking to Ryan about is you and Pearl and trying to work out what happened next,' she says, her eyes shining. 'Is there time for another instalment?' Anila lifts out her phone from the top pocket of her polo shirt and checks. 'I've got half an hour, then I'm back on duty down at the exercise field.'

She perches herself on the edge of an unwanted bedroom stool. Happy Tails' budget doesn't run to anything more than second-hand furniture, a fridge Claire got off eBay, and Katie's old kettle from home. The contents of the room are eclectically mismatched, from the circular teak table with one leg shorter than the others to the chest in the corner where they keep the tea, coffee and sugar so it doesn't prove too much of a temptation to the other animal residents of Happy Tails, the mice. Claire had made it her goal to apply for funding from every source she could find to spruce up the pens and the staffroom, but she hadn't had any luck.

'I can't wait,' Anila says excitedly, not even stopping to flick on the kettle. 'We had just got to the part where Pearl is helping you to read.'

'I remember.' Nate smiles.

'I had no idea you ever struggled with it. You always look like you've got it covered. All the forms we have to fill in here and the information we have to read in the new starters' book. I've never seen you have any problems at all.'

'Pearl made sure I could do it. Didn't give up on me once. I'm not sure anyone else would have been so patient.'

Anila sighs contentedly.

'And so, you fell in love?'

'We did,' he says. 'In the most unlikely of circumstances, and much to my mother's disappointment. She never liked Pearl or her mother. She often took unreasonable dislike to people. She wished her own life had turned out differently. I didn't ever see her happy with the one she had.'

'But it didn't stop you from spending time with Pearl?'

Nate shakes his head. 'No. If anything, it made us cherish the time we spent together.'

'It's hard for me to imagine what it was like then,' Anila says. 'Can you tell me?'

So, before he returns to his position on reception, Nate takes them both back to 1975.

1975

The navy sky was full of stars. So many it was impossible to count them. The day's warmth still filled the evening air. It was too close even to consider wearing a jacket, so he wore his favourite outfit of flared jeans and dark blue three-button T-shirt.

The queue ran right the way around the cinema building and halfway along the street. People talked, smoked and some of the women fanned themselves with a newspaper they had to hand in the line, all content to wait their turn in order to enter the air-conditioned coolness of the auditorium and enjoy the latest film. Nate wasn't particularly interested in the main feature. He was too preoccupied thinking about Pearl. Inside, they took their seats in a row filled with two other courting couples and a group of four women who talked incessantly about the lead actor, a man they all loudly appreciated. The plush red seats were soon fully occupied as people took their places, the lights dimmed to darkness and the film began.

Nate reached for Pearl's hand and wrapped his fingers around hers. He didn't want to let go. In the darkness, he couldn't tell where his hand ended and hers began. She leaned into him and stayed there with her head resting on his shoulder. He felt happier than he'd ever done before, as if his life was finally on the right track. They sat like that for what seemed an eternity but was in fact just the first half of the presentation.

During the interval, the bright lights came on in the auditorium and he walked down to the usherette standing at the front. He bought ice creams for them both and carried them quickly back to their seats, so they wouldn't melt. In addition, he bought cool drinks for them to sip in the second half. The heavy black curtains in front of the screen swished back, the feature began again, and after they'd finished their ice creams and drinks, they moved closer and held hands once more. When the film ended they were the last to leave.

On the way home, they took their time on purpose. Each step he took beside her reminded him he didn't want to go back to Victoria Street. He wanted to stay out all night with Pearl. They'd talked about the film and realised they'd both been too distracted to pay much attention to the plot. It soon became apparent they hadn't been watching it as avidly as they might have. So, instead, they talked about the future. A teaching career for Pearl. For him, a job in an office somewhere nearby. There was so much to look forward to.

They stopped under a streetlamp. He pulled her close, and when she looked up at him, his heart beat so fast he didn't think it would ever slow down. He felt her breath on his cheek, her hand in his. He kissed her then, very tenderly under the stars and the navy-blue sky and thought only of the many happy years he was certain they had ahead of them.

PEARL

The sun melts over the moor like a crimson candle in a dish.

The French doors at Highview are flung open wide and a breeze ruffles the edges of the white paper napkins placed ready on the kitchen table.

Her heart feels light; not even the flutter of hostess nerves can diminish the wonderful sense of occasion. She checks on the surprise in the larder and is relieved to see it hasn't suffered in the heat and looks just the same as when she prepared it four hours earlier.

'I've brought some tealights,' Derek says, coming in through the back door. 'They're citronella . . . in case of wasps. You can never be too careful.'

'That's true,' Pearl agrees.

Molly is busy setting glasses for water and wine on the table. She looks up and smiles at the sight of Derek standing just inside the French doors with handfuls of lemon yellow candles to light on the patio.

'Hey. You OK?'

'Yeah, this looks amazing.'

'It's all Pearl's hard work. I'm just adding the final touches.'

'Where's Connor, Mol?'

'He's in the shed. He wanted to make sure the garden looks its best for when everyone arrives. He's putting the mower away and tidying up.'

Molly had arrived hours ago, thrilled her mother could look after Tommy because it allowed her to give Pearl all her attention. 'The makeover of all makeovers,' she had promised, and Pearl had felt her heart skip a beat at the thought of it.

Now, en route to fetch a box of matches from the front room to light Derek's tealights, Pearl glimpses her reflection in the hallway mirror. The face looking back, she notices, is almost unrecognisable. The way the new hairstyle frames her face, the shade of light brown eyeshadow Molly applied so carefully that makes her eyes look bluer than ever, and the lipstick the colour of peonies that warms her lips.

When Michael and Annie arrive with their two youngest boys, they bring bottles of red and white wine, and Michael explains that he is the designated driver for the evening, much to Annie's delight. Amber is out with her boyfriend, Annie explains. Pearl hopes she is having a lovely evening; it is such a wonderful night to be young and in love.

'And I'll apologise in advance if I may, for these two,' Annie says. 'They've been so excited about coming . . . I mean, more excited than usual.'

Aaron and Cain nod ceremoniously, like two small Beef-eaters catching sight of the Queen on duty, before they run off, out of the French doors and into the garden. Seconds later, their delighted shouts can be heard all around. 'You hide first, I'm counting!'

'Leave the strawberries,' Annie calls out to them, antici-pating their wonder at seeing fruit not wrapped up in supermarket packaging but instantly accessible and grow-ing wild. 'I'm sorry, Pearl. I hope they don't eat them all.'

'They're very welcome to help themselves. I'm not sure how many are left. Unfortunately, the crows have taken a huge liking to them,' she smiles, remembering how they danced and flapped their wings at the sight of the wild, red fruit growing just feet away from their home.

With everyone arrived, Pearl lifts dishes out of the oven and Derek and Connor carry to the table bowls of olives and plates of garlic bread, creamy pasta, and salads made of tomatoes and buffalo mozzarella and fresh green leaves. Annie and Molly sip glasses of chilled Pinot Grigio, and Michael passes around napkins. Pearl watches everyone merrily helping themselves, wanting to remember this moment, bottle it up, and keep it close.

'This is delicious,' Michael says. Pearl notices he is dressed in a smart shirt and has made a considerable effort to look spruce.

'So good,' Molly agrees, looking up. 'Can you pass me some more bread, Derek?'

'The diet's on hold,' Annie confirms. 'I'm not even thinking about getting on those scales in the town hall right now.'

Plates emptied of food, they hold their glasses in the air and it's Connor who leads the toast.

'To Pearl!'

'To Pearl!' everyone cheers in response, and their happy voices fill the room. Before long, everyone is singing 'Happy Birthday'.

While they sing, Cain slips out of his chair, hurries round the table and comes to stand next to Pearl. The young boy has hair the same striking shade of red as Derek's and eyes the colour of orange-blossom honey.

'Pearl?' He pulls on her long silk skirt, like someone practising bell ringing. 'Do you have anything we can play with outside now?'

'I have a cricket set in the larder if that's of any use,' she offers.

'What's a larder?' Cain looks confused.

'It's the cupboard in the pantry, just through that open door.' Pearl points to the small side room off the kitchen.

'Can I go in there?' he asks.

'Of course.'

'Toys!' he says, disappearing through the doorway. 'I'm coming to get you!'

She waits for his response.

'Pearl?' Seconds later, Cain steps back into the kitchen with an accusatory look on his face. He reminds her of a smaller, less Scottish version of Detective Donnelly. 'There's a thing in your larder . . . and it isn't a cricket set.'

'Is it a cake?' she asks.

Cain shakes his head seriously. 'No.'

Pearl's expression is one of genuine surprise. 'Isn't it?'

Cain sighs like he's addressing a very elderly, deaf relative. 'No, it's a gat-ox.'

Pearl laughs. 'Yes, strictly speaking, I suppose it is. Would you like a piece?'

'Yes!' Cain punches the air before running around the kitchen, bringing his knees up to his chest like an Olympian warming up before a major event.

'Cain?' Annie says, exasperated. 'What are you up to now?'

'Having gat-ox.'

'It's gateau!'

'Gate-oh!' he shouts.

'Are you allergic, Cain, to anything?' Pearl says.

'Nope. Not nuts or stuff,' he replies, before rushing to the door and shouting out into the garden where his brother is running rings around the bird feeder. 'Aaron, get in here, there's a massive Gate-oh and we can have some of it!'

Before Pearl has time to organise dessert plates, her friends are out of their seats just as fast as Annie's boys, all eager to sample the chocolate cake that has Cain so excited.

'And take some home with you,' Pearl offers. 'Please, I'll never eat it all.'

'Have you ever thought about going into business?' Derek asks, once he has finished his piece. 'This would go down a storm at the farmers' markets and in the local shops. Especially in this size, and different flavours.'

'I'd never really thought about selling them, to be honest.' The idea of having a job at all seemed so far out of reach, but one where she can bake from home sounds instantly more achievable.

'I really think it would work,' Derek says. 'I think the demand's there for quality cakes like this.'

'I'd buy them, and I know plenty of others who would too,' Annie agrees.

'Me too,' says Molly, still eating.

While everyone helps to clear the table, Connor disappears into the hallway and returns with a carefully wrapped present.

'Happy birthday, Pearl.'

As she takes the slim package from him, she tries to guess what it might be, before discovering a product inside she never even knew existed.

'You just switch it on here,' Connor says, as she pulls aside the rose-patterned paper and finds a Kindle inside. 'It means you don't need any more shelves. You can read as many books as you like on the screen.'

'And no need to put them away in boxes in the reading room,' Annie smiles.

Pearl is lost for words.

As she holds her gift, Michael raises his glass in a final toast, and everyone joins in. 'Many happy returns, Pearl!' What a night it's been.

After cake and several glasses more wine, Annie is yawning, and Michael looks like he might doze off in his chair. Three crows land on the patio and fly away again almost immediately, having had their fill of cake crumbs and energetic small boys. When it's time to leave, Aaron and Cain pile in the back of Annie's people carrier, alongside Derek, with Michael in the driver's seat and Annie alongside. Cain waves from the open window, his face covered in chocolate.

'Thank you, Pearl, for such a wonderful evening,' Annie calls from the passenger seat. 'Next time we come over, we'll cook and bring the food!'

Michael waves and starts the engine.

Standing just outside the door clutching her Kindle close to her chest, Pearl watches them go and hopes there will be many more next times to come.

PEARL

The following morning, she wakes later than ever before and hungover. It's a small price to pay. She smiles at the memory. Looking in the mirror in the bathroom, she sees Molly's carefully applied make-up has smudged in places and disappeared into her face in others. She will remove it completely later, but for now all that's needed is a strong cup of tea.

After two cups, Pearl slips on her cleaning tabard and makes a start on the washing-up from the night before. Everyone had offered to help before they left, but she hadn't wanted to waste time clearing up when they could make the most of enjoying the evening.

As the sink fills with water, she adds washing-up liquid in generous quantities and tiny bubbles filled with rainbow colours float briefly in the air. They smell pleasantly of apples.

Outside, a napkin lies abandoned on the patio. It is unmoving, no breeze to lift a corner or curl it on one side. There is no sign of the crows in the baking heat. No doubt they have given up waiting for their breakfast and gone in search of something dead and rotting on the moor.

Life feels different today, Pearl realises, and not just because she has had the benefit of a substantial lie-in. Today she feels a sense of peace. She doubts she will ever get to Zumba or Weight Watchers at the town hall, climb a mountain, or travel down the Nile, anytime soon. But she is taking steps in the right direction. One at a time. Across the patio. Past the roses. Down the garden. Maybe further still. She thinks of Brighton, London, and all the places even further afield she has visited virtually on Travel Tuesdays.

Today is the first day of her sixty-first year. The start of a new decade of possibilities.

In the spirit of adventure, she crosses to the radio and tunes in to a new channel. She listens to an energetic-sounding young man who is 'pumped' to be delivering a host of fresh sounds. Pearl looks about the kitchen, at the haphazard arrangement of dirty plates and glasses, empty wine bottles and chocolate crumbs on the floor. Turning up the radio, she opens the doors and lets the heavy infectious beat fill the room and float outside in the direction of the trees.

After six high-tempo tracks, the kitchen is restored to its pre-party state, with just a small pile of dirty crockery stacked neatly by the sink still to be washed up. Pearl rewards herself with another cup of tea and the remaining piece of gateau from the tin. Its chocolatey sweetness fills her with renewed energy, and her third cup of tea revives her even more. Crossing to the dresser in the corner, she retrieves the Adult Education brochure from the drawer. Flicking through the pages, she finds the section that she hopes will change everything. After folding over the top of the page, she puts the brochure safely back in the dresser drawer.

Outside, the crows line up on the patio, side by side. They warily eye the stray napkin lying on the stones. She fetches a bag of monkey nuts and throws a handful to them. While they bulldoze the shells with their beaks, she waits for Connor to arrive.

A new era is about to begin. A new start. She has so much that she needs to say.

CONNOR

*There's a plant that grows in the central reservation of the
M5. It survives without being cared for or watered and,
despite its size, can grow in nothing more than a crack in
the concrete or the smallest patch of soil. It thrives despite
the fumes from cars and lorries passing by and is a wonderful natural habitat for butterflies. The Buddleia davidii
is a truly remarkable shrub and, in some countries, is
believed to be a symbol of new beginnings.*

It had been her favourite flower of all. Sarah used to make
a point of making sure he took in the tall, sage-green stems
and long purple flowers, every time they headed up the
motorway on their way to their annual holiday in Tenby.
Summers on the beach, sandy sandwiches, getting changed
under a towel, and building sandcastles with his father while
his mother slept in the sun.

She used to say, 'If that plant can grow on concrete surrounded by all this traffic, anything is possible.'

And he'd stared out at the buddleia and believed the
same.

★★★

At Fern Crescent, Connor finds his father in the study
collecting files to take back to work.

'We should talk about Mum's grave,' Connor says. 'When I'm gone someone will need to replace the flowers and look after it.'

'I'm quite busy, could we talk about this later?' His father looks tired again. 'I've got some work to catch up on.'

'And I've places to be too. A job I need to get to.'

He'd promised Pearl he'd help with the clearing up after last night's party. She'd rung to thank him again for the present and said she hadn't woken up until late. He'd admitted he'd done the same.

For a moment, Donald says nothing in response.

'Dad? We need to talk. We haven't really . . . ever since Mum died. We should try, I think she'd want us to.'

'And I should get going for work.'

'Can't we sort this out?'

'What is there *to* sort out?'

'Everything.'

Donald shifts uneasily in his new dress-down uniform of chinos and polo shirt. It looks odd on him and has done since the day he started wearing it because Yvo suggested it. 'I have a client meeting this morning. I'm sorry, I'm going to be late.'

Connor stands his ground. Aware also that he is standing between his father and the door. 'Can't we just talk tonight then, you and me? After work.'

Donald sighs.

'I'll be in the office until eight. I have emails and calls to catch up on after the bank holiday. I'm two days behind. I won't be leaving before then.'

'I'll come to the office.'

Looking resigned, his father nods. 'Then I will see you at eight.'

★★★

When Sarah was in the hospice, the nurse who looked after her had taken the time to sit with Connor and his dad, offer them coffee and talk about what was going to happen next.

'Hearing . . . it's the last sense to go,' she'd said, getting up and tucking in a corner of sheet that had dislodged itself. 'It's good to keep talking, even if it looks like she's sleeping. Chances are she's picking up every word.'

He thought about what the nurse said and, when she left the room, he began talking about anything that sprang to mind – like a change in the weather and how he was meeting Molly and Derek later.

Before the next visit, Connor wrote a list at home of things he wouldn't want to forget to say to his mum when the time came. Important things like how much he loved her, how he was so grateful for her always being there, like every time he cut his knee as a kid or needed to talk when he was older, and how he promised to look after the garden, always. He held the list for the entire duration of the next journey to the hospice, worrying it might be reduced to a papier-mâché mess by the time he arrived because his hands were so clammy with nerves. While he checked it over and over, Donald drove, unblinking and silent at the wheel.

The same nurse had greeted them at the door and showed the way to the room where Sarah was lying in bed with her eyes closed.

'Your mum's comfortable now,' she said. And as she was leaving, asked, 'What's that?' looking at the piece of paper in his hands. 'Is it a list?'

Connor nodded. 'It's all the last things,' he said, his voice sounding small in the bare room.

'Are you going to read it out?'

He nodded.

She smiled. 'I think that would be a good idea.'

Donald followed her out, saying he needed some air.

After the nurse had closed the door quietly and Connor could hear her talking to his father in the corridor, he read the list out, finishing with how he couldn't imagine the world still going on if she wasn't in it.

He sat in the room and waited.

Then he prayed for a miracle with his eyes closed.

But when he opened them, Sarah Matthews had gone.

NATE

The car park is almost empty of visitors.

Nate parks his car in between Katie's hatchback and Claire's impressive sports motorbike. There are a few discarded Happy Tails flyers on the ground, left after the busy Bank Holiday weekend. He picks them up and carries them inside.

In the Happy Tails reception area, Wayne is filling out paperwork, Katie is manning the phones and Claire is on the computer. Stan and Eric are curled up asleep together in a camouflage-patterned oval dog bed at her feet.

'Nate? Come and have a look at this?' she says, beckoning him over. 'Did you want to help choose?'

'If I can help, I'd like to,' he says. 'Frank deserves the best.' He takes in the long list of potential new owners on the screen.

Claire turns and studies his face, with a look that most men would find terrifying, but Nate doesn't anymore. 'Or . . . *Nate*,' she says, 'you could take him home to yours. As a Happy Tails team member you're entitled to first refusal.'

'Did you just make that up?' he asks.

'I might have,' she says. 'But it doesn't change the fact that I think you should definitely consider it. Frank would love it too.'

Nate shakes his head. 'I couldn't.'

'Bloody hell, Nate, why not?' Claire asks, blankly.

'Because he'd miss out on a proper family home.'

'You could be his family.'

'But it's just me. No one else.'

'Nate,' Claire sighs. 'You do realise that's all Frank actually needs? Someone there for him, one to one. He'll get that with you . . . and you can bring him to work with you so he's never alone. How many people can do that?'

'Not many,' Wayne interjects, whilst simultaneously stroking a bearded dragon. 'Go for it, Nate, you'll never regret giving him a home.'

At Claire's insistence, Nate collects Frank from his pen and takes him down to the exercise field for a run.

In the early-morning sunshine, Happy Tails' most sought-after resident spins around chasing a butterfly and then a bee, tail wagging and tongue lolling out of the side of his mouth. It's easy to see why he's won over so many visitors' hearts, not to mention those of the staff members, each and every one. He races over the exercise equipment without any encouragement, up one side of the balance beam and down the other, through the see-through plastic tunnel set out on the grass, and in and out of the poles sticking out of the ground at the bottom of the field, like a sheepdog going for gold. He's lean and as nimble as a collie. As enthusiastic as one too. At the end of it, he is out of breath, happy to lie on the patchy grass and close his eyes. Nate fetches a fresh bowl of water, filled from the outside tap, and lays it on the ground for Frank to drink from, imagining what it would be like to wake up to that wagging tail and unending enthusiasm. To go for walks together around the town, in the park, and across the fields. It would mean neither of them would ever be alone again.

Frank pushes at Nate's hand with his muzzle. His nose feels warm and comforting. Nate strokes the dog's head, smoothing the short, golden fur away from his eyes, and pictures his trusty companion coming to work with him, sitting by his side in reception, and heading out on walks along the path with other dogs, Anila, Katie and Wayne.

'What do you think then, Frank?' he says. 'Shall we make a go of it?'

Frank's tail thumps against the ground.

'Fancy a new home at Weatherly Gardens?'

Frank looks back, his mouth open, taking in air after his earlier exertion. To Nate, it looks like he is smiling.

'Come on, then,' he says, and Frank gets up.

Back in reception Claire and Wayne are both waiting.

'Well?' Claire says, unable to stop smiling. 'This is it. Is Frank getting a new home or am I ringing round all these people?'

Stan and Eric wake up at the sound of excited voices and start running around the reception area, their feet sliding on the tiled floor.

'It's now or never.'

Wayne is smiling too, there's even a glint of tears in his eyes. 'He'll never let you down, Nate. Dog like Frank, he'll always be there for you. Why wouldn't you give him a home?'

Nate decides there really isn't a reason he can think of. Nobody telling him he can't, in fact, two people telling him he really should. Nobody else to consider but himself and Frank.

'It's a commitment for sure,' Wayne continues. 'But look what you get back, and the walks you can go on together . . . an adventure in themselves. I've always seen it like that.'

Nate thinks of his empty flat. Quiet and still.

Seeing the look on his face, Claire gets up from the desk and crosses to him. 'Come on, shall we do the paperwork?'

Stan and Eric stop running about and look up at her. Nate notices how focused they are on her. Close as family.

'Yes,' he says, already imagining walking through fields, taking trips to the beach, relaxing on the sofa at flat nine Weatherley Gardens in the evenings, all with Frank by his side. 'Yes, I'd like to fill in the adoption forms.'

'Good decision,' Claire says. 'Here, you can use my pen.'

PEARL

Connor arrives looking like he has the weight of the world on his shoulders. Hopefully, she can change that.

At the sink, they stand side by side and wash the last of the crockery left over from the party.

'I'm going to talk to my dad tonight,' he says, as she cleans plates in the bowl of warm soapy water and passes them to him one by one for drying. 'I'm finally going to meet him at his office in town.'

'If you'd like to talk about it afterwards, I'll be here. Watching *Detective Donnelly*.'

'We've got some catching up to do on that last series.' He smiles.

'We have. The last one's as good as the Christmas special. It's got car chases and explosions and it's filmed in Belarus.'

'I'm up for that.'

'Will you be OK, Connor?' Pearl thinks of how much there is to discuss between father and son. So many ways the conversation could be derailed or brought to a complete standstill, all without having covered the most important ground.

He nods. 'I just need to explain . . . everything. And to listen. I'm sure Dad's got things he needs to say too.'

'I'll be keeping my fingers crossed for you.'

Pearl finishes the plates and moves on to the large pan she used to boil the pasta. It's her favourite on account of its size. You can cook blackberries in it for freezing, plenty of them, all ready for baking in pies or defrosting and having on their own with a little sugar.

'Connor?' she says, trying to keep her voice steady. It wouldn't do to give the game away too soon. 'This came in the post a few days ago.' She dries her hands on a spare tea towel, crosses to the dresser and takes out the booklet from its drawer. She tries to do it without smiling but doesn't quite manage it. 'I don't suppose you could read section seven for me, could you? Only I haven't got my glasses.'

She hands Connor the brochure and he starts to flick through it. First going forward too many pages, and then back, he finds the page with the corner turned over.

'A landscaping course?'

'That's the one,' she says.

'I've seen these advertised,' he replies, scanning the description. 'The college is great. One of the best.'

'Well then?'

He nods. 'I'd sign up for it in a heartbeat if I could. If things were different, you know. One hundred per cent.'

Pearl can barely contain herself. One hundred per cent. That says it all. No better way to put it. She feels enormous relief for not having discarded it in the recycling bin.

But he closes the booklet and puts it down on the worktop, looking regretful. 'I don't have the money to pay for a course and I can't stay at home to do it anyway, not with Yvo and Dad and the way things are. It's a nice thought, though,' he adds. 'Thanks for keeping it.'

He picks up the booklet and taps it on the worktop, once and then twice. 'Shall I put it back in the recycling?'

'Yes. Thank you.'

★★★

It doesn't take long to look up the details on her computer. There's a hefty sum in the bank account, thanks to Ray. Enough to keep her in weekly grocery shops and pay the bills for the rest of her days at Highview. And more than enough to pay for a landscaping course at a local college.

Bank account checked, Pearl hurries along the landing in her slippers and down the stairs to the kitchen. Seeing Connor sitting on the lawn, she crosses to the open French doors and steps out onto the patio. She feels a wave of excitement bubbling up inside her, and it's such a powerful feeling it's almost impossible to control.

'Did you want me to put the kettle on?' he says.

'Yes, we could do that, but I'd rather run an idea past you first if I can?'

'An idea?'

'Yes,' she says again, looking down and realising she hasn't even taken the time to change into her walking shoes, the urgency of what she needs to say is so great. 'And I think it's a good one, even if I say so myself.'

He looks bemused.

'In fact, it's something I should have thought of doing weeks ago.'

'OK. I don't understand.'

'Connor . . .' She smiles.

'Pearl?'

'I want to talk about the future.'

He waits.

'Well, more to the point, I was wondering if you would like to have the second bedroom at Highview as your own. Now that it's empty of all the recycling, it's quite large. I was wondering what to do with it and it was the obvious solution. And we could move in the bed from the spare room. I could put in a desk too. And you're more than welcome to use the computer, although I'm sure you have something considerably more twenty-first century.' Pearl stops, thinking of their first proper introduction either side of the French doors. 'I'm rambling, again, I know. Always, when I've got something important to say, I want to do it quickly,' she says. 'But if you'd like to, that would be—'

'Pearl, are you serious?'

'Very much so,' she replies. 'Deadly, in fact. I'd like to offer you a room, and I'd like to pay for your college course. To study landscaping. I probably should have said that first.'

Disbelief changes to obvious relief as a smile stretches across his face. The joy of seeing him suddenly awash with happiness is overwhelming. But he's also shaking his head at the same time. 'But, Pearl, I can't let you do that. I can't let you spend all that money.'

'I don't think there's a lot you can do to stop me. Not really. We could ring the college this afternoon if you like?' she says, feeling so energised by the idea she can barely stand still. 'Find out if there are any places left for the next term and come up with a plan . . . for a different kind of future.'

'Bloody hell. Are you sure?'

'One hundred per cent.' Pearl smiles, feeling the phrase fits so many situations, particularly important ones like this.

'I can't believe it.'

And then he's stepping forward and wrapping his long arms around her, and he is saying thank you, over and over again. She wraps her much shorter arms around him in return and hugs him close. And, comfortingly, it feels like the most natural thing in the world. This boy she almost didn't let in. Thank goodness she did.

'You've saved my life,' he says, his voice choked with emotion. 'Just when it was all about to go wrong.'

And standing on the patio in the glorious sunshine, she knows he has saved hers too.

CONNOR

The office of Matthews Solicitors is tucked away down an alleyway between the estate agent's and a shop selling silver jewellery, incense sticks, and homemade soaps. There's a sign in the window advertising Tarot readings on Thursdays. The High Street is quiet now the tourist season is ending, slowly but surely. Soon, Westdown will go back to its ordinary existence, roads will be clear of caravans and coaches, and next week the local children will return to the primary school at the top of the hill to begin a new term. It has been a summer like no other, one he will never forget.

Parking his car and walking up the road towards the office, Connor thinks about new beginnings. Turning down the alleyway, he hopes the conversation he is about to have will bring about a change. One that will enable them to get back to being the father and son they used to be two years ago. It feels like the last chance.

When he opens the door, Donald is studying legal documents at his desk. He looks exhausted, and much older, as if for him the process of ageing has accelerated in the last two years.

'Dad . . .'

'Ah, Connor.' His father takes his glasses off and rubs his eyes. 'Is it eight o'clock already? I'm sorry, would you mind if we do this another time? It's been one of those days.'

'What I've got to say won't take long,' he says, feeling ready to keep talking if he has to.

'All right then,' Donald sighs. 'Take a seat.'

Connor feels his heart beating erratically. On the way into town, he'd rehearsed what he was going to say. An explanation of how Pearl has offered him the opportunity of a lifetime: to follow a course of study he wants to do more than anything, together with a place to live for as long as he needs it.

Now, sitting in the office, with the water cooler bubbling every few seconds in the corner, the words don't come as freely as he'd anticipated. His throat feels dry when he begins, 'I think we should talk, Dad. I mean, properly.'

'Yes, I remember you saying so this morning. We've covered the issue with the train ticket to York, haven't we? It's non-refundable unfortunately, so . . .' His father looks genuinely clueless. 'I'm not sure what else there is to discuss?'

'It's not about that, and . . . actually . . . there's everything to talk about.'

And then he feels it – the anger that always surfaces whenever he encounters his father's refusal to discuss anything important. Like a dam breaking, a tidal wave of anger is released inside.

'Like Mum not being here anymore and you getting together with Yvo. That would be a start.'

'Yvo?' Donald looks none the wiser, which is even more infuriating.

'Yes, Yvo! Why can't you see how difficult that's been? How weird it is having every room in the house painted in unusual colours, not to mention everything that's not nailed down being changed, and plenty of stuff that is. You just invited her to come and live with us without even saying a word to me. One day I went out and then when I got back she was there! And on top of that, for the last two years you've been like the Invisible Man. You're never around.'

'Connor, I—'

'No! Let me speak.'

For a moment, Donald looks like a beaten man. There are deep lines around his eyes that Connor hasn't noticed before and his skin looks grey under the spotlights in the ceiling.

'We've not talked about Mum's illness, ever. But I need to . . . we need to,' he says, feeling the anger still riding high. 'Why can't we? Other people do. Other fathers and sons.'

Donald sighs and pinches the bridge of his nose as if he's trying to stop a nosebleed. 'I don't know what to say.'

'You can't just avoid it.'

'No, I mean, I don't know how to even start talking about Sarah,' his father admits. 'Please, Connor. I want to explain, I do, but—'

The telephone on the desk rings. His father ignores it. Connor knows that ordinarily Donald would immediately have taken the call. But now, it's as if he can't hear it.

When it stops, he says, 'I'm glad you didn't take that.'

His father nods. 'I won't if it rings again, I promise. I really need to explain without any interruptions.'

Connor wonders how many late nights his dad has worked for clients that they expect to be able to get hold of him here so late in the evening.

'When Sarah died, I really didn't know how to cope with it. I still don't know,' Donald admits. 'I loved her and when she became ill, it didn't seem real, any of it.' He shakes his head sadly. 'I can't even fully remember the day of the funeral. Just bits of it, like driving in the front car and the hymn we all sang at the end. Nothing in between. Not the service in church or the time I must have spent speaking to the vicar before it began. I think I've blocked it out. It's no excuse . . .' he adds quickly. 'But I couldn't deal with what was happening.'

'But I needed you, Dad and you were never around. Have you any idea what that was like?'

'I do,' Donald says quietly. 'And I am sorry.'

'And Yvo?' Connor asks. 'What happened?'

Donald looks down at the papers on his desk as if they might help him say the words he needs to say. 'We met and found we had things in common, realised we enjoyed each other's company. Suddenly the days weren't so dark. She was understanding and I genuinely believe she has only ever wanted to help . . . us both. Yvo's a good person.'

'Yvo isn't Mum, though, and never will be,' Connor replies, knowing he sounds unnecessarily bitter but needing to say it anyway. 'She can't just come in and turn everything upside down.'

'I honestly don't think she is trying to do that, or to replace anyone,' Donald replies. 'I think she cares and is doing the best she can to show it. Yvo has done nothing wrong.'

'Hasn't she?'

'No. But I think I have.'

'Are you just saying that?'

Donald shakes his head. 'No. I should have spoken to you, right at the beginning . . . explained everything that was going on with me, and let you talk about how you were feeling. I realise now you must have needed me, and I wasn't there for you. And I am sorry. Deeply sorry, in fact. Look, can we try and start again?'

Connor takes a deep breath. 'Dad, before we do that, you need to know something else.'

'Yes?'

This time Connor doesn't falter. 'I'm applying for a place at college to study landscaping. I have somewhere to stay and I'm moving out.'

Donald looks completely thrown.

'I don't understand.'

'If we'd talked more, I would have explained sooner. I know now, Uni isn't for me, and I don't want to go all the way to York.'

'But it's arranged.'

'I'm sorry,' Connor says. 'I know it's not what you want to hear.'

'All I really want to hear is that you're happy,' Donald says. 'That's what any parent wants.'

'But I haven't been that for a while. A long while actually.'

Donald nods sadly. 'I can see that now. I had thought moving to York and going to university would be a fresh start for you . . . away from Westdown. New faces. A chance to start over somewhere completely different without the memories.'

'I like the memories, Dad,' he says. 'And I like Westdown. I have friends and a future here. Different from the one you imagined but it's the one I want. I don't need to leave here to be feel better.'

'I thought you might want to follow in the family footsteps.'

'I don't, can't you see that?'

'I'm beginning to,' Donald says quietly. 'You were right, we should have talked before.'

Connor looks out towards the street.

'It's getting dark.'

'It is. I should close up.'

'Dad, what happens now?'

Donald stands up and looks around for his keys.

'I was thinking, would you have time for a drink at the Traveller's Rest?'

Connor realises it's his turn to look surprised. 'Shouldn't you call Yvo?'

'I will when we get there. And then we can talk . . . properly.'

At the open door, Donald sets the alarm, punching in the four-digit code, while Connor waits on the empty pavement.

'There's a new fishing rod for sale up in the hardware store. It's on special offer,' Donald says, turning away from the door. 'I was thinking about going down tomorrow in my lunch break and having a look.'

'There are some decent ones online too,' Connor replies.

'We can check them out on my phone when we're in the pub.'

'Dad, you did hear me when I said I'm not going to York?'

Donald nods.

'And you and Yvo? I didn't mean what I said earlier, about replacing anyone, I was just angry.'

'I know,' Donald says. 'And for now, we're just taking it slow. And perhaps cutting back on the decorating.'

'One step at a time,' Connor adds, thinking of Pearl walking slowly across the garden.

'That's exactly it,' his father replies.

Then, under the watchful eye of a fox standing outside the Co-op, father and son walk together side-by-side, up the hill towards the welcoming lights of the pub.

NATE

The sky breaks when he's lying in bed. The few first drops patter on his skylight window, lightly to begin with and then so hard it makes him think of Katie and her wet washing. He hopes she hasn't left any of it out on the line overnight.

Next to him, in a new dog bed on the floor, Frank snores quietly in his sleep. It's a comforting sound. A reminder he is there. Nate makes a silent promise that he'll look after him as long as he's alive. As Nate lies looking up at the rain hammering on the skylight, Frank begins to run in his sleep, his back legs almost catching up with his front, as he chases rabbits in his dreams.

Nate's mobile phone on the bedside table pings with a message. It's from Anila.

> *Can't wait for the final instalment of the story! See you at work. A x*

Nate thinks about Pearl. The ending will be the hardest part to tell. Frank stops running in his sleep and lies still and relaxed, his soft ears flat on his head, his paws no longer scrabbling for imaginary ground.

The rain hammers on the roof harder now. It's coming down like stair rods, people used to say. Just like the day the rains finally fell in 1976. Everyone cheered, people danced in the street in the downpour, and the whole nation looked forward to the end of water rationing. People no longer feared that fires would rage unabated on the open commons and destroy the forests, testing fire crews to the limit. The long, dry summer had come to an end.

Nate turns over and closes his eyes. How to tell Anila the end of his story? The summer of 1976 changed their lives forever, his and Pearl's. Two innocent teenagers who didn't know what was about to happen. It's so difficult to know how to begin the final chapter. But begin he must, with the day he has never been able to forget.

1976

They lay side by side on the grass alongside the pool, their skin scented with chlorine. All morning they had luxuriated in the feel of the cool, silken water on their limbs, neither of them wanting to leave. They swam several lengths before stopping at one end. Face to face, he could see her eyes were the colour of water, not the sort filling the Lido but the shade of a clear, sparkling ocean. She gazed at him, and he wanted to stay in that moment forever.

They played like young kids, not teenagers, bombarding each other with double-armed waves of water and racing one another to each end, arms windmilling in the water, legs kicking, laughing as they went and trying not to swallow water in the process. Nate chivalrously accepted defeat when Pearl beat him resoundingly.

After they had finally managed to tear themselves away from the water, they stretched out on the wide grassy space next to the pool. Crickets called nearby, and out on the road there was the distant rumble of afternoon traffic.

Overhead, an aeroplane nosed its way into the clear cerulean sky.

'Someone's off on their holidays.' Pearl lay back and shaded her eyes with one hand. 'I wish I was on that plane.'

'There can't be anywhere in the world hotter than here right now.' Nate turned his head to look at her. 'If it's sun you're after, you're better staying right here. Costa Del Guildford Lido.'

Pearl smiled. 'It's got a ring to it.'

'It's on the jet-setters' map now,' Nate said. 'The world's top location for your summer vacation. A pool, sunbathing, blue skies. What more could anyone want?' He felt so happy.

Pearl raised herself on one elbow and gazed down at him. His brown hair was now completely dry and curling away from his face.

'Are you staring at me?' he asked, looking deep into her eyes.

'Yes, I am,' she said, smiling.

'Why?'

'Because I can't believe you're here with me.'

'Why wouldn't I be?'

'I don't know,' she said. 'Sometimes I think we can't be this lucky.'

'But we are,' he said, pulling her to him and feeling the warmth of her body against his.

The air had stilled. There was just the heat of the sun and the rest of the day before them to enjoy.

'I love you,' Nate said, feeling his heart swell. True love that could last a lifetime. He'd never experienced such a captivating feeling as this. As he tenderly stroked Pearl's hair away from her face, he made a wish. That they would always be this way. That nothing would ever change.

'I love you too,' Pearl replied. 'And I always will.'

PEARL

She'd listened to the weatherman's forecast on the radio and later to the sound of heavy rain coming down, on the roof, the path, and the corrugated iron on the outhouse.

She imagines the bleak moor and its landmark prison, appearing even more dismal in this gloomy light. The moor is a place apart, home to crows and convicts alike, unpredictable and wild. A landscape people aim to conquer with compasses, maps and waterproof clothing, and on occasion fall foul of in a terrifying way. It has been the downfall of many an ambitious walker, caught unawares by the climate and the moor's uniquely confusing topography. Pearl had often watched the rescue helicopters from the kitchen window, hovering overhead, lights flashing brightly in all directions, signalling that help is on its way to those disorientated by the mist or the creeping darkness, lost in an expanse of harsh, undulating land the size of London.

It's when she listens closely that she hears it, drawing her like a moth to a flame. *Drip, drip, drip*. In the dark, she puts on her slippers, pulls her cardigan around her shoulders and hurries along the landing. It's louder under the yellowing loft hatch. This is the place Ray often stood to smoke while staring out the landing window, his nicotine-filled exhalations rising above him and staining the square of wood on the ceiling. The new sound, one she hasn't heard before, is coming from somewhere in the roof. It's not the bang and clank of the old heating pipes, or the creak of the well-trodden boards. Not the sounds she's used to. It's a different noise, solid and repetitive. It's water, and worryingly, it is finding a way in.

CONNOR

His ringtone shatters the sleep-filled silence at Fern Crescent.

Pushing himself up, he reaches down to the floor and pats his hand around on the carpet until he finds his mobile. He turns it over and manages to crank open one eye. It takes him several seconds to register the name on the brightly lit screen.

'Pearl?'

'I'm so sorry to ring so early . . . or is it late?'

'Is everything all right?'

'I think I've got a leak. I'm sorry,' she says again, sounding disorientated. 'It's coming from the loft.'

'Don't be sorry. I'm on my way.'

Dressing quickly, he thinks about the roof at Highview and the missing slates. Michael has been meaning to fix it but has been delayed. There's not a moment to lose. The less water gets in, the less chance Pearl's possessions in the loft will turn black with mould and need to be thrown out.

When he arrives, she is standing in the doorway in her nightdress, cardigan and slippers.

'Shall I bring a bucket from the kitchen?' she offers.

'That'd be great. Sounds like it's the water coming in through the missing slates. I'll get up in the eaves and have a proper look around.'

He pictures a stream of freezing, dirty water running through the gap.

Pearl returns with a bright orange bucket.

'Will this be big enough?'

'It'll be fine. Hopefully, there won't be too much coming through. Anything you want me to bring down while I'm up there?'

'I don't know,' Pearl admits. 'I've never actually been up there.'

Picturing old curtains and suitcases splashed with rainwater, Connor takes the stairs two at a time then uses the chair from the spare room to stand on while he reaches up and releases the hatch to the loft. Sliding it to one side, he sees a concertinaed ladder. Pearl watches from the landing while he pulls this down then climbs up with the bucket swinging from one hand.

'I'll put the kettle on,' she says. 'And I'll look for another bucket just in case we need two.'

As Pearl disappears down the stairs, he reaches the top of the ladder and steps into the loft. He hears it then. The water dripping on a solid surface. For a few seconds, he has to let his eyes adjust to the darkness before he switches on the light on his phone to see more clearly. At first the space around him looks similar to most other lofts – a cardboard box of old LP records, an artificial Christmas tree with baubles still attached, and an old rocking chair with enough dust on it for someone to write their name in. Beside this lies a tall lamp with a maroon shade. The material is ripped on one side and it's missing a bulb. On the other side, coming through the roof, there is a tell-tale

sliver of thin early dawn light illuminating the exact location of the missing slates. He treads carefully over to the
edge of the boarded area, bending down under the eaves
and crabbing his way towards the source of the leak. When
he gets closer, it becomes instantly clear why there is such
a noticeable sound. Beneath the hole is a plastic storage
container, its closed lid as tight as a drum. The indented
top is now brimming with silvery water. Kneeling down on
the bare boards, he touches the side of the box, feels the
hard plastic, bowed slightly because the contents crammed
inside have caused it to bulge.

The plastic container is filled with envelopes, and lots of
them, squashed in until there's not a centimetre of space
left. Some are pale yellow, some office brown, some a simple white. Taking particular care not to splash more water
onto the boards, he lifts the lid of the container and angles
it towards the bucket to let the water run off, before gently
laying it back on the floor. He slides the bucket under the
leaking roof where it can collect the rainwater before turning his attention back to the box. The envelopes are packed
tightly together and look like they have been stored inside
for some time. He takes out a yellow envelope from the top,
holding it carefully in his hand. It feels dry and crisp, the
edges curling like a fallen leaf. Judging by the thin, almost
translucent paper it must be old. He checks the date stamp.
7th November 1976.

Written neatly on the front is Pearl's address. All the
others are addressed the same way. There must be dozens
of them. A hundred maybe.

Lifting each one out, he makes several piles of letters around him until he is surrounded. By the light of his torch, one thing becomes clear. He double-checks to be sure and is then certain. Not one of the neatly written envelopes has ever been opened. They are all sealed just as securely as the day they were posted.

On the back of the yellow envelope there is a name and address, a single-line prompt to return the letter should it fail to reach its destination. But they haven't been returned. The sender's information is written in the same even, clear handwriting as the address on the front.

Nate Williams, 17 Victoria Street, Godalming, Surrey GU7 1JM

PEARL

She turns to see Connor in the kitchen doorway. He is carrying a large plastic box. It's difficult to see in the early-morning light and without her glasses, but it looks like it is filled with old paper. Perhaps some of Ray's old business letters or communications with the bank.

Connor carries it over and places it on the table.

'Was this in the loft?' Pearl asks, lifting her glasses out of her cardigan pocket and taking a seat. 'I'm sorry, I don't recognise it.'

He looks surprised and a little dazed. Pearl wonders if he might have hit his head on the eaves.

'There are envelopes inside and every one of them is addressed to you,' he says, still looking unsure. 'But they haven't been opened. Pearl, do you know anyone called Nate Williams?'

She must not have heard him correctly. Why would Connor be talking about Nate?

For several seconds, it's difficult for her to breathe.

★★★

'Pearl, are you OK?' Connor asks, coming round to stand by her side, his face a picture of concern. She must look like a rabbit in the headlights, she's sure. Shock will do that to a person.

'Are they really from Nate?' she asks. 'Every single one?'

He nods compassionately. 'I checked. Every one.'

'After all this time,' she hears herself saying. 'It's quite a shock.'

'There's loads of them,' Connor says. 'I reckon nearly a hundred.'

'I didn't think I would hear from Nate ever again.'

'Are you sure I can't get you something?'

'No . . . but thank you.'

Connor stands waiting and she realises she must still be looking a sight.

'I knew Nate a long time ago, before we moved to High-view, but we lost contact . . .' she is struck anew by memories of all those lonely days in her room, waiting for news '. . . and I thought the letters he'd promised to send me had simply never been written. You see, we were very much in love once, but the last time I saw him was a very long time ago.'

She stops talking suddenly. It's hard to take this all in.

'It looks like he actually tried really hard,' Connor says. 'To keep in touch.'

The box of letters sits between them on the table.

'Yes, he did, didn't he?'

'Shall we open the box?'

Pearl nods.

When Connor tips the envelopes out, they slide onto the table's solid wooden surface and are soon completely covering it.

Pearl reaches out and touches the one closest to her. It's the colour of milk, its surface creased with age.

Nate's handwriting is a comforting sight: the gentle slant of each letter, the solid commas, and the full stop at the end. Pearl remembers him sitting beside her in the library in Godalming, with a pen and an old notebook, writing down words from a book to help him remember for when he needed to read them again. She hears his voice repeating them now and sees his kind brown eyes smiling back at her, his expression filled with all the relief he was feeling.

The envelope is postmarked 20th October 2013. She tries to imagine the confusion Nate must have felt. For how long did he write these unanswered letters, and at what point did he give up, believing she no longer cared? Looking at the letters spread out before her, it feels like the years are rolling away: 1999, 1989, 1979 . . .

'My dear Nate,' she says, quietly, feeling her heart ache in her chest. 'I'm so sorry. If I'd seen these, I would have written back in a heartbeat. Nothing could have stopped me.'

Turning the pale envelope over in her trembling hands, Pearl opens it slowly and begins to read the first letter from Nate.

> *10th August 1976*
> *Dear Pearl,*
> *I am writing just as I promised I would. I miss you so much.*
> *   Please know what happened that day we went to the Lido will never change how I feel about you; it only makes me want to love you even more and give you all*

that I can. I hope one day, when you have settled in at Highview, I will be able to see you.

Do you have a telephone, Pearl? Please write and send me the number. I will call as soon as I get it. I've kept the piece of paper with your address on it in a drawer in my bedroom where I know it's safe.

My mother has been talking to everyone about what happened. I'm sorry. She seems to think there is another story behind it. I know you told the truth. I don't listen to what other people say. I think of you every day.
Pearl, I will be waiting to hear from you.

Sending all my love,
Nate xxxx

CONNOR

He had offered to stay. Pearl had looked so shocked about the letters in the loft and then equally as grateful when he said he'd sleep in the spare room, he'd gone outside and brought his rucksack in from the car and helped her to make up the bed. It was clear the discovery of the unopened envelopes had affected her deeply. He could see that from the way she held them so carefully and smiled and cried at the same time when she read the written pages inside.

Sitting on the bed in the spare room, he sends a quick text to let his father know he's not going to be home for a couple of days. A text comes back asking if he's all right and if he needs to talk about it. He replies that he'll explain everything next time he's back at Fern Crescent. For now, there's something more important he has to do.

Turning his attention to tracking Nate down, he begins an immediate search on his phone. Online there are plenty of listings for people called Nate Williams. There's a musician about a third of Nate's age with a tattoo of a dragon on his neck, a forty-something accountant from Leeds who does battle re-enactments at the weekend, and an influencer with a gym addiction living in Manchester who has half a million Instagram followers to his name. None of them are the Nate Williams he's looking for. There's nobody of that name about sixty years old and living anywhere in the UK, let alone Surrey. Connor sighs, gets up and goes downstairs.

In the kitchen, Pearl has made a separate pile of letters on the chair.

'I've read these ones,' she says. 'I think it's going to take me some time to go through them all.'

'I had a look for Nate online,' he says, wondering if this is the time to deliver further bad news. 'But I can't find him.'

Pearl still looks worryingly bewildered by the unusual find in the loft.

'Why would anyone put his letters up there? I feel kind of bad for him?' Connor adds. 'Actually, really bad for him.'

'I don't know,' Pearl says. 'I can't imagine why my mother or Ray would ever want to do that.'

★★★

Outside, a new morning is beginning. Soon it will be light, and the strange night they have had will be over.

He makes a fresh cup of tea for them both, eats some cake, and thinks about the lack of an email or phone number for Nate online.

'We could write back to him at this address?' Pearl says, holding a yellow envelope in her hand.

Connor looks at all the unopened letters still lying on the kitchen table.

There really is only one piece of information available that'll be any use in finding where Nate is now, he realises, only one place they can sensibly start to find out if he's still in the country. But how long would a letter take to arrive? What if the return address no longer exists? What if Nate has left the country? Clearly, Nate meant a great deal to Pearl, and Pearl meant the world to Nate. They should at least have the chance to meet. Nate could have moved, emigrated to New Zealand, who knows where he lives now. Nothing ventured, nothing gained. Pearl has had to wait forty-three years to receive a letter from Nate. She shouldn't have to wait any longer now the letters have been found.

'I was thinking . . .' he says, aware he hasn't planned any of this in detail as yet, 'I was thinking I might take a trip.'

'Where to?' she asks.

'Well, I thought it might be a good idea if I took a train to Godalming.'

NATE

He attaches Frank's lead to the collar and checks the new name tag is clearly visible.

FRANK WILLIAMS
FLAT 9, WEATHERLEY GARDENS

Underneath is Nate's mobile number etched into the small metal disc, just in case. He wouldn't ever want Frank to be lost and nobody know where he belongs. Besides, Claire is always reminding new owners who take a dog home from Happy Tails that it is a legal requirement these days.

Outside Weatherley Gardens, the air is colder. Clouds gather overhead, making the sky darker than it would usually be in the late afternoon. Nate sets out along the pavement in the direction of the nearest field and Frank walks obediently on the lead alongside him.

The way to the field is past a building site where new homes are springing up like the daisies that used to cover the rough ground before them. Nate walks around the side of the site, past the diggers and tradesmen's vans, down the public footpath and out onto open land. He lets Frank off the lead and watches as he runs this way and that, stopping to sniff the ground before running off again. He meets a woman who says hello and tells him Frank is a gorgeous dog. He thanks her and says her Jack Russell looks very dapper in his tweed coat. Nate realises you can never be lonely with a dog. There's always someone you meet with a shared interest, and that shared interest can easily spark a conversation.

Once Frank has had his fill of running around the field, Nate attaches his lead once again and heads across town to Victoria Street. Amy and Doug live there now, an Australian couple in their early thirties who have worked wonders on the place. Amy made a promise to Nate, even though they had only known each other a short time. A promise he was incredibly grateful to hear.

Frank stops to sniff a lamppost at the top of Victoria Street. Unmoved to add his own mark to it, he is happy to trot on to the next interesting-smelling spot, with only the slightest of tugs on the lead.

They walk down the street of redbrick terraced houses, each with a different-coloured front door. Bright blue, yellow, then green. Number seventeen is down towards the tall redbrick wall at the end that has a sign on it saying NO BALL GAMES. There wasn't a sign like that in the street when he was growing up. Back when he was a boy, they didn't have games consoles or DVDs. Kicking a ball against a wall, Nate remembers, was good fun and as exciting as it got for entertainment.

Number seventeen has a modern, dove-grey door and a planter outside complete with an olive tree. The house stands out from the rest. Amy and Doug have worked hard to improve the curb appeal.

Standing outside with Frank, he resists the urge to knock on the door. Through the front window, he can see the television is on. Perhaps Amy is home. But he won't knock and disturb her. He looks down at Frank and the dog wags his tail in response.

He glances back at the television in the front room of the house where he grew up. Amy would have let him know if mail of any kind arrived for him, he is in no doubt about that. The happy couple have lived in Nate's childhood home for ten years now and Amy checks in with him every so often just to say hi, but there has never been any news of a letter for him. She has his mobile number and email address just in case. When he sold the house after his father died, he redirected his mail, but had only been able to do so for a year. If a letter were to be posted, this is the only address it could come to. All he's ever hoped is that one day it will.

CONNOR

The irony of it is not lost on him: catching a train to Godalming on the same day he was supposed to be catching one to York. Looking around, he sees the carriage is full of people on their way to work. Some are balancing laptops on their knees, others have their eyes closed, catching precious moments of extra sleep before the working day begins. In a seat on the other side of the gangway, an elderly woman is knitting. A ball of turquoise wool balanced on her fabric handbag jiggles in time with the movement of her hands. Her husband is dressed in a cream linen suit, a white shirt, and a red tie. He is reading the *Daily Telegraph* and appears to be stuck on the crossword. In front of them is a man dressed in a high-vis donkey jacket, drumming his fingers on a hard hat on his lap. As they whip through a tunnel the carriage is momentarily plunged into darkness.

Out the other side, coming into the light, Connor digs around in his rucksack for his headphones and plugs them in. He chooses one of his favourite tracks. It's a song he used to listen to whenever he felt low. After the funeral especially. It has an uplifting beat and a good message and helps him through difficult times.

He turns it up and thinks of Pearl, how she has offered him a chance of a future he could never have imagined for himself. He remembers the steps they have taken together out into the garden. Pearl's bravery and her kindness. He hopes he can find Nate, more than anything else, and is counting on him still living at the same address.

After twenty minutes the train slows to a halt at a station; there is a familiar shrill whistle and then the hum of a standing engine, doors that open and slam shut, as well as the inevitable wait to get going again. He closes his eyes and fights sleep, but with so little rest in the last two days, he cannot resist.

***

It is the guard's announcement that wakes him.

'Reading!' the man says, walking up and down the aisle. 'Passengers change here for Guildford and Godalming.'

Connor gets up and wipes his eyes, feeling disorientated. He follows the knitting woman and elderly man along the gangway and out of the train.

He waits on another platform and catches another train, and then at Guildford he does the same again. Different carriage, different people. After four hours he finally arrives.

At the entrance to Godalming railway station, and still feeling like he's in a dream, he stops to check the address on his phone.

There is a line of black cabs waiting with their engines running outside. He walks to the head of the queue and opens the door of the first one.

'Victoria Street, please.'

'Right you are,' the taxi driver replies.

As the taxi moves off, Connor stares out of the window at the passing rows of houses and unfamiliar streets. It's a long way from the wide-open spaces of home, the moorland, and the faces he knows.

'It's just down here,' the driver says almost as soon as they set off. He indicates right and turns down a narrow street. 'Do you want me to wait?'

Connor shakes his head. 'No, thanks. Keep the change. I probably should have just walked.'

He hands over a ten pound note and the taxi driver says, 'Cheers for that,' before doing a three-point turn and driving back towards the entrance to the main road.

The house across the street has net curtains at the window. A young boy flips his head underneath, fascinated by the arrival of someone new. Connor looks at the boy, who pokes out his tongue then quickly disappears.

Connor sets off down the street in search of Nate's address.

Number seventeen nestles towards the end of a row of redbrick, two-up, two-down properties. To either side, the houses look the same, but number seventeen has a modern, light grey door and a potted olive tree. He takes a moment to check the address just to be sure as a window opens above him and a woman calls down.

'G'day, mate. You all right there?'

When he looks up, he sees her waving from the top window. She has tanned skin, shiny white teeth, and long blonde hair. It hangs down either side of her face and spills over the window ledge.

'Hi. I'm looking for Nate Williams. Does he live here, please?'

'Oh!' she says. 'Hang on. I'll be right down.'

When she opens the door to him, he sees she is wearing a tie-dyed T-shirt and denim shorts. Her face is covered in freckles.

'So, you're looking for Nate?' she says, beaming like someone who has won the lottery and is receiving a cheque for a million in person. 'I'm not going to lie to you, I didn't think this day would ever come, right? It's pretty exciting!'

'Have I got the correct address?' Connor asks, feeling confused. 'Is Nate here?'

'Ah, well, not anymore. He used to be,' she says.

'So, is he still in the area, then?' Connor asks, hoping he hasn't just taken a four-hour train journey only to have to turn around and go straight home having achieved nothing.

'Oh, yeah, he's here, all right. Not right here in this house, but still in Godalming,' she smiles. 'Hang on a sec, I'll get you the address.'

She disappears and returns with the details on a piece of paper. Connor takes it and checks the address.

'Thanks. I really appreciate this.'

'No worries. And can you tell Nate hi from me too?' she asks. 'He's always checking in to see if anyone has arrived looking for him. Been doing it for years. It means an awful lot to him this. Although he hasn't ever really said why. It's his business not mine. Can you let him know I'm happy for him that someone finally showed up? He's a good bloke,

Nate. Sold us this house for a lower price than he could have. We'd never have been able to buy it otherwise.'

Connor nods. 'I'll let him know.'

'Name's Amy, by the way.'

'Thanks, Amy. I'm Connor. So, is it far to Nate's new place?'

She shakes her head and laughs. 'Not really, it's that close you can walk it from here in about ten minutes.'

NATE

There's a blocked gutter that needs clearing at the bottom end of the pens. After the downpour two nights ago, a pool has formed, swilling around the base of the drainpipe. Katie has already put a yellow plastic hazard sign in place: WARNING SLIPPERY SURFACE.

'Take it easy, up on that ladder, Nate,' she says, in her usual motherly tone. 'You sure you'll be OK? I can shut up reception and divert the phone? Put my foot on the bottom?'

'I should be fine,' he says.

'You sure? I'll keep an eye on Frank then,' she says, looking down at Nate's flatmate asleep on a striped blanket at her feet. 'I really don't think he's going anywhere.'

'I don't either,' Nate replies, seeing the dog is already snoring peacefully. 'I won't be long.'

Out in the yard, he fetches the ladder from the staffroom and contemplates the task in hand. At the top of the drainpipe, he can see the offending clump of leaves and moss. He props the ladder against the wall, climbs to the top and sets to, pulling out debris and clearing the gulley. Within half an hour he's cleared the entire run and put the pile of leaves and moss into the bin behind the first row of pens.

When he returns to reception, Frank wakes up and looks delighted to see him as if he has just returned from a long trip. Katie is finishing a call.

'Yes, the toy poodle? He is still available for rehoming . . . Just one minute, please.'

She looks up and starts waving at him frantically with her free hand, like she's just seen a great white shark in the car park, and mouthing the words, 'Hang on!'

Nate hopes it's not another gutter that needs clearing of sludge.

He waits for her to finish the call, and when she does, she says breathlessly, 'You've had a phone call.'

'Have I?'

'You have. Just now. From someone called Amy. Lovely accent. Australian. She was very excited. She says a visitor came to the house and can you call her urgently?' And then, 'Nate, are you OK? You look a bit . . . pale.'

★★★

Katie calls Wayne on his day off, who agrees to come in and man reception while she drives Nate and Frank back to Weatherley Gardens.

'You sure you're feeling better?' she asks, reaching out to put a comforting hand on Nate's and then returning it to the steering wheel as she turns a bend. 'You gave me quite a fright. One minute you looked OK and then you went as white as a sheet.'

Nate nods. 'I'm OK, thanks, Katie. Just had a bit of a shock.'

'Well, you know, if there's anything I can do to help . . . if you're in trouble in any way, you just ask, Nate. We're all friends at Happy Tails.'

Nate shakes his head and gives her a reassuring smile. 'It's nothing like that. It's just . . .'

Sitting in Katie's car, with child seats in the back, a half-eaten packet of Wotsits and an ABBA CD case on the floor, he wonders how he could explain. When he'd rung Amy straight back, she'd said it was a young man who'd arrived at her door.

'Well, whatever it is,' Katie says, bringing him back to the now, 'you do what you have to, Nate. But just know you're not alone. And take your time. We've got the centre covered.'

'Thanks, Katie,' he says, seeing the turning for Weather-ley Gardens ahead. 'It's just here.'

She drops him off in front of the block of modern apart-ments and lets Frank out of the boot, with the promise that she'll pick them both up in the morning so Nate can collect his car from Happy Tails.

'And you'll be OK?' she asks, looking worried all over again.

'I will,' he says, wondering who the young man is that Amy has directed here to meet him. 'I'll be back in tomorrow.'

'Right, then.'

Katie drives away, strains of an ABBA hit already blast-ing out through the sunroof.

Feeling nervous, Nate rounds the corner of the building, using one hand to hold Frank's lead. He's not sure what to do with the other and decides to keep it ready for shaking that of his young visitor. He sees him sitting on the steps to the lobby, just as Frank pulls himself free and charges over.

The young man with tanned skin and light brown hair smiles as the dog runs up to him and gives Frank a gentle rub on the head.

Nate walks over, and the young man gets up. He's tall, has a rucksack over one shoulder, and a ready smile.

'Hello,' he says, and Frank wags his tail at the sound of an unfamiliar voice. 'I'm Connor, are you Nate by any chance?'

'Yes,' he says, nodding. 'Yes, I am.'

'I'm a friend of Pearl's,' the young man says. 'And I'm so glad you're here. Is there somewhere we could talk?'

PEARL

From the kitchen window, Pearl watches a pale sun cast its crystalline beams onto the moor through several breaks in the cloud. She thinks of how her view through the window will continue to change as the seasons come and go. The reds and golds of autumn will soon be here, and then the chill winter when the crows will lose their cover of leaves in the oaks, and she will see them so much more clearly, looking back at her expectantly.

When the doorbell rings, she gets up and hurries to answer it, still feeling out of sorts after the events of last night and today. Molly is standing on her doorstep, wearing a shiny, purple Puffa coat, a green satin mini-dress, no tights, and lace-up boots. Her loose curls hang down over gold hooped earrings. Annie is standing alongside her holding a packet of biscuits and a bottle of wine.

For no reason other than lack of sleep and the shock of finding Nate's letters, Pearl begins to cry.

Molly immediately steps to her side and wraps a protective arm around both shoulders, engulfing her in the smell of freshly washed clothes and a scent that is both musk and floral. 'Pearl, what's gone on?'

'Shall we go in and sit down?' Annie asks, looking equally concerned. 'How many are there?'

Pearl searches for a tissue up her sleeve but finds there are none left. 'It's probably easier if I show you. It's just through here.'

At the kitchen table, Annie and Molly silently take in the sight of the envelopes piled on the table and chairs. Over cups of strong tea and a large brandy, Pearl explains about Nate, and all the years she waited for a letter to arrive and how all along there'd been a box of them left in the loft.

Annie sighs, picking up one envelope and studying it like a detective looking for clues, then another. 'Why would anyone hide them away?'

'And you never even knew?' Molly adds, her dark eyes searching Pearl's.

'No,' she says, taking another sip of brandy and feeling its warmth in her throat. 'And now Connor has gone in search of Nate. He took a train to Godalming first thing this morning.'

'Has he rung with any news?' Annie asks hopefully.

'Not yet.'

'He might already be there.' Molly gets her phone out of her Puffa coat to check.

Pearl contemplates the day he must be having. 'The train journey alone takes four hours.'

'You should have been allowed to read these. They are addressed to you.' Molly shakes her head in disgust, dark curls bouncing wildly around her shoulders. 'You should at least have got the chance to write back.'

'I don't really know why my mother and Ray kept them hidden,' Pearl sighs. 'It could only have been them, there was nobody else in the house.'

'Do you mind if I have a brandy?' Molly asks.

'I'll get the bottle,' Pearl says.

'You take it easy,' Molly says, flagging her down with a wave of her hand. 'Top up?'

Pearl nods, deciding it might be the only way she'll be able to sleep tonight. There are so many unanswered questions still filling her mind.

When she looks back at Annie, her friend is holding two envelopes that seem to be stuck together.

'Hang on. There's a loose piece of paper in between these two blue ones,' Annie says, peeling them apart. 'It's sandwiched right in the middle.'

With the tip of her tongue sticking out the side of her mouth as she concentrates, Annie lifts out the piece of yellowing paper very carefully. 'It looks quite old. I don't want to rip it.'

When Annie extricates it and passes it to her, Pearl unfolds the paper slowly, taking care not to cause any damage to the fragile sheet. The handwriting on the note is unmistakable. She recognises it immediately.

'It's from my mother, Lana!'

Smoothing it out on the flat surface of the table, she reads the short note before silently passing it back to Annie for her to read too.

Annie lets out a deep sigh, and seeing the sad expressions on both their faces, Molly reaches out to hold Pearl's and Annie's hands in hers.

'Is it bad news?' she asks. 'Is it about the letters?'

'It is,' Annie nods. 'Oh, Pearl, I'm so very sorry.'

My Dearest Pearl,

I hope you can find it in your heart to forgive us both. We hoped to protect you as best we could. It's all we wanted after that terrible day in Godalming. I'm so sorry.

When Mrs Williams was so cruel to you after you telephoned to speak to Nate, you looked like you had lost what little strength you had left. You had been through too much. Ray and I said we would never let anything hurt you so badly again. We made a promise to each other.

I hated seeing you so lost and afraid every day. I tried to find help but every time we did, nothing seemed to work. Do you remember, Pearl? I couldn't risk anything making it worse. A reminder of what had happened and how it made you never want to leave the house and go outside.

Please understand, we never did this to hurt you. My dearest girl.

I wish we had known what to do for the best. In the absence of that, we did what we thought would help.

If you are reading this, you will have found the box of letters. We never opened them or read what they said. We hoped, if you ever did, that enough time would have passed for you not to feel any sadness because of what could be written inside.

Lana and Ray xx

After Molly has read the note also, Pearl folds the piece of paper carefully, her heart aching at the news. So many years and she had no idea Nate had wanted to reach her. So many years she could have known that he still cared.

Mrs Williams's refusal to let her speak to her son on the telephone had set in motion a tragic sequence of events. Nate's letters had been hidden to protect her and eventually he had stopped writing, that much is clear from the last postmarks. But not before he'd tried for many years. No doubt he finally stopped in the belief that she had moved on, even though that couldn't have been further from the truth. In turn, she had assumed he had found love, and eventually resigned herself to never hearing from him again.

It was tragic, each action had rippled its effects across time.

'Oh, Pearl,' Molly says. 'That woman, Mrs Williams . . . she can't have realised what she'd done. We need Connor to find Nate, and now.'

And as fresh tears begin to fall, Pearl feels herself enveloped once again in a now familiar hug that smells comfortingly of Persil Automatic and patchouli.

CONNOR

They talk for so long it begins to get dark outside.

Nate introduces Connor to his next-door neighbour, Anila. When Nate tells her that Connor knows Pearl, she looks genuinely made-up.

'Nate's been telling me their story,' she says. 'It's so romantic. I can't believe you're here! Sorry, I should have said before. Can I get you some food, or something to drink?'

Connor smiles. Anila seems very welcoming and kind. He's glad Nate has a friend like her with him now. Connor's unannounced arrival at Weatherley Gardens was clearly a shock, judging by the look on Nate's face when he arrived.

'I'm OK, thank you.'

'Well, just let me know if you change your mind.'

When Nate had asked him if Pearl was well, he had said she was. Nate had wanted to know as much as Connor could tell him, and he'd explained about the letters and the fact that Pearl was so upset to learn they had been kept hidden from her in the loft.

'But why?' Nate asked, and Connor realised he couldn't answer that.

A man called Ryan arrives, tired and hungry from a strenuous day applying cat's eyes to the middle of the A26 near the Surrey–Kent border. He is sent out immediately by Anila to the local Chinese takeaway and returns with tinfoil containers full of steaming chow mein and egg fried rice.

While they eat at a compact kitchen table in Anila's apartment, they talk about the letters and how they had been kept in the loft at Highview.

'There must have been a reason.' Anila looks confused then says, 'We never did get to the final part of the story where Pearl moved away, Nate, did we?'

Connor waits. It's the answer to the question he hasn't wanted to ask for fear of intruding on Pearl's past. The reason she left Godalming and relocated to the moor. Her life before he met her is her own business, and he's always respected that.

He watches Nate struggle to answer, darkness clouding his eyes, a memory that seems to haunt him even now.

'Nate?' Anila whispers.

Ryan shifts uncomfortably in his chair at the table. This is a difficult moment for everyone but for Nate most of all.

'It should never have happened. I don't think I will ever forget it,' he says, looking like all the life has drained out of him.

And Connor realises then he must tell Nate everything, without missing parts out.

'Nate, there's something you should know about the way Pearl lives. I'm sorry but this might be even more upsetting for you to hear than what happened to your letters.'

'Please tell me,' he says. 'I only want to help Pearl.'

★★★

Ryan and Anila offer to drop him back at the station and Connor gratefully accepts. The last train is leaving in twenty minutes. Nate comes along too, and they say goodbye with a handshake and the promise to stay in touch.

'I can't thank you enough, Connor,' Nate says. 'It means the world to me, simply knowing Pearl is safe. You've done a brave and good thing coming here today and I'm very grateful to you.'

'I'm glad it was good news,' Connor says. 'I'm not sure what I would have done if it hadn't been.'

'It would never have been anything but,' Nate reassures him.

'Will you come to Devon to see Pearl?' Connor asks, wondering what happens next.

Nate nods. 'Just as soon as I can get my car from the rescue centre.'

'That soon?'

Nate nods. 'I hope so.'

'I'd better go, now,' Connor says. 'I think that's my train about to leave.'

'See you in Devon.'

'Bye Nate.'

In the empty carriage, he finds his seat and sits back as the last train of the evening travels at what feels like supersonic speed in the direction of home, walled by the darkness outside.

He checks his phone for a signal and is glad of the four bars showing. At the earliest opportunity, he rings Pearl.

When she answers, it sounds like she is on the other side of the world.

Reasons To Go Outside

'Connor?'

'Hello?'

'Is that you?'

'Pearl, I found Nate,' he says, noticing his signal wavering unpredictably as the train speeds along.

'Hello . . . Connor?'

'Pearl, I found Nate,' he says again.

'Oh, Connor. What did he say? Is he well?'

'He is.'

'Are you on the train?'

'I am.'

'Connor, I found another letter, it's from my mother and Ray – I will tell you about it when I see you. Annie and Molly came over, but they've left now and it's late. You must be tired?'

'I'm OK. I'll drive straight over as soon as I get back,' he says, exhilarated not exhausted now the reality of the situation is kicking in. Nate is alive and well and will soon be on his way down to Devon. All the tiredness in the world can't dampen the positivity he is feeling.

And then the train shoots through a station and the signal is lost.

NATE

When they arrive at Happy Tails in Ryan's car, it looks like Wayne and Katie have forgotten to switch the lights off, because the reception building is lit up like a Christmas tree. It's a blessing in disguise, Nate realises, as he, Anila and Ryan make their way across the grass and along the path. At least they can see where they are going.

As they walk, they make arrangements concerning Frank.

'Are you able to look after him until I come back?' Nate asks.

'Of course, no problem at all,' Anila replies. 'I've still got the spare key you gave me. I'll go and fetch him when we get back and put his bed next to ours.'

When they open the door, they are greeted by the anxious faces of Katie, Wayne and Claire.

'What are you all doing here?' Anila asks. 'It's the middle of the night!'

'Katie said Nate collapsed and we were all worried,' Claire replies. 'Really worried.'

'I didn't say collapsed exactly,' Katie clarifies. 'I said he looked a bit peaky.'

'Whatever,' Claire says. 'We were worried. I messaged everyone and we decided to meet up here just in case we were needed. Nate, are you OK? Katie said you had to go home urgently. Are you in trouble? Is it the law or the tax office?'

Reasons To Go Outside

'I didn't say in trouble with the tax office or the police,' Katie qualifies.

'It's been a bit of a night,' Anila says. 'But you could have phoned us, we would have explained.'

'We tried calling,' Wayne says. 'But your phones are off.'

Nate checks his and Anila does the same. They notice they've both got a series of missed calls.

'How are you feeling, Nate?' Katie asks.

'Better, thanks,' he replies.

Claire comes around to the front of the reception desk, looking as purposeful as always. 'Nate, if you're in some sort of trouble, honestly . . . we've got your back.'

'Nate's not in any trouble,' Anila explains. 'He's just got to drive to Devon . . . tonight. He's had news about an old friend. Not bad news, it's all good.'

She looks at Nate as she says the words, and he nods, a silent agreement between friends for her to tell the rest of the team about the situation in his absence. Because right now he has too much on his mind and a three-and-a-half-hour journey to make.

'Nate, is it worth heading off now?' Ryan says helpfully. 'There's roadworks on the A303 at the moment and a diversion in place.'

Nate thinks about Connor, and Pearl, and the long journey ahead of him driving through the night. Nodding at Ryan, he says, 'I'll get going then. Thanks Ryan.'

'You're leaving now!' Claire asks. 'But we still don't know what's going on.' She looks lost for a moment, just like she did the first day they met when she sat on the floor in the pens and pulled Eric and Stan to her.

'Don't worry. Anila will explain.'

'Good luck, Nate,' Ryan says, reaching out and shaking his hand, just as Nate had shaken Connor's at the station. 'I hope all goes well with the drive and when you get there.'

'I'm here, and I will have my phone on this time, Nate, I promise,' Anila adds. 'I'm going to be keeping everything crossed. It's the final chapter of the story . . . isn't it?' she says, smiling with tears in her eyes.

From behind the reception desk, Katie looks content to wait for her to explain. 'Wherever you're going, Nate, take care. It'll be chilly tonight. Maybe even a frost.'

Wayne lifts his hand in a wave. 'Good luck, mate.'

'Thank you,' Nate says, wishing they could all join him somehow, but that's not possible, he knows, because the centre must open tomorrow as usual. Happy Tails will always keep going, for the sake of all the residents, new and old. It's why his friends give their time for free and are happy to do it.

As he walks out of the brightly lit reception and over to his car, he thinks about the journey ahead, the roadworks on the A303, the possibility of delays. But most of all, as he drives out onto the road, he thinks of Pearl.

PEARL

It's Annie who reaches her first.

In the darkness the house is cold and worryingly silent except for the insistent ringing. Over and over, it doesn't stop, like a trapped budgerigar flying around downstairs in the hallway. What is that noise? It's so early. Not anywhere close to morning.

Getting out of bed and hurrying downstairs, Pearl forgets to put on her slippers. The cold stone floor bites at her feet. Where have the hours gone? Has Connor been knocking at the door unable to get an answer? Is this him now, ringing her on his mobile? When he called from the train he'd said he would come straight to Highview, but it had grown late, and eventually she'd gone up to bed and fallen instantly asleep. She moves from side to side. The air is as chilled as the floor beneath her feet. In the kitchen, Nate's letters are still piled on the table.

'Hello?' Pearl answers the landline, her voice cracked by interrupted sleep. 'Hello, Connor, is it you?'

'Oh, Pearl!' She isn't expecting it to be Annie. Her friend sounds desperate, her voice drained of its usual upbeat cheeriness. Worryingly so. 'Pearl, I'm so sorry. I can't believe it . . .'

Her voice breaks off, followed by the sound of sobbing.

'Annie?' Pearl asks, her mouth suddenly dry.

On the other end of the line, Michael takes over. 'It was an accident.'

She hears him saying words then, words that don't seem to make any sense ... *on the road up to the moor* ... *a speeding car that didn't stop* ... *multiple injuries* ... *airlifted to hospital* ... *critical condition.*

'I don't understand.' Pearl shakes her head and rubs her eyes, thinking she might still be asleep.

Annie takes over. 'I've got a friend who works in A&E. She's going to get you in to see him.'

'It's not strictly allowed,' Michael manages, his voice nowhere near as steady as usual. 'Supposed to be only family, but Connor ... he was asking for you, Pearl, in the air ambulance. The paramedics relayed the message to Annie's friend in A&E.'

'How soon can we get there?'

'We're on our way to you now,' Annie says, 'Hold tight. Michael is driving as I speak. I'm holding the phone.'

She imagines making the journey to the hospital, suddenly pictures the distance from her front door down to the road, and the miles they will need to travel in the van after that. 'But ... Annie ...'

'I know.'

'But the journey?'

'Don't worry, we've got help,' Michael and Annie say together. 'We've had a huge response on Facebook. We really weren't expecting it.'

Pearl hears Derek's voice in the background and then Annie and Michael are saying, 'We'll be there as soon as we can.'

'I'll be waiting,' she says, feeling her voice fading.

In the chilly hallway, Pearl pulls her wool cardigan closer around her shoulders, but it does nothing to stop an icy feeling from running down her back and soaking into her bones. The walls draw in. She can't hear anything, and she doesn't exhale. Instead, she holds her breath inside because suddenly she's sinking below a watery surface. The weight of it is pressing her under, further, colder, deeper, until finally she feels herself descend to the bottom, to where there is nothing but complete darkness.

NATE

Nate turns off the M5 and heads along the A30, all the while listening to a traffic alert on the radio about an earlier accident. A collision involving two cars on a country lane. One person seriously injured and airlifted to hospital. The road is still closed. There are diversions in place.

According to his sat nav, he is about seven miles from Highview. Feeling he might need to take a moment and have a breath of fresh air, he pulls over in a layby overlooking the town and opens the window. He remembers Westdown, nestled in the moor. The memory of its thatched cottages and picturesque High Street is still clear in his mind. He decides he will tell Pearl as soon as possible about how he drove here twice as a young man, desperate to see her, and how he was turned away on both occasions by Ray and Lana. He remembers they said she was resting and how important that was given what had happened. If only he hadn't taken no for an answer. If only she had been able to read his letters. How different their lives would have been. The recollection of it motivates him to keep going. It won't be far now.

As he's about to turn the key in the ignition, he hears it: engines racing, tyres rumbling, the sound of a convoy approaching from behind. There are vehicles of all types: a bright red postal van, a yellow VW camper with a surfboard on top, a sign-written pink car with *Cherry's Hair Salon* on the side, followed by cars of all colours and sizes behind . . . *one, two, three, four, five, six, seven* . . . racing past, all led by a white van. When the road is clear, Nate shifts his car into first gear and joins the line of traffic.

The procession leads him up a winding road and onto the moor in exactly the same direction as his sat nav is instructing him. In the darkness, a tall, white wooden signpost looms into view like a scarecrow, followed by snatched glimpses of ponies grazing at the sides of the road, shadowy figures with their noses to the ground. Nate follows the line-up as it turns off the main road onto a narrower lane that twists and turns, dipping and then rising, climbing higher and higher. Half a mile further, in the location the sat nav has directed him to, the vehicles start to slow and one by one pull up on the verge. When the passengers get out, bright lights from their torches and mobile phones dance in the blackness like fireflies. More vehicles arrive and soon he is surrounded by as many as fifty men, women and children, walking and talking, some calling out instructions on where to stand. It reminds him of an event like a charity run or a sponsored walk; it has the same sense of anticipation, supportive atmosphere, smiling faces and friendly welcome. But he has no idea of what is really going on.

Nate meets a man with a lined face and brick dust in his hair.

'Sorry, we didn't have enough time to fully brief everyone over social media,' the man says. 'Did you want to find a space in the line?' He reaches out and offers his hand. 'And thanks for coming . . . we really appreciate the help of every single person who's turned up tonight.'

Nate shakes the man's hand as a woman near the front door of the house calls out to him: 'Michael!'

'Sorry, I need to go,' the man says. 'Thanks again, though.'

Slowly, the crowd takes up position on both sides of the path. They are lining it from the front door to the garden gate. Given the hour and the temperature, they all look to be in remarkably good spirits.

'There's a space here, mate.' A man, holding hands with another shorter man, is looking at Nate and pointing to a gap in the line. He squeezes along to make room. 'I'm Scott,' he says. 'I run the newsagent's in town. And this is Jack. When we saw the message go up we just got straight in the car.'

'Nate. I just got here.'

'Nice to meet you, Nate.'

'Forty-three years,' a woman with a smooth blow-dried bob of creamy blonde hair is saying. She is standing a little further along the path. 'Just makes me want to do everything I can. I've got everything crossed.' She bites her lip in concern. 'Come on, Pearl,' she says more quietly, looking up to the front door. 'Come on, girl.'

'She'll do it, Cherry,' the old man with white hair standing next to her says. 'She will. Connor's been taking the steps with her.'

'That's the spirit, Jim,' the woman says, slipping her arm through his. 'Come on, everyone, let's link up.'

'Nate?' Scott says, offering his arm.

Scott, Jack, Nate, Jim and Cherry join together, followed by other people in the crowd. Soon everyone is happily linking arms. Nate notices in particular a tall Black girl holding a toddler, on the other side of the path. Her eyes are fixed on the front door.

'Everyone ready?' the man with brick dust in his hair calls out, and the crowd respond with a cheer. 'Yes! All ready!'

It's a wonderful sight. So many people all here to help Pearl leave her house. Connor had explained about the agoraphobia. But why Pearl has to do it right now in the middle of the night, he isn't sure. He thinks about telephoning Connor on his mobile. Perhaps he's somewhere in the crowd and they can talk. He'll know what's going on.

When they'd said their goodbyes at the train station, Connor had promised that he would see Nate soon.

PEARL

When she comes to on the hall floor, there is the sound of voices outside.

She runs upstairs and dresses as fast as she can, before coming back down, slipping on her mother's shoes and opening the door. She looks out at a multitude of unfamiliar faces, edging the path like borders of tall flowers, grown especially for the occasion. The people fall silent immediately and turn their faces towards her. At the far end, beyond the gate, Michael's van is parked with the passenger door open and the engine still running. Grey smoke leaves the exhaust and disappears into the cold air. There is no time to wonder how many people are standing in the front garden.

The closest person to her is Annie. 'We're all here for you, Pearl,' she says.

'I'll get back in the van, so we can go straight away,' Michael says from where he's standing nearby.

'Take your time, Pearl. One step at a time!' someone calls from the crowd. A man.

'Come on, Pearl, you can do it!' It's a different voice next. A woman.

'We're here for you, Pearl.'

Other voices join in.

The first step is the hardest.

It seems to take forever, like that first step out onto the patio with Connor.

She hears the voices more clearly now, willing her on.

'It's all right. One foot in front of the other. All the way.'

'Keep going, Pearl.'

'You're doing great.' Molly is there with Tommy, and next to her is Derek. His face is tear-stained and pale. She can tell he wants to speak but can't find the words. They are all thinking of Connor.

Pearl closes her eyes for a second. One step. Then another. There's no going back.

When she opens them, she sees a woman wearing a multicoloured woolly hat.

'You're doing great,' she says. 'That's it. Brilliant!'

'Come on, Pearl.'

The ground beneath her feels like alien territory, uneven and unsteady, moving of its own accord. It's like walking on a conveyor belt. Each step requires her full and undivided attention. She looks down, remembering how she did the same over forty years ago when she first arrived at High-view. There are still the same explosions of emerald-green moss sprouting from the cracks in the path.

Then everyone is cheering. Loudly. Jubilantly.

'You're almost there!'

The voices grow even louder. 'Not far now!'

'Connor needs you, Pearl. One more step!' It is encouraging; the wall of sound on either side, shielding her, carrying her forward.

Must keep going. Pearl recites the words in her head. *Keep moving forward.*

And suddenly, Annie and Molly are wrapping her in their arms at the end of the path and the crowd are applauding. 'Pearl! You did it!' Annie cries. 'We're at the van!'

Nearby, she sees the pony-tailed postman who delivers her mail wipe a tear from his eye.

Michael offers his hand and Pearl takes it gratefully. He helps her into the van and shows her how to pull the seat-belt out and strap it across her safely. She stares out at the jubilant crowd just briefly, all the people from the town who have turned out to help.

She doesn't see the man waiting patiently on the far side of the path, sandwiched between the old gentleman with a head of pure white hair and the two young men hugging each other ever so tightly.

'We should get going,' Michael says urgently, and Pearl nods, lost for words.

'Ready,' he says. 'We should get going,' he adds, and Pearl nods, lost for words.

As the van pulls away, she feels her stomach lurch with each change up in gear. The first time she has ridden in a vehicle since she sat on the back seat in Ray's car count-ing seconds on their way to a new home. The feeling is as unnerving now as it was then.

They dip down towards a wider road and rumble over a cattle grid. 'Can't we go any faster?' Annie asks.

Michael shakes his head in reply and remains silent.

Pearl swallows the terror she feels and looks out at the blackness.

All that matters now is getting to the hospital. Nothing else is more important than that.

★★★

Michael parks in the nearest available space to the entrance of A&E.

'You go in. I'll feed the meter,' he says. 'I'll be right here, waiting.'

Walking through the entrance to the hospital with Annie by her side, Pearl sees that nobody notices them even though she's shaking so much she can barely put one foot in front of the other. But she keeps walking regardless, past the people with legs and arms in casts, a man in a wheelchair, and a woman holding a little boy with a saucepan stuck on his head. There isn't a moment to waste.

'He's along here.' Annie's friend, an emergency department nurse, greets them both at the double doors on the other side of the reception area.

Annie says, 'Thanks, Janice, for this. I wouldn't usually ask for a favour but . . .'

'It's OK.' The woman nods. 'Supposed to be family only,' she explains to them both. 'But I'll get you in. You'll have about five minutes.'

Pearl nods.

'It's this way.'

Annie leaves them at the double doors and Janice guides the way, leading Pearl along a white corridor, through another set of double doors, and down another corridor with a sign pointing the way to the Intensive Care Unit.

'Connor has multiple injuries,' she says, as she walks and talks. Pearl imagines Janice must have to do this more often than not. 'He's in an induced coma so he won't respond, and . . . ' she turns to look at Pearl. 'He won't look like he usually does. I just wanted to warn you. He's not moving, and he won't respond to you,' she adds. And then, more gently, 'The doctors are doing everything they can. I'll keep Annie updated, as soon as I know anything more. I know there'll be plenty of people who'll want to know how he's doing.'

Through another set of doors, they come to an open area with a reception desk. There is a doctor dressed in scrubs, as well as nurses dressed in the same uniform as Janice. They all look extremely busy. Out the other side of this area, they continue along another corridor.

'He's just down here,' Annie's friend says, bringing them to a stop outside a private room with a closed blind over the window. 'Five minutes,' she adds. 'I'm sorry it's not more but I shouldn't even be doing this. The dad's already been in, but he's gone to get a coffee and a consultant will be speaking to him after that. I'm looking after Connor for now, so this is it. These few minutes are all you have, I'm sorry it can't be anymore.'

'No, you've been so helpful already. Thank you.'

'I'll leave you to go in.'

The nurse hurries away and Pearl sanitises her hands at the wall station alongside the door before slowly pushing it open.

Inside the room, it's quiet. But there are still the everyday noises from outside to which other people are accustomed but, Pearl realises now, she isn't. Doors closing, footsteps walking, people talking, and the continuous drone of a ventilation unit operating somewhere above or below, she can't tell.

He lies in the hospital bed completely still. His head and arms are covered in bruises, a smear of blood stains the base of his neck. She wants to wipe it away but knows that is impossible. A collection of monitors surrounds his bed like electronic nursemaids, the noises they emit proof that they are helping to keep him alive. And there's a powerful smell of disinfectant that she can almost taste.

A plastic band around his wrist has his name and date of birth printed on it. It confirms he is eighteen years old. Pearl imagines this must be the hospital where Connor was born and given a similar tag, a smaller version tied around his ankle so there could be no mistake to whom he belonged, in this sprawling building with so many corridors and rooms, and acres of tarmac for a car park.

She looks around at the pale blue walls and shiny grey floor, before sitting down on the chair positioned alongside his bed. It must be where his father was sitting earlier.

Afraid to touch him for fear of dislodging the cannula piercing the back of his hand, she puts her own hands together and rests them in her lap.

'I'm here,' she says. 'Oh, Connor, I hope you can hear me.'

The constant beep of the monitors marks the disappearing seconds.

Pearl's hand reaches out and her fingers touch his. Tears begin to roll down her face.

'Please don't go. There is a wonderful life ahead still to come . . . I promise you.'

Outside, it is suddenly quiet. Elsewhere in the hospital, she knows, people are lying in their beds, looking forward to going home. In other parts of the hospital, there are successful operations being carried out, babies being born, lives being saved. In other parts of the hospital there is hope.

She loses track of time. It could be seconds or minutes, she isn't sure, but someone enters the room.

When she turns, she sees it is Janice. The precious moments have slipped away.

'Connor's father is on his way back with the consultant. I'm sorry, I know it was shorter than expected but that's all the time we have.'

'What will happen?'

'We just have to wait. That's all I can say. He has been in a major accident and has a significant head injury . . .'

For a moment Pearl thinks Janice is going to add more and decides she doesn't want to hear these words. Painful, final words that there is no coming back from. A statement of hard fact about what will happen next that she can't unhear.

'We have to go.' Janice looks away down the corridor to check who is coming.

They walk quickly along the corridor, through the open area with the reception desk, down another corridor, then another.

'The exit is just through here.'

'Thank you, for letting me see him,' Pearl says.

'I'll have to go straight back.'

'Of course.'

As Janice walks away, Pearl pushes through the double doors that lead her back out into a waiting area made up of a square of wooden chairs and two vending machines. One of them has a ripped piece of white paper Sellotaped to its glass front. The words 'Temporarily Out of Order' are written on it in black pen. The overhead lights are harsh, throwing their glare on every sharp corner and rough edge. She wants to close her eyes to the lights. Sink into a chair and wait.

Annie appears and rushes to meet her. 'How is he?'

Pearl shakes her head. 'It's not good.'

They stand not knowing what to do for the best.

'I think we should go now. Janice said she will ring if there's any news,' Annie says.

'Yes,' Pearl agrees. 'Let's go home.' They follow the signs for the hospital exit. As distressing as it is to walk away now, there is no other choice.

***

Feeling devastated, they pull up outside Highview in the early hours of the morning and sit side by side in the van.

'Do you mind if we just sit here . . . for a few moments?' Annie says. 'I don't think I can move.'

Pearl nods and Michael leans forward, looking out through the windscreen into the gloom. He switches the van's headlights on to full beam, illuminating the verge running alongside the fence and picking out a single car. It's a medium-sized silver hatchback, parked up ahead. All the other vehicles have disappeared.

'Someone's still here.'

They stare out into the darkness at the lone car just as the security light at the side of the front door is triggered by a movement.

Standing in the spotlight is a man.

'Who's that?' Annie says, peering out into the night.

'It's one of the volunteers from Facebook, and the car owner, I'm guessing. Poor bloke. He must have been sat here in the dark.'

Pearl moves closer to get a better look, before one hand shoots to her mouth.

'Pearl?' Annie says, looking directly at her and taking in her shocked expression. 'Is that . . .?'

Pearl feels the floor of the van fall away under her feet like she's suddenly been jettisoned into space.

Michael moves to open the driver's door. 'I should probably go and apologise. Let him know it's time to go home.'

'Hang on a minute, Michael,' Annie says, pulling him back by his jacket.

'Why?' he asks, sounding baffled. 'It's freezing out there. He'll catch his death of cold.'

'He's not one of the volunteers off Facebook.'

'Who is he then?' Michael asks. 'Are you sure you don't want me to get out?'

Pearl shakes her head. 'I don't think that'll be necessary.'

'Michael, that's not some bloke,' Annie says. 'I think that's Pearl's Nate.'

NATE

It is cold enough for hats and scarves, but they don't feel the chill. It reminds him of the November night they first met, the sight of her standing under the streetlamp, and her favourite book lying on the ground.

He looks across the path to where Pearl is standing now, his heart beating rapidly in his chest. As the van she arrived in disappears down the road, he hopes the overwhelming emotion of meeting each other again after all this time won't cause him to clam up completely.

'Nate . . .' When she says his name, they could be two teenagers once more, standing in the glow of the streetlight in Godalming. 'You're here?'

'I came as soon as I could,' he says, wanting to wrap her in his arms and hold her tight, but knowing at the same time it could seem odd after so long without seeing each other. 'I wanted to get here and tell you, Pearl, that I never stopped thinking about you. Not for a single day. Connor told me about the letters. I only wish you could have been able to read them.'

'Oh, Nate, I wanted to. I sat in my room for days and waited for them to arrive. But I've read them now. All of them.' And then, 'So much has happened since then.'

'I saw what it took for you to get to the gate.'

'Were you in the crowd all along?'

He nods. 'I was willing you on. And you made it.'

'For Connor.' He watches her face fall.

'A man with white hair told me about the accident. I am so sorry.'

'Seeing him lying in the hospital . . .' she says, tears beginning to form in her eyes. 'It was so sad.'

When her tears begin to fall, he steps forward. Very slowly and gently, he takes her in his arms as he has wanted to do since he saw her get out of the van. She leans into him, and he feels the warmth of her body next to his as her head rests against his shoulder. 'It's going to be all right,' he says.

Nate thinks of the white-haired man called Jim who had relayed the details of the crash after Pearl left for the hospital. The news of Connor's injuries upset Nate greatly. He had stood as the crowds dispersed, frozen and unmoving, hoping it was all a big mistake.

They fall silent for several moments, wrapped in each other's arms, not quite believing they are here. Standing on the grass outside Highview, he doesn't mind the freezing air, or the cold seeping into his bones. Being here with Pearl is all that matters.

'What can I do to help?'

Pearl lifts her head to look at him. In the half-light, he notices her eyes are still the same ocean-blue he remembers. 'Can we go inside? There is so much to talk about,' she says. 'Don't you think?'

He nods. 'There is.'

'And you can stay a while?'

'As long as you need me.'

'You don't have anyone to get back to?' she asks, her expression changing to one of concern.

He shakes his head and smiles at her.

'Nobody,' he says. 'Nobody at all unless you count Frank.'

PEARL

In the kitchen, she sits at the table and Nate offers to make the tea, finding his way around, boiling the kettle, looking for cups, and explaining about the Labrador he has rehomed from the shelter where he works.

'Anila and Ryan are looking after him while I'm gone,' Nate says. 'They live next door and are a great couple. It was Anila who suggested working at the animal rescue centre in Godalming after I was made redundant. I'd been with the insurance company for forty-two years before that.'

Listening to him talk, Pearl realises there is so much they have to catch up on. Years of experiences, people and places that have played an important part in Nate's life as well as her own. She is keen to hear his news and thinks about what she will say in return. There is the subject of her agoraphobia, the steps she is taking to overcome it, as well as Connor and his plans for the future, her new friends, and so much more. But there is plenty of time, she reminds herself, they have all the time in the world to finally catch up.

He pours a cup of tea and hands it to her. Pearl wraps her hands around it, grateful for the brew's familiar comforting warmth.

A gentle silence fills the space between them, until Nate says, 'Pearl, before his accident . . . Connor explained to me about the letters. He said he'd found them in the loft and that they'd been kept up there for years, hidden away.'

He looks crushed by this.

'I am so sorry,' she tells him. 'Ray and my mother thought they were doing the right thing. They were afraid I might find them upsetting . . . '

'I would never hurt you, Pearl. I promise you,' he sighs, reaching out and taking her hand in his. It's been so long but his touch still feels comforting and warm, just like his arms did when he wrapped them around her earlier.

'I know you wouldn't. I always did.' She smiles sadly, remembering the telephone conversation with Mrs Williams the summer they arrived at Highview. 'But it was a sentence your mother said when I telephoned to speak to you that convinced Lana and Ray to hide the letters away. She said you had moved on and that I wasn't to ring again because of what had happened that summer. So, I didn't.'

Nate's face registers his anger. It passes just a quickly. 'I wish I had known. My mother could be cruel. No doubt, in her mind, she thought I'd be better off, but I wasn't. That's why I kept writing. When I didn't get a reply after so many years, I assumed you'd found love and started a family of your own.'

Hearing him say the words makes her think of looking after Tommy for Molly, and the children and grandchildren she will never have, and it brings fresh tears to her eyes.

'All these years we were convinced to believe a lie,' she says, wishing she hadn't telephoned that day, then Lana and Ray might have felt differently. 'All these years when we could have been together and found our own way.'

He nods in agreement before saying, 'But it's not too late, is it?'

Looking up at the kitchen clock, Pearl notices the time. It will be getting light soon, and the dawn chorus will begin.

'Will you really stay, Nate?' The words leave her lips before she's thought about them. 'I'm sorry. I realise you might have made arrangements to stay in a hotel . . .?'

He shakes his head. 'I just jumped in my car and drove. But, of course, I can book into a B&B in the town if you would like me to?'

'No, could you stay here? Would that be all right?'

'I will, for as long as you need me,' Nate says. 'My flat is fine. Anila has said she will keep an eye on it for as long as I need her to.'

Pearl feels a wave of relief wash over her. He is here, by her side, just like when they were young. The only love she ever knew or needed.

And when he holds her in his arms again, she closes her eyes and feels all the sadness of the years they have lost start to fade.

NATE

He has never fed crows before, but when it is officially morning he finds himself rolling hard-boiled eggs onto the patio in the same style as elderly men playing bowls on a green.

They seem extremely appreciative, the crows, nodding and pecking, and not being put off by him standing so close.

He sees Pearl watching him. 'They like you,' she says, smiling a happy but tired smile. It had been late when they'd eventually retired to their separate beds. They'd talked until it was light and slept for only an hour. 'I think they can tell you're an animal person. I'll bring some monkey nuts. They get very excited at the sight of those.'

Nate looks out at the view, past the patio occupied by hungry crows, the wall and the oaks, and thinks of Frank and all the residents of Happy Tails rescue centre. How they would love to be let loose here on the moorland, running free and making the most of all the new smells and open space. It is such a wonderful place and Highview is positioned right in the middle. It's with a heavy heart he realises that Pearl hasn't been able to enjoy the moor as she might – walking for miles, breathing in the fresh air and taking in the magnificent views. It's a hillwalkers' paradise but for all these years it has been beyond her reach. Not for the first time since arriving, he feels the loss of all the experiences they might have shared together if life had taken an alternative path: a wedding day with confetti floating in the breeze, a cosy home they could call their own, a family that would expand and surround them as they grew older. He sighs at the thought of it and rolls a final hard-boiled egg out in the direction of the crows.

In the early hours they had talked, neither of them wanting to sleep. There is so much yet to discover, about how Pearl has lived her life, her hopes, her dreams. When she told him about The Fear he listened, and when she cried he held her close to him once again.

Pearl brings a handful of nuts, and he feeds the crows their favourite treat one at a time until they start to flap their wings and dance around the patio.

'That's their way of saying thank you . . . now they're full,' Pearl says, and he watches as first one and then another fly away to the row of oak trees at the edge of the lawn. 'Would you like to see the garden?'

'I'll get my shoes,' he says.

With Pearl standing on the lawn, he walks down as far as the vegetable patch, sees the sprouting heads of broccoli and lettuce and the strawberry plants that have grown but no longer bear fruit. He takes his time to marvel at the galloping vine bursting out of the greenhouse, and the substantial outhouse built at the back of the house. He steps inside it and sees how neatly Connor has left it, with rows of gardening equipment, spades, forks, a hoe and two outdoor brooms all in their place. There is a metal bin half-full of ashes, and orderly shelves stacked with weedkiller, grass seed and petrol cans.

The air inside is warm despite the cold morning and it smells comfortingly of cut grass.

On the wall, above a wooden work bench, is a list of vegetables planted in the patch. On the table there is a short pencil, broken at the end, and some left-over packets of radish seeds.

When he leaves the outhouse, he walks back to the patio where Pearl is waiting. He can see her face has lost its smile from earlier, and her eyes are shadowed by a new concern.

'Pearl, what is it?'

'It's not good news,' she says, shaking her head in despair once again. 'Annie's just phoned. It's Connor. He's developed an infection.'

PEARL

Two weeks later, she wakes with a start and rushes down-stairs. Ray used to say, 'Like a cat on a hot tin roof,' she remembers, which, in her opinion, doesn't cover the half of it.

It had been the same every day since Connor's accident. Pearl anticipated the telephone ringing so often, she began to hear it in her sleep. The hospital staff are continuing to help him fight the infection that causes his temperature to spike and puts his life severely at risk.

Each day Pearl hopes for better news, but as yet there is nothing more from Janice at the hospital.

With a despondent sigh, she takes off her slippers and leaves them by the telephone table for when she returns.

Nate waits by the front door.

'Shall we try a little further today? What do you think? Maybe the gate?' He is keeping her mind off the situation. Keeping her going.

Every day since the accident, with Nate by her side, they have walked a little further down the path. Each time, she battled The Fear. Only the thought of Connor lying alone in hospital drove her on. He is her reason for each step that she takes. Out of the front door and down the path, with the gate ahead for a guide, and the open moor beyond as her ultimate goal. She hopes he knows she is walking. *Don't give up, Connor. I won't.*

'Are you ready?' Nate asks.

'I'll just tie these and get my coat.'

The week before, Nate had spent a whole morning in an outdoor shop in Plymouth purchasing them both sturdy walking boots and a new coat for Pearl. The three-in-one layered garment has lots of features she'd never come across before and had no idea could be included in a single item of clothing: a waterproof membrane, hydro-seal zip, and a storm-resistant hood.

With her new coat fastened up, she slips her feet into the new boots. With both planted firmly on the path, she walks a little further than the day before.

Before them, under the grey and white sky, the mighty tors of Dartmoor rip through the earth. Her aim is to climb to the top of the nearest one. A journey to the summit.

'We'll be up there soon enough.' Nate's words echo her unspoken thoughts.

'It's a bit further than the gate.'

'But we will make it.' He reaches out and she takes his hand. Their fingers find each other and hold on tight. The air is cold, but his skin feels warm. His touch anchors her to him.

She can almost smell the grass covering the moor, coarse and strong like a thick, green carpet. To step on it would be invigorating; to roll around on it like the ponies do, even better. She didn't ever imagine she could feel this way again but it's happening.

Today their view is unbroken by dog walkers or passing cars in the far distance. Just earth and sky. Green and concrete grey. Overhead, a buzzard hovers, expectantly searching for prey, and on the path, a beetle crosses in front of her feet, its black bullet of a body rocking from side to side as it navigates the deep cracks in the concrete.

When they reach the gate, they stop to lean on it and take in the view.

'A step further?' Nate asks. 'Through the gate.'

Pearl nods. 'And then onto the moor and back,' she says decisively.

'And tomorrow?'

'Tomorrow we will go even further.'

***

After lunch, Annie telephones again, this time with more hopeful news.

'They're not sure, but they think the infection is under control,' she says with huge relief. 'They'll let us know. It's still very uncertain but a slight improvement.'

'Oh, Annie. Is there anything we can do?'

'No, I don't think so,' she replies, sounding tired. 'Apart from wait. I won't say "don't worry" because that would be completely pointless,' she adds. 'How is it going there? How's Nate?'

'He's well,' Pearl replies. 'We're going to try and walk up to the top of the tor,' she adds, knowing if she tells Annie, it will encourage her to go through with it even more. 'We're doing it for Connor.'

'That's amazing! He'd be so proud if he knew, Pearl. He would. And I know he's still fighting, he is,' Annie says, her words broken up with sobs. 'I must stop crying, I'm sorry. I'd better go; the twins need their dinner and I'm due on shift at The Willows.'

Before she goes, Annie promises to pop round with Michael the following week.

'So, he can finally fix that roof.'

Pearl imagines the new slates going on, closing the gap where the rainwater came in. Before autumn ends and the weather changes.

'Take care, Annie.'

''Bye, Pearl. See you soon.'

Molly is the next to telephone.

'Do you know if we can visit Connor yet?' she asks. 'It's so hard, just waiting.'

'It is, but we can't see him because of the infection.'

'When will we hear, do you think?' Molly sounds desperate, and Pearl wishes she had better news.

'I'll speak to Connor's father,' Pearl promises.

'Has he been in touch?'

'No,' Pearl replies. 'But I'm sure he's just as shocked and upset as we are. He's already lost his wife, now he could lose his only son.'

'He must be wrecked.'

'I think so.'

'I'm finding each day so hard, just thinking of what happened. Tommy is sad too. It's like he knows, Pearl.'

'Please give him a hug from me. And ring me whenever you want.'

'Is it all right if I call again tonight?'

'I'll be here.'

'Thanks, Pearl.'

'Take care.'

'You too.'

Donald Matthews sounds tired when she rings, like she has woken him from a long sleep.

Pearl stands in the hallway, with the receiver in her hand, and Nate fetches her a cup of tea. From what Connor has said, she feels she knows so much about this man who owns the solicitor's practice in town. Connor's closest relative.

'Hello, my name's Pearl . . .'

'Hello, Pearl.'

'I hope you don't mind me ringing. I know your son, Connor.'

'I'm glad you called,' he replies, much to her surprise. 'I'd hoped we could have spoken before. I'm sorry, it's been a difficult time.'

'I understand.'

'Connor spoke to me before the accident about the future he'd chosen and your help. He looked happier than I'd seen him for a long time . . .'

His voice trails away like a ferry leaving port.

'I realise now how much I'd lost touch with my son,' Donald says, his voice laden with regret. 'I lost the opportunity to tell him so much that I wanted him to hear.'

'Donald, is there anything I can do to help?'

'No but thank you.'

She hears it in his voice, that determination to continue regardless, to keep a stiff upper lip.

'If there's anything at all . . .' she says.

He takes a deep breath followed by a sigh. 'Thank you, that's kind. We were getting back on track, you know . . . beginning to.'

After they have talked for longer than Pearl anticipated, about temperature control, antibiotics and treatment plans for coma patients, Donald says he will call just as soon as the hospital gives them the all-clear to visit.

'There are lots of people,' Pearl says, thinking of Annie and Michael, and Derek and Molly. 'Perhaps we could visit in shifts?'

'I think that would be beneficial,' Donald agrees. 'The consultant at the hospital said it is important for Connor to hear the voices of those he is close to around him . . . even to feel their touch. Both of these things have been proven to make a difference in some cases.'

Pearl wishes she was at the hospital right now, holding Connor's hand and telling him all about the garden at Highview, and how so many people care about him.

'I'll ring,' Donald says. 'Just as soon as I hear back from the consultant in charge.'

NATE

In the evening, Nate telephones Anila. In the background, he hears Ryan saying hello.

'Shall we video call instead? I can get Frank in the picture too, then!' Anila offers. 'I'll ring you straight back?'

Soon her friendly, familiar face is smiling at him on the screen and Ryan is fetching two glasses of wine for them both in the background, while Frank follows at his heels.

'Hi, Nate, how's it going?' Ryan says, filling the screen with his presence.

'Good, how are you both?'

'I'm well. It's busy at work but I do have news.'

'Ryan's been promoted!' Anila says, jumping in. 'We think we might just be able to sell up and get a house.'

Nate smiles. 'That's incredible! I'm so pleased for you both.' They look so fresh-faced, young and in love.

'It will seem strange not being at Weatherley Gardens anymore if we move,' Anila says. 'It already feels completely weird not having you next door. It's not been the same and Frank's missing you like mad.'

Frank sticks his nose up to the camera and his nostrils cover the screen.

'Hello, boy,' Nate says, realising how much he misses Frank's soft snores and constant companionship. 'I hope he's behaving himself.'

'He sleeps on our bed!' Anila laughs, as Frank moves away to investigate something interesting on the floor. 'Ryan goes nuts, but secretly I think he's the one who invites him up.'

Ryan shakes his head in a feeble attempt to deny it.

'Is there any news on how Connor's doing?' Anila asks.

Nate shakes his head, thinking of the difficult conversation he had with them both after the accident. They had liked Connor instantly just as Nate had, and been devasted when he'd told them about the extent of the injuries. 'No more updates, unfortunately. We're still waiting to hear.'

'Is it still OK for us to come down?' Anila asks tentatively. 'It's just, we're so desperate to see you and to meet Pearl.'

'Of course, we can't wait.'

Frank gives a loud bark as if he wants to remind everyone he's not to be left behind when the time comes, just as another call comes through on Nate's phone.

'It's Claire.'

'No problem, you go, Nate, and I'll ring tomorrow. Give our best to Pearl,' Anila calls back. 'We're thinking of you all.'

Taking the call from Claire, he asks how everyone is at Happy Tails.

'Fine,' she says. 'Well, we will be when we get a temporary volunteer to fill in.'

'I'm sorry I'm not there,' he says, knowing that being one person down will have left a gaping hole in the already stretched rota at the rescue centre.

'Don't be!' Claire replies stunned. 'You're right where you should be, Nate, without any doubt. I thought that as soon as Anila explained everything. Second chances at happiness don't come around very often, but when they do, you have to bloody well grab them with both hands. Don't worry, we'll be absolutely fine.'

Nate realises he can't put off telling Claire what he has decided any longer.

'And if I don't come back to Happy Tails?'

She wastes no time in reassuring him. 'Then we'll get a permanent volunteer to fill in and Melissa and I will come down to Devon to see you as often as we can. And Wayne, and Katie. We'll all come!' she adds. 'You can't get rid of us that easily.'

'Claire?' he asks.

'Yes, Nate?'

'I never did thank you for that first day. It meant more to me than I could say at the time.'

He hears her breathing on the line, steady and even. 'Truth is, Nate,' she says, 'we were lucky to have you. I knew that as soon as I met you.'

For a moment neither of them speaks. It feels like the end of something, but not completely.

'Goodbye, Nate,' she says.

'Goodbye, Claire.'

After the call, he takes a moment before going in search of Pearl and finds her standing on the patio in the dark, looking out towards the moor. On the fence, three crows stand staring back intently as if expecting her to speak.

He will stay. He knows that. He knew it even as he was driving down from Godalming. If Pearl will have him. She has said she would like him to stay for as long as he can. That will be until his dying day. They have discussed so much of their lives already, the past, present, and future. But there is one day about which they haven't spoken. It is the most important one, for all the wrong reasons. He knows, they both need closure and must put it in the past for good.

She turns as he walks towards her. 'I was just thinking,' she says. 'Shall we walk to the top of the tor tomorrow?'

'I'd like that,' he replies, hoping a new day might bring the opportunity they need. 'And perhaps we'll take a picnic with us in the rucksack for when we get there.'

PEARL

With a resolve that makes her tie the laces on her walking boots faster and tighter than ever before, Pearl pictures the summit. The explosion of granite rock, stones piling one on top of another, a view she has never seen before. One she knows will be undeniably breath-taking.

In the kitchen, she puts homemade Bakewell tarts and a flask of tea in their new rucksack, while outside Nate runs the mower over the grass.

'I'd like to do whatever I can to keep it looking good . . . for when Connor comes back,' he calls from the lawn, and Pearl hopes that day will come. It is better to hope. No news is good news.

Annie telephones and they talk about everyday things, like broken washing machines and a delicatessen that's opened in town.

'Michael loves samosas and chorizo, and they sell both,' Annie explains, and Pearl knows her friend is just trying to keep her mind off the thought of Connor lying alone in the hospital.

'I've spoken to Donald,' Pearl says. 'He is going to talk to the doctors and let us know when we can go into the hospital and visit.'

'Thank God,' Annie says. 'It's been torture, hasn't it?'

'It has. But hopefully we'll be able to sit with Connor soon.'

'Pearl, it still feels so unreal.'

'I know. Even now.'

With their rucksack packed, Pearl and Nate set off. First down the path, through the gate, across the road and onto the moor. Today, the air is crisp and fresh. She feels it on her face, pinching the end of her nose, a reminder of colder days still to come.

Today, The Fear is being beaten again. Every time it rises, she challenges it head on, calls it out. Do your worst, she says, feeling more empowered than ever before. I'm ready for you.

As they walk, she looks ahead to the place they want to be at the top of the nearest tor. Her focus. The place where they will talk. 'How long will it take us to get up there?'

'About an hour or so,' Nate says, relaxed. 'Maybe a bit more if we stop on the way or choose to take it a little slower.'

Hand in hand, they begin to climb the grassy hillside. He asks her if she's feeling all right and if she needs to stop. But she feels fine. It's in his nature, she knows, to think of others and not just of himself. It makes him easy to love.

Overhead, a buzzard calls, looking for food, always with an eye on the ground. They climb higher and two sheep dart away in surprise as they round a corner. The sheep hurry down the hillside, their tails wagging like dogs' as they go. The grass under her feet is rough and tough, and either side of the unofficial track there are great swathes of purple bell heather.

Further up, Pearl sees this give way to banks of bracken, swaying gently in the breeze. Some fronds have changed from green to yellow and gold. The seasons are changing. Like life. The days come and go. And today, both their lives will change, hers and Nate's. When they stop at the top and look down at how far they have come.

Halfway up, the path twists and turns. They climb higher. Pearl stops to catch her breath and Nate does the same. And then they are walking on again, towards the summit. Steady steps. No rush. Plenty of time.

As they climb further, Nate tells her stories about working at Happy Tails, funny stories that make her laugh, like how Katie was always getting the names of owners and dogs copy and pasted incorrectly in contact emails and how she had once written 'Dear Spud, we are delighted to let you know Marjorie Daniels is now available for rehoming.' The time passes quickly as a result and before she knows it, they are almost at the top.

Nate stops, his cheeks flushed with the exertion of the climb. 'It's not far now.'

As they reach the next turn, they fall silent. Both lost, Pearl realises, in their own thoughts. She thinks about how she will say what needs to be said. To talk about what happened all those years ago and then leave it behind at the top of the tor with the granite rocks and the crumbs from their Bakewell tarts.

The Fear, she knows, arrived that day in 1976. It saw its chance and took hold, never leaving her side, confusing her mind and convincing her she could never be safe again. It controlled her. But not anymore. She needs to be strong for Connor. Looking out as she walks, Pearl feels her head clear. It is time to leave The Fear behind at last. Just one final step is all that is needed.

At the top, Nate unpacks the picnic, and they taste the sweet, sugary topping of the Bakewell tart, and bite into its soft pastry base. The tea they drink is strong and hot. They'll need its warmth, Pearl knows, for their descent.

When they have finished eating, Nate moves closer and puts his arms around her. She is sure there is no better time to talk than now, looking out at the most amazing view she has ever seen, better than all the images on the computer screen from a host of Travel Tuesdays. Pearl inhales a deep breath and takes it all in – patchwork fields of different greens, sewn together by hedgerows and stretching for miles, a wisp of smoke lifting from the chimney of a distant farm, and further down the hill, a flock of sheep with purple identification marks sprayed onto their backs are grazing peacefully.

Feeling warm and comfortable, she moves closer to Nate, and he responds by pulling her to him.

She looks up and he kisses her forehead.

'Ready?' he asks.

'I am,' Pearl says.

NATE

The summer of 1976

He left her at the bottom of the road where it split to go back into town or up to The Heights. She was smiling in the sunshine, her hair still wet from swimming at the Lido. To him she was the most beautiful girl in the world.

She waved goodbye, turned and walked away.

And because he believed Pearl would come to no harm on her way, he did the same.

PEARL

1976

She knew Mr Stanbury by sight and had spoken to him on several occasions. He had a gaunt face, thinning hair, a wife but no children, and he belonged to the same church as Nate's mother. Mrs Williams spoke of him highly. Ray owned a haulage company and Mr Stanbury worked in the office there. Pearl heard Ray telling her mother Vincent Stanbury's marriage was *on the rocks* because his wife had run off with a car salesman. Pearl didn't allow herself to think too much about it. She knew him but not enough to comment on such a story. Her thoughts were otherwise taken up with ideas for the future, for her and Nate. They'd sat on Burys Field, the day before, and talked for hours about a teacher-training course at a college in Guildford for her and a job in an office in Godalming for Nate. They stayed in the shade on Burys Field, under an enormous oak tree, while nearby, a woman was sitting in the sun under a white lace parasol. Very soon, she sought the shade of a tree as well. It was just too hot to sit out in the open for any length of time.

A week later, money started to go missing from the petty cash at Ray's haulage firm. There were discussions among the men in the yard. They said without doubt it was Mr Stanbury who had taken it, and Ray believed them. He fired Vincent Stanbury on the spot while the men looked on.

Pearl saw Mr Stanbury driving around the town in his mustard-coloured car with a dent in the front wing and couldn't help but feel sorry for him. He had lost his wife and his job. Ray said he had it coming. There was something unpleasant about Stanbury, he said, and he wasn't to be trusted. Pearl didn't like to judge people. It wasn't her way.

On the day she and Nate went to the Lido in Guildford, Pearl wore a new skirt that was the palest blue and fell just above her knees, and a white broderie anglaise top with no sleeves that exposed her arms. It was hotter than the days before. They said on the news that the temperature was at its highest for the whole summer. The sun spilled its rays down on their world, and she couldn't imagine it ever ending. This summer had been more perfect than any she had known. Like a perpetual holiday. And with Nate by her side, anything was possible. He made her feel she could swim the Channel if she wanted to, not just a length of the Lido. His love gave her the confidence to believe in herself, in a way she hadn't felt able to before.

On the way home on the bus, they sat on the back seat and held hands, laughing like ten-year-olds before falling into each other's arms and just being. Water dripped from Pearl's hair onto her light blue skirt, leaving a tell-tale patch of darker material where it fell. The windows were open but there was no cool air to be had. It was just as hot outside as it was in, but they were happy in the heat.

At the bus stop in town, they got off and headed in the direction of Victoria Street. At the bottom of the hill, they said goodbye. He took her in his arms and kissed her and Pearl thought about how she couldn't wait to see him again the next day. He turned and walked away. She watched him. He waved to her from the bottom and then he was gone. She began to walk up the hill towards The Heights. Bees buzzed in a nearby flower bed, a television played in a house near the road, and she smelled someone's dinner cooking through their open windows.

When she was halfway up the hill, she felt faint. They'd been so busy swimming and talking they'd not stopped for any food or drink the whole day. That hadn't been wise. She steadied herself against a low wall. What was it Ray used to say? 'Mad dogs and Englishmen.' She must be truly mad to be walking about in this heat, up the hill, towards home.

When a car pulled up alongside her, she noticed it was Mr Stanbury behind the wheel. The street was empty. Just her, Mr Stanbury, and the mustard-coloured car with the dented front wing idling in the street. He was perspiring and dabbing his forehead with a handkerchief. She thought of him losing his job and his wife. When he offered her a lift, she remembered he was a religious man and hoped he wouldn't ask her the last time she had gone to church. She said it wasn't much further and she could easily walk it. He laughed even though this wasn't funny and said he could save her feet the trouble. She felt that not to accept would seem unnecessarily rude of her, not to mention a little churlish. It was just a short distance, after all. If he talked about church she would think of something to say, Pearl decided, then thank him at the top and get out.

Inside the car, her legs stuck to the leather seats and there was a sour, tainted smell in the air. Pearl looked around for the source and soon realised it was the stale odour of whisky on Mr Stanbury's breath. Every time he spoke it grew stronger.

He drove up the hill while talking about the Ten Commandments, and then about the car salesman who had coveted his wife. He said he hoped she rotted in hell and told Pearl, with increasing anger, how he also wished the same on Ray for ruining his life.

'I'll make him pay,' Mr Stanbury said. 'In a way he'll never forget.'

She noticed flecks of thick, white spittle fly from his mouth as he spoke. Suddenly, the interior of the car seemed smaller. Pearl hoped she could get out soon. Not much further now. She should have walked. Mr Stanbury's voice grew louder, and he began to use words no one would say in church. He said his wife was an evil whore and that she'd made a fool out of him before the entire congregation. He said all women were cheap like her, no matter who they were. Pearl saw the driveway to Ray's house appear on the brow of the hill, and breathed a sigh of relief, but as they approached it, Mr Stanbury simply accelerated and kept going.

They drove for miles before they stopped. Pearl peered outside. They were parked down a secluded track next to a dense, dark wood where tall fir trees blocked out the sun. When he laid his hands on her, the touch of his fingers burned her skin, but the only mark was left inside. She closed her eyes rather than look at his face and waited for the pain to end. Afterwards, he told her to pull her new blue skirt back down as if she had been the one to lift it up to her chest. When he drove her back to Ray's house as if nothing had happened, she glanced down at her arms and legs. They didn't look like her own bones and flesh. It was as if they belonged to somebody else. She wished she could be back with Nate then, at the busy Lido, or sitting on the bus from Guildford, laughing and holding hands. It felt like it could be days ago and yet she knew it had only been an hour or so earlier.

Vincent Stanbury didn't look at her when he stopped the car, and he didn't speak to her when she got out. She stumbled at first, but when she found her feet, she ran as fast as she could. All the way to Ray's house, through the door, and safely inside.

***

A policewoman arrived at the house and told Pearl her name was Mary. She said she was a WPC and had been doing the job for just four weeks. She wore a navy uniform made of scratchy wool that smelled damp as if Mary had once been caught in the rain and been unable to get her smart uniform completely dry afterwards.

She asked Pearl to tell her what happened. Lana sat nearby while Pearl talked. Mary said Pearl was incredibly brave and had given a good and useful account. Ray paced up and down in the kitchen. He threatened to kill Vincent

Stanbury with his bare hands, and Mary said that wouldn't be a clever idea. She didn't write down anything Ray said in her small notebook with the black leather cover, only the words Pearl spoke. Pearl was glad. If Ray killed Vincent Stanbury he'd go to prison for life.

Mary said she would pass on everything Pearl had said to the officers at the station.

Vincent Stanbury was questioned later that week but released without charge. He had said the account given was a product of Pearl's wild and vivid imagination. He had laughed and asked to see the evidence. The police had none.

Mary delivered the shocking news.

'I'm so sorry,' she said.

Their lives became chaotic and surreal. Vincent Stanbury walked about the town grinning like a Cheshire cat. He read a lesson in church, drove his car the wrong way down a one-way street without getting a ticket, and seemed immune to the law. When Ray decided he'd had enough of the injustice and would make good on his threat to hurt Stanbury, Lana found a house as far away from Godalming as she could. It was called Highview, in the middle of a moor in the West Country. They'd never visited the place before. It was to be a fresh start.

For Pearl, The Fear arrived on the day she sat in the front seat of the mustard-coloured car with the dent in the wing, and from that day it never left her. She felt the need to stay inside, and apart from the journey from Godalming to Devon on 1 August 1976, she did exactly that. Being inside prevented her from ever meeting someone like Vincent Stanbury ever again.

NATE

They sit looking at the breathtaking view and completely lose track of time, wrapped up in their brand-new waterproof coats, content just to be.

When two more hikers arrive at the summit, they say hello and talk briefly with them about the climb, before giving up their top-of-the-tor seats and heading off down the hill.

'Shall we go home or walk a little more?' Nate asks, so proud of Pearl he can barely speak.

Seeing tears in his eyes, she takes his hand and smiles. 'Let's head home,' she says. 'I could get the fire going. It's starting to get cold.'

Nate wipes the tears from his eyes. It is time to move on.

They greet other walkers they pass on the way down, and he wonders how many people make the trek to the top to look at the view and reflect.

They retrace the same twisting path through the gilded bracken and the swathes of colourful bell heather, to where it levels out and eventually becomes flat. Ahead is a walk that takes them through a flock of grazing sheep, to the road, the gate, and the path to the front door of Highview.

He feels, suddenly, like he's walking on air, lighter than usual, his walking boots supporting his feet and ankles effectively, just like the man in the outdoor clothing and equipment shop said they would.

Inside, they take off their coats and hang them on the coat stand in the hall before easing off their walking boots and putting them by the front door. Ready for another hike on the moor sometime soon.

In the kitchen, he makes tea. He enjoys being in this house, with its French doors opening out onto the large garden, the cavernous hall with rooms leading off it, the spare room with the comfortable bed. When the kettle boils, he makes two cups of tea and brings them into the front room, placing them on the coffee table by the sofa. Pearl has already lit a fire with kindling and firelighters and is laying a seasoned log gently on top.

'It won't take long to get going,' she says. 'It is so cosy in here when it does.'

After tea, they sit and watch television. He asks if she'd like to watch her old favourite crime programme. She was very keen on it when he first arrived but lately, he's noticed, seems less so. Instead, she chooses a comedy programme. A stand-up comedian on stage is telling jokes. His enthusiasm and winning smile as he walks this way and that before his audience begin to take effect on them both. The people watching him on-screen smile and laugh, focused on him completely.

'Yesterday,' the comedian says, 'I saw a man drop his game of Scrabble all over the pavement. Can you believe it?' The comic walks another length of the stage. The audience waits for the punchline. 'So, I asked him, "What's the word on the street?"'

Nate feels it in his stomach first, rumbling up, reaching his mouth, and then pushing at his lips to get out. And then he's laughing and can't stop. He looks at Pearl and she is laughing too, her eyes shining brightly. Before long they are both wiping tears from their eyes.

'I needed that,' she says, and Nate thinks how good it is to see her finally unburdened of the hurt and fear of the past. 'What was his name?'

'I'm not sure, but I could watch it again,' Nate agrees. 'He's got the audience on their feet!'

The crowd in the theatre are clapping and whistling, and the comedian is taking a bow; his work is done for the evening, he has achieved his goal of entertaining the appreciative audience and lifting them away from the strain of everyday life for an hour or two.

'Shall I get some wine?' Nate asks.

'Yes, I think we could do with a glass . . . or two. I have some that I ordered in my last delivery. It's in the pantry.'

He notices when he comes back into the room that she's turned off the TV, stacked the newspapers and television guide neatly on the coffee table. In the waste bin he can see a solitary VHS tape in its distinctive video case, 'Detective Donnelly' printed across the top. Despite its age, it looks like it has rarely been used. He says nothing about it. They drink two glasses of wine each, sitting snuggled together on the sofa in front of the roaring fire.

In the late afternoon, as the fire is finally dying, he takes her in his arms just as he did at the top of the tor. In the quiet, she asks him a question.

'Nate, what happened to Vincent Stanbury? Is he still alive?'

For a moment, a flicker of worry shows on her face.

Nate shakes his head. 'No. He died several years ago now.' He takes a moment before saying. 'He passed away in prison where he was serving a sentence for rape . . . a long one.'

He sees the confusion in her eyes. He wasn't going to say anything. It's the final part of the story. The reality that people like his mother and even the local police had refused to see until it was too late.

Nate pulls her closer and holds her tight.

'There was a young girl at the church. She told a friend Stanbury took advantage of her when he gave her a lift home in his car. The police investigated thoroughly. Stanbury didn't bank on them using the new form of DNA testing that was available to them on some of the evidence. It was enough to convict him.' He shakes his head and takes a deep breath. 'Vincent Stanbury thought he could get away with committing crimes against young girls. But he didn't. Not in the end. He had to face up to what he'd done and after that people at the church looked at him very differently,' Nate says finally. 'In fact, everybody did.'

★★★

When darkness falls, they climb the stairs to bed. She takes his hand, and he follows her into the bedroom. When they are lying side by side he holds her close once again, and they look out of the window at the diamond-bright stars in the black sky.

'I'm looking forward to tomorrow,' she says into the stillness.

'New beginnings.' He feels her fingers touching his on top of the covers and the warmth of her skin. He looks down. Just like that night in the cinema when they were younger, he can't see where his fingers end and hers begin. They were starting out then, just like they're starting out again now.

'I love you, Pearl,' he says. 'So very much.'

'And I love you, too, Nate,' she replies. 'I always have.'

PEARL

Donald rings two days later.

'He's stable, Pearl. The antibiotics worked!'

Pearl feels her heart lift. 'Is he awake?'

'No, but there is some more good news,' he says. 'We can visit. In pairs. Two at a time . . . sorry, I didn't mean to clarify that so needlessly, it's just I'm a little sleep-deprived. Anyway, we can. For fifteen minutes.'

Pearl takes it all in, before saying, 'Will you be going this morning?'

'Yes, first thing . . . and I wondered if you'd like to join me?'

'I would. Thank you, Donald. Shall I meet you there?'

'Yes, let's do that. I'll see you soon.'

At ten o'clock, Nate drives Pearl to the hospital. It's easier now The Fear has disappeared.

Nate parks in the enormous pay-and-display area and buys a ticket.

'I'll be waiting here,' he says. 'Take all the time you need.'

He gives her a hug and that's all she needs to set her on her way, through the automatic doors and into the reception area. She can see the hospital looks different today compared to the night of the accident. The lights are brighter; there are more people about, waiting for appointments, and attempting to outsmart the broken vending machine.

Donald is waiting by the doors leading through to the Intensive Care waiting room.

Connor had said that he was a very tall man with a stoop, so he is easy to spot.

'Donald?'

'Hello, Pearl? It's good to meet you.' He smiles, the same wide smile as Connor's, instantly putting her at ease. 'The consultant said we can go straight up.'

He opens the door for her to walk through ahead of him, and Pearl resists the urge to explain she has been here once before on the night when Janice risked her job and Annie stood outside and Michael waited in the van.

'Just remember to breathe,' she says, as she walks.

'Absolutely,' Donald replies. 'I keep having to tell myself that all the time lately. It feels as if I might forget to do it otherwise.'

Pearl feels her face reddening. 'Sorry, I didn't realise I was thinking out loud.'

'Don't worry, it's good advice,' he says. 'We're just in here.'

He pushes open the door and they go in.

Inside, Connor lies unmoving in the centre of the bed, wired up, and with every mechanical assistance surrounding him to keep his organs functioning.

Donald takes it upon himself to manoeuvre chairs into position on either side of the bed and they sit, just quietly at first. Pearl takes a deep breath; it's difficult to see someone so young and vibrant lying so still and so pale. Connor was always so active, digging and mowing, working in the garden from dawn 'til dusk. It was what he wanted to do. What each of them would give to see him doing that now!

'I should have known what he was feeling,' Donald says, breaking the silence. 'After Sarah died. How hard it must have been for him. Instead, I buried myself in work. I'm not making excuses, but . . .' He stops and fiddles needlessly with his car keys. 'The thing is you can't get the time back. If it's taken away there's nothing you can do.'

Pearl looks at Connor, half expecting him to answer his father. To continue the dialogue they have begun. But he lies still, eyes closed, unaffected by the conversation taking place around him.

'He is my only son and yet I let him down. I'm not sure what sort of father that makes me.'

Pearl waits, wishing with all her heart that the driver of the speeding car that night had taken a moment longer to look down the road, long enough to see the lights of a rusty old Fiesta driving towards him.

'Connor,' Donald says, dipping his head towards his son's ear, 'My boy. Don't give up . . . please.'

He looks at Pearl, his eyes desperately searching hers. 'I don't know what I'd do if . . .'

He pauses for a moment then says, 'The consultant was talking about the future. If Connor doesn't regain consciousness . . .'

Pearl takes a deep breath. 'We mustn't give up.'

'You're right, of course.'

She hopes Connor knows they are there. She can't bear to think about how horrifying it might be for him to be trapped inside a body that won't move, unable to respond in any way, maybe even able to hear everything that's going on around him, but incapable of responding in any way. Reaching out, she gently rests her hand on his.

'I walked to the top of a tor yesterday, the one you can see from the kitchen window at Highview,' she says. 'It really is a wonderful sight, looking out across the moor. Cold but wonderful,' she smiles.

There's a row of calluses on his palm, no doubt from digging the vegetable patch. She touches them, feels the rough skin, then squeezes his hand gently, mindful of what Donald had told her about patient response to touch. She must do all she can.

'And there's the vegetable garden and the blueberry crop,' she says. 'So much has happened in the garden. Nate keeps the grass down, but he's hoping you'll come back soon and show him how it's done properly.'

Intent on updating him with all the developments, she doesn't notice it. Sitting across from her in the hospital chair, Donald doesn't see it either.

It's the slightest of movements. Imperceptible to the naked eye. But it's there. The flicker of an eyelid. And then it's gone.

CONNOR

It's too bright to open his eyes. He can tell by looking through his eyelids. It's like someone has brought the sun into the room.

His head aches, there's a pain, but it's dulled. And there's something sharp piercing the back of his hand. It's hard and his skin feels sore around it. When he tries to move his head, it feels twice the size it was before, too heavy to lift off the pillow.

The accident comes back to him in flashes of shattered memory. The road disappearing in front of him, the speeding car in the corner of his eye, and the sound of glass breaking all around. Each moment is slowed, each sound amplified ten-fold.

He can feel someone holding his hand, but he can't see them. He tries to open his eyes, but he can't do it. Still, it's too bright, and he's too tired. The exhaustion is like nothing he's ever known. Even when he'd run up to the moor from Westdown and back three times with Derek for a bet, he'd never been as drained as he is now.

He sighs, hearing his own breath leave his body. It mingles with the sound of distant voices, each muffled like he's hearing them from underwater. There's a weight on him, a pressure holding him down. Not somebody but something.

This feels like hell. Trapped inside a body that won't move when you want it to. So, he just lies there and prays it will change. Prays it will get better soon.

★★★

It's dark when he wakes again. The sun has left the room.

He can hear the consistent beep of a hospital monitor, feel the sharp needle in the back of his hand still, and when he manages to open his eyes, there's a woman standing beside the bed whom he doesn't recognise.

'Connor?' she says gently. 'Connor, my name is Janice, I'm a nurse in the emergency department here at the hospital. You've been in an accident.'

When he tries to move, she helps him. When he manages to sit up, she doesn't let go of his arm. He sees all the equipment in the room: the monitors, the drip, the metal stand it is hooked to.

'Connor, can you tell me your surname?' the nurse asks.

'Matthews,' he says, gulping as he tries to form the words. His throat is dry and scratchy.

'Would you like some water?'

'Yes, please.'

She fills a plastic cup from a jug on the bedside table.

'Here, take it steady.'

After several small sips, she says, 'You're doing really well, Connor, but I need to ask you some questions.'

'OK.'

Can you tell me the name of someone in your family?'

'Sarah Matthews.'

'That's great. And who is Sarah?'

'She was my mum.'

The woman nods. 'And anyone else in your family?'

'There's my dad, Donald.'

'Good, that's good.' She smiles.

'And how old are you, Connor?'

'I'm eighteen.'

He draws in a breath and wishes he hadn't. His head hurts with every movement, no matter how small.

'Take your time,' the woman says.

He thinks about the dulled pain and how much medication he must have been given to keep it that way.

He opens his eyes a little wider. The nurse looks like she's about to ask more questions. Harder ones that he might not be able to answer. Ones that will show there's a problem.

'Can you remember what happened on the night of the accident?' she says.

The images dart into his mind once again. 'Only bits of it. I know I was driving. There's another car and a road . . .'

He stops, realising he can't remember anything more. 'That's it.'

She nods. 'Don't worry, that's perfectly normal.'

Hearing the word 'normal' gives him hope. He might not remember what happened, but he knows what year it is and what his name is. He moves himself up the pillow and sits straighter against the metal headboard of the hospital bed. 'Am I going to be OK?'

'Your condition is better than we expected, but I'll need to get the consultant in now to have a proper look at you. He'll check you over. And then you'll need plenty of rest.'

'Can I go home?' he asks.

'Not yet,' she says. 'You'll be with us for a while.'

Connor realises he has no idea what day or time it is.

'How long have I been here?'

'It's been almost three weeks,' the nurse tells him. 'You've been unconscious the whole time.'

'I don't remember any of that,' he says, feeling anxious. 'Not even lying here in the bed.'

'It's OK,' she reassures him. 'That's normal too.'

She pauses.

'So, if you're feeling all right, I'll get someone who can tell you a bit more about what's been happening to you. Would that be OK?'

She lets go of his hand when he nods his answer, and he wonders if he dreamed the feeling of someone touching his fingers when he couldn't move. Someone talking about a garden.

That touch and those words.

He lies back and slowly the memories return. Special memories. Ones he never wants to lose, like walking out onto the patio at Highview with Pearl, one step at a time, the journey up to Godalming to find Nate, and the talk in the pub with his father. There are people waiting for him, he knows it now. Family and good friends who believe in him.

Then he feels it. A flood of joy running through his veins, his heart, his lungs. The sheer relief of being alive. He senses a sudden urgency to get up and go. To make the most of each day. To get out of bed, run out of the hospital and start living. There's not a moment to lose. His life could have been over in a moment, but instead, there is a future waiting, and it's one he can't wait to begin because something tells him it's finally going in the right direction.

PEARL

It had only been a summer. A summer that turned into autumn while they waited for news of Connor's progress. But it has changed her life.

She is wearing a new dress; it is a beautiful shade of forest green and fits her perfectly. It arrived the previous day, wrapped in brown paper and delivered by Rick, the postman. He stands and talks when he delivers her junk mail and bills now, his headphones consigned by choice to the pocket of his bright red shorts. He has a little girl called Ella, Pearl has learned, and is newly married. Just the week before, Pearl surprised him with a box of freshly baked cupcakes for Ella's fifth birthday party.

Anila, Nate and Ryan are talking, with glasses of wine in their hands. It's been wonderful having the young couple to stay at Highview and getting to know them. They have all enjoyed long walks on the moor with Frank and two delicious meals at a pub five miles away. It had a roaring fire, and baked Camembert and moules marinière on the menu.

There is so much to enjoy, so many more walks to be had, places to visit, and an opportunity to travel further afield too. Nate has booked a holiday in Tuscany for them, but not before they both sat at the computer in the spare room and experienced a few of the sights virtually. It reminds her of Travel Tuesdays.

At Nate's feet, Frank lies dozing, having spent the morning chasing the crows, whom he has no chance of ever catching. They lift themselves into the air at the sight of him approaching, long before he's had a chance to get anywhere near.

In the corner, Derek is chatting to Molly. Today, Molly's mother is looking after Tommy. Pearl watches Derek and Molly talking, filling the house with their happy voices and laughter. She is so grateful to the beautiful girl for transforming her appearance, and to Derek, for his inspiration. If it weren't for his enthusiasm and encouragement, she wouldn't even have considered setting up a business of her own. Her very first job. Now, she has orders coming in from cafés and hotels every week, and travels with Nate to the Farmers' Market where she has her own stall. On the side are some of her new creations, ready for when everyone is hungry later on. Raspberry and peach Battenberg, a Spanish orange cake which is gluten-free, and a blueberry and passion fruit tart.

Aaron and Cain are eyeing them greedily, waiting for the go-ahead to tuck in.

'I'm watching,' Annie tells them, giving Pearl a knowing smile as she does. 'Why don't you two run off some more energy in the garden? We're not quite ready yet.'

'Can we take Frank?' Aaron asks.

'You'll have to ask Nate,' Annie tells them. 'And don't interrupt if someone's talking.'

Aaron nods, as if he's already sworn an oath of silence.

'Anila said there's dogs that still need homes at Happy Tails,' Cain fills in. 'So can we have one, pleeeeease?'

His mother laughs. 'We'll see.'

Clearly not taking it as a flat no, Aaron and Cain approach Nate and wait for everyone to stop talking.

'Is there any word from Donald yet?' Annie asks. Pearl shakes her head.

'Not yet, but I don't think it will be long.' She checks the clock on the wall. 'He said it would be before three.'

While everyone helps themselves to more wine, tea and soft drinks, Pearl crosses to the dresser and opens the drawer. Lying inside is the college brochure with the details of the landscaping course and an application form ready to be filled in for the following year. All the paperwork that is needed to help Connor follow his dream of one day creating gardens that people will love and enjoy. And he will achieve it, she has never been more certain of anything in her life.

Outside, the peaceful moor lies below a pale sky strewn with streaks of pure white cloud. When she steps through the French doors and out onto the patio, she feels the cool October air on her bare forearms. Usually, the merest hint of a chill and she'd be reaching for her cardigan but not today. Molly has worked her magic with the hairdryer and her make-up kit and Pearl is as grateful for this transformation as she was for the first. They have become close. Molly is learning to drive, and Michael is teaching her, so that she can drive to Highview with Tommy, without relying on a lift from anyone. Just last week, Derek dropped her off at the house and she and Pearl sat and talked together for hours.

In her new pair of smart low-heeled shoes, Pearl makes her way down to the vegetable patch at the bottom of the garden.

Nate has given it a weed and a tidy-up the day before and it is looking neat and cared for, as are the lawns and the vine in the greenhouse. Nate has picked all the grapes and set up his own wine-making area in the outhouse, and everyone is looking forward to the first bottle. They both wanted the garden to look just as it did when Connor left it. They didn't want him to think all his hard work had gone to waste. She takes a deep breath, inhaling the cold fresh air, and thinks back to the first time she saw him, his thin frame, baggy T-shirt and hair that refused to go where it was supposed to.

Turning around, Pearl goes back into the house. It won't be long now, and she doesn't want to miss the call from Donald.

Inside, she hears the telephone ringing. She hurries through to the hallway, and everyone in the house is suddenly silent, even Aaron and Cain.

'Hello?'

'I'm on my way,' Donald says on the other end. 'Won't be long. Is everyone there?'

'Yes, we're all here. We'll be standing at the gate.'

'Should be about twenty minutes.'

'OK. See you soon.'

Glasses of wine in hand, the adults make their way out of the front door and down to end of the path, followed by Aaron and Cain, happy to wait outside and not wanting to miss Connor's arrival. Once they reach the gate they gather together, standing close, talking, and laughing. It's impossible not feel elated. On a day like today.

'This is it,' Molly says. 'Everything's going to change now, Pearl, isn't it?'

'Will you tell him?'

Molly nods. 'When he's fully recovered, we'll have a proper talk about us, but I know I'll need to give it some time.'

None of them want to overload him. The doctors have said to take it slow, especially for the first few weeks.

When the car appears, they fall silent. Pearl feels Nate's reassuring presence beside her. He is holding her hand, and Frank sits on the grass beside them. Anila and Ryan are holding on to each other, and Michael is looking at Annie's red eyes and offering her a dusty handkerchief.

'I'm sorry,' she says, dabbing her cheeks. 'I said I wouldn't but now the car's here . . .'

At the sight of Donald's Volvo, so close, Pearl feels the tears welling in her own eyes.

First Ryan and Michael start cheering and clapping, then everyone joins in, and as the car draws nearer, she can see him sitting in the passenger seat, her friend, his arms wasted from bed rest, his body that will need filling out. Not a problem. She has cake.

He has defied all the odds, survived when none of the medical staff thought he would.

Pearl feels her heart might break all over again. But Nate is by her side. Her rock, she knows he will always be there.

'It's OK,' he says.

She nods her agreement, smiling through the tears.

When Connor gets out, he closes the passenger door of the Volvo and walks to the gate. As he draws closer and looks around at the group, she can see his eyes glistening with tears too. Happy tears.

Overwhelmed with joy, she says the first thing that comes to her mind. 'You must be hungry?'

'Yes,' he laughs. 'As always.'

'How about we get the kettle on and have some cake?'

'Like old times?'

'Like old times.'

'Welcome home!' everyone cheers, and the sound of their rousing toast rises through the cooling October air, to the familiar group of crows flying in perfect formation overhead.

ACKNOWLEDGEMENTS

I first had the idea to write a novel about a woman who never took a step outside her home after interviewing a mother of two living with agoraphobia. The meeting had a profound effect on me. But it wouldn't be until many years later after a move to Dartmoor and the completion of several creative writing courses that the novel would find its way into the hands of literary agent, Judith Murray. And I'm so glad that it did. Judith is not only an extremely kind, supportive person, she has a wealth of experience and is everything anyone could ask for in an agent. Simply put, without Judith and the team at Greene and Heaton, I wouldn't be sitting here today with the opportunity to thank all the wonderful people who have helped *Reasons to Go Outside* reach readers all over the world.

I'd also like to say a huge thank you to my publishers, Hodder & Stoughton, in particular, Kimberley Atkins, my editor, for her unending faith and enthusiasm for Pearl, Nate and Connor's story; Amy Batley for reading drafts again (and again, and again!); book illustrator Joanna Kerr; designer Natalie Chen, who produced the extremely beautiful cover and illustrations; Callie Robertson for her marketing genius, and the many people who have worked so hard behind the scenes, handling everything from proof reading to printing.

Thank you also to good friends: Nat, Robyn, Anushia, Lisa, Boo and Matt, Dave (for repairing my old laptop every time it stopped working and I thought I'd lost every word), and the lovely Lynn Curtis. And finally, a very special thanks to my gorgeous family: Peter, Ethan, Evie, and Milo – my constant four-legged writing companion. I love you all so much.

reasons
to go
outside

Esme King is a former news journalist and an award-winning short film writer and director. She was inspired to write her first novel *Reasons to Go Outside* after interviewing a woman with agoraphobia. Esme lives in Devon with her husband, two children and rescue dogs, Monty and Milo.